# What Money
# Can Buy

# What **Money** Can Buy

Sidney B. Silverman

iUniverse, Inc.
Bloomington

# What Money Can Buy

*iUniverse books may be ordered through booksellers or by contacting:*

*iUniverse*
*1663 Liberty Drive*
*Bloomington, IN 47403*
*www.iuniverse.com*
*1-800-Authors (1-800-288-4677)*

*ISBN: 978-1-4620-3076-7 (sc)*
*ISBN: 978-1-4620-3077-4 (dj)*
*ISBN: 978-1-4620-3078-1 (ebk)*

*Library of Congress Control Number: 2011909966*

*Printed in the United States of America*

*iUniverse rev. date: 07/14/2011*

I started this book in mid-October 2008, at about the time our twin grandchildren Eleanor and Benedict were born. When I told Irene I proposed to dedicate the book to them, she protested: "Our other grandchildren will feel slighted."

I dedicate this book to all our grandchildren, Daniel, Noam, Leo, Tamara and especially Eleanor and Benedict.

*A*ddicts are disdained by society, scorned by friends, and ostracized by their own families. They are accused of being weak, lacking self-control and willpower. Those who can afford it are carted off to detox centers where psychotherapists delve into their destructive habits and they attend twelve-step meetings from morning till night. Those who cannot afford treatment make up a special underclass: the homeless, the street people, the bums. They end up dead well before their time, swept away from the gutter like detritus.

There is another kind of addict—those who spend their lives pursuing money. They are as obsessed with wealth as alcoholics are with wine. To them, a million dollars is petty change. In the 1980s, rich meant a "bill," shorthand for $100 million. By the twenty-first century, the bar was raised to $1 billion.

For the money addict, the most sought-after prize is not a Nobel but inclusion in the Forbes 400.

Unlike other addicts, the money worshippers are rewarded by society. They are granted honorary degrees, appointed to presidential committees and boards of universities and charities. The haughty maître d' bows as he escorts them to the best table. The super-rich travel by private jet and chauffeured limousine to Shangri-la. They are welcome everywhere.

How do I know? I was one of them.

There is an adage: every great fortune is built on at least one criminal act. I committed none, suppressed my darker inclinations, did my duty, and respected the law. Though not everyone agrees.

How do you do? My name is Henry Josef Wojecoski.

# 1

*W*alk along any big city street and you'll likely see a mother or nanny pushing a twin stroller. Today, one in every thirty-two births is of twins, up more than 65 percent from the days before fertility drugs. Mary and I were born on April 6, 1949. Our double birth was traceable to genes.

We grew up in the working-class town of Riverhead, New York, down the road a piece from Southampton and, to be specific, in a plain wooden two-bedroom bungalow on Pulaski Street between Claus and Marcy in the heart of Polish Town, a fifteen-block section that actually exists on the map. It's not just local slang for where poor Polacks hung their hats.

When they bought the house, the proud owners thought they would never outgrow it. But when Elizabeth returned from the hospital with her two babies, she told Andrew, "We're going to need a bigger house, with three bedrooms and two baths. Henry and Mary will each need a room. They can share a bathroom, but not ours. We should start planning now."

"Don't worry," my father said. "It'll be a long time before these two cashews know their heads from their tails. When they need separate rooms, I'll fix up the attic for Henry and install a bathroom in the basement." When I was eight, he did just that.

"Don't call them cashews! We knelt and prayed together every night for their safe deliverance. How quickly you forget. Those earlier miscarriages were awful. The doctor doubted I could carry one child. With two, he predicted a certain miscarriage. Andy, I tell you it's a miracle, bestowed upon us by Jesus. I thank

Him every night for the twins. I've heard you do the same. Jesus gave us a complete family, a boy and a girl."

If our birth was a miracle, Jesus was paid back.

In celebration of the miracle of birth, Andrew and Elizabeth added to the many devotional symbols already in our house. A picture of our Lady or our Lord and a crucifix hung in each room. Scattered throughout the house were small statues of the saints. A pair of rosary beads adorned a small table near the front door. A bottle of holy water sat on a counter in the kitchen, which we used to bless ourselves before going to bed. I never remember a meal at which grace was not recited. Meat, our favorite dish, was verboten on Friday. We called on St. Anthony when we could not find something. We blessed ourselves when we passed a church and bowed our heads at the holy name of Jesus. We observed all religious holidays and never, except when sick, missed Mass.

As a kid, I accepted that Poles dominated Riverhead and did not question how it came about. Once I married Peggy, the origin of the Polish community was unmasked. In 1870, her great-grandparents, Francis and Regina Kuszniewoski, left their village of Mala Wies, a part of Poland ruled by Russia, and emigrated to America. They were farmers in the old country, and Riverhead was a farming community. The farms needed workers, and the Polish immigrants needed work. The Kuszniewoskis were the first Polish immigrants to settle in Riverhead. By 1910, three hundred thousand Poles had followed in their wake. Peggy's grandmother on her maternal side, Veronica Sendlewski, was the first child born locally of Polish-immigrant stock. "Well, the Kuszniewoskis and the Sendlewskis," said Peggy, "were not the Cabots and the Lodges, but among the Polish community on the East End, they were royalty."

Although our country treated the new immigrants poorly, relegating them to low-paying, backbreaking jobs (the ones no one else wanted) and making fun of their intellect and dress, the Poles were fiercely patriotic. Flags flew on every national holiday, and the men enlisted, rather than waiting to be drafted, to fight in every war. The Riverhead Veterans of Foreign Wars had so many Polish members that it could rightly have been called the Polish American Veterans of Foreign Wars.

What caused the mass immigration? Perhaps their lives were even worse in their native land. But then why did they hold on to the old ways? Take church, that most important institution: Although there was an established, traditional Catholic church in Riverhead ready to accept the new arrivals, they founded their own, St. Isadore's Roman Catholic Church of Riverhead, led by a Polish-speaking priest. Packed on Sundays and religious holidays, attendance was also high for dances, picnics, suppers, and trips to Radio City Music Hall at Christmastime. The church served as the center for religious and social life. My parents sang in the choir: Andrew, a bass; and Elizabeth, a mezzo soprano. They met at a rehearsal for a Christmas pageant and courted for six months before marrying.

The Irish and Italians prayed with their fellow Americans, intermarried, and moved up the social ladder. Not the Poles of Riverhead. They prayed in their church and, locked in their working-class jobs, passed them on from father to son. It was a rare father who said, "My life is dreary. I'm at the bottom of the heap. I want my children to have a better life." Instead, they thanked Jesus for their hardscrabble existence; pushed their sons to become plumbers, carpenters, house painters, electricians; and encouraged their daughters to marry on the same social level.

It was weird that we were so insular when at our doorstep lay a world of privilege and opportunity.

Our home was 8.6 miles from the estate section of Southampton, where the houses were adorned with diamonds as big as the Hope. On my one-speed Schwinn bicycle, I could make the trip in fifteen minutes with the wind at my back, and they were the most glorious minutes of my life, except for when I actually arrived in this land of mansions and endless emerald green lawns and beaches whose waters stretched across the entire ocean.

How did I know so young that I wanted to live in luxury—that I *had* to? I will go to my grave not knowing the answer to that. I just knew. Maybe I was born knowing. Or maybe my father, the plumber, and my mother, the bookkeeper, secretly pointed me in that direction, while telling me all the while to embrace my heritage and to avoid the rich as though they carried the plague.

"What do they know?" my father would say. "They need to be waited on hand and foot because they're helpless. They're pathetic."

"Count your blessings that they need you to fix their plumbing," my mother would chime in. "Without them, where would we be?"

God, how I hated to listen to his bitterness and her always counting her blessings—for our little box of a house where nothing special ever happened. The people in Southampton did not speak this way or live the way we did. They didn't whine; they didn't have to count their blessings to be reminded of anything, because their good fortune was everywhere in evidence—and in plenty of places I couldn't see.

Angry and eager to leave as I was, growing up in Riverhead, I witnessed the passion of blue-collar families in caring for and improving their homes. Awareness of this trait, and putting it into practice, enabled me to amass my fortune.

My parents thought Riverhead was God's country, a place no sane person would want to leave. But they had no ambition and were content to stay imprisoned in their little world and endure boring, hard work. Their dull lives affected their appearances. Andrew, a veteran of World War II, was not what an objective person would call handsome. His features were prominent, his head came to a point, and his hair was thick, unruly, and all over his body. Years of maneuvering on his hands and knees through crawl spaces had stooped his shoulders and turned his skin dull and gray. In my mother's kindness and affection for him, she'd say, "As a young man, he had movie-star good looks. If he had wanted to, he could have made his fortune in Hollywood."

In a wedding photo taken when my mother was eighteen, she looked bright-eyed, pretty, and pleasantly plump, a very different look from the haggard woman I grew up with. She grew heavy, her blonde hair turned gray, and her face was lined with decades of hard work and financial worries. She looked old to me, older even than the mothers of my friends, and this sometimes made me sad even as a child, but I'm not sure if it was sadness for me or for her.

She impressed Andrew in a different way. "The first time I heard that canary sing and got a good look at her, I knew she was for me. Over the years, she has gotten better looking." He bragged that while in the army, before he met my mother, he "carried on with Frenchies, Brits, and fräuleins." Then he softened the blow. "None could hold a candle to this all-American rose."

Although Mary and I were two peas from the same pod, we looked and acted differently. She had a well-shaped nose, big blue eyes, and honey-colored hair. She was tall and slim. The signs were clear: she would blossom into a beauty.

I was wide and thought I was ugly. My shoulders were broad; my arms, hands, and feet outsized. I never could understand why girls liked me. I thought about the "Frenchies, Brits, and fräuleins" who swooned over my father. Would they fall for me? We looked different, I thought. Maybe I was wrong. At my confirmation, the priest said, "The apple doesn't fall far from the tree." Priests don't lie.

Mary was a reader, an A student, and class valedictorian. I was an athlete, a three-letter man, and football was my passion. I played fullback on offense and linebacker on defense. In my senior year, I was the captain. I started on the basketball team and played center field in baseball. My grades were good for a jock, even though I spent little time hitting the books. I was popular. Maybe even the most popular, according to the yearbook.

Mom didn't worry about me but she did about Mary. "She reads too much. She'll ruin her eyes. She'll never get married. Men don't like girls who are too smart. That's why she never has a date. If she continues in her ways, she'll die a spinster."

Her complaints were directed at me as well as Mary. "Mary helps you with your schoolwork; why don't you help with her social life? Fix her up with dates. Take her to parties. If I had not had a well-rounded social life, I would never have snared your father."

"Maybe you'd have landed a better fish." I thought I was being funny.

"Don't you say anything against your father. You do that too much. I want you to stop."

In defending him, she offered the same excuse. "He works hard doing dirty work to support us." She was so earnest you would think no other father slaved away. She spoke about his service in World War II and called herself dull compared to the "women of the world" he met during the war. He talked so often about his longing to return to London and Paris that she believed he would have been happier working as a plumber in those cities than in Riverhead. I almost believed circumstances, not Andrew's nature, were at fault. She assured me Andrew loved me, though she admitted he had difficulty showing it.

My father and I had a bad relationship. As a kid, I laid the blame at his door; he struck me as ridiculous. For example, he celebrated the anniversary of VE Day by dressing for dinner in his army uniform. After we recited grace, he stood holding a glass of water, and year after year, he made the same toast: "To my fellow brothers in arms, the valiant soldiers who died to make the world safe." He listed the dead he claimed to have known, but from year to year, the first names of the departed changed and so did last names. When he couldn't remember a name, he made it up. Some service for his fallen comrades!

Andrew may have noticed the bored looks on Mary's and my faces as he uttered his foolish speech for the umpteenth time because, when we were fifteen, he threw us a curve ball. To get our attention, he mentioned—mercifully without specification—the victory of his fellow soldiers over European women. "Those Frenchies were hot stuff. My god, the things they did to please soldiers. The English dames pretended to be oh so proper, but they were wild. The hottest of all were the Germans. We conquered them but not their women. My buddies and I agreed: we beat the Nazis but surrendered unconditionally to their gals."

Our mouths agape, we burst out laughing. Mary, who had studied French, rattled on in that language while gazing soulfully at Andrew. Then she translated: "You great, big, handsome Yank. My hero. You've saved France. Come with me to Paris and claim your reward."

Mary impersonated an English woman, speaking with a part cockney, part Oxbridge accent: "King George VI is throwing a party in Buckingham Palace for all you American blokes. There'll be plenty of proper English women there who won't behave properly. The king's daughter will fall head over heels for you. Women named Elizabeth generally do. You're definitely the princess's type. Tall and silent. Who knows? You may become the consort to the next ruler of England."

For the finale, Mary gave the Nazi salute; said, "Heil Hitler"; and sang, "GI Joes are strong and mean but cannot conquer us fräuleins."

Mom and I howled with laughter. Even Andrew smiled but ruined it by adding glumly, "That's not the way it happened."

The following year, he stuck to the old script.

It did not feel like a happy household to me at the time, despite the essential stability. We were fed and clothed and taken to church. We had friends and Thanksgiving and Christmas dinners, and we did not fight all the time. But Mary and I were both so different from each other, and we were both so different from our parents, that I felt sometimes that I had come home from the hospital with the wrong family. Sometimes, but not always.

# 2

"*N*o" is overused by two-year-olds. They don't really mean it; it's a way to assert independence. When I was two and urged to sit on the potty, I announced, "I sez nope." Weeks later, the potty and I were friends.

The summer I turned fourteen, I said nope to working another summer for my father. This time, I meant it. I was sick of being pushed around, working long hours, and not being paid. When I said, "There are laws protecting children," my father shouted at me, "I feed you—and you eat more than me—put a roof over your head, buy you all kinds of things I never had, and what's the thanks I get? You want to send me to jail! Here, I'll pay you what you're worth." He handed me a penny. "That's pay not for one day but for the whole damn summer."

On school vacations, Andrew took me with him on jobs and constantly criticized my work in front of others. "Henry is the cleanest kid. He never has to take a bath. Why? My boy doesn't do dirty work and never breaks a sweat." I could never satisfy my father. And he never found a word of praise for me.

One sweltering evening, I sat on the front porch in case a breeze wafted by. I was avoiding my attic sanctuary where it might be a hundred degrees. I had spent the day working for my father, and like so many of those days, we fought like bitter enemies. I was resting; he was watching TV. I guessed the program was over when my father appeared in front of me. He looked menacing. I was not frightened. He barked a lot but never hit me.

"Look at my hands," he said, shoving them in my face. "They're the hands of a working man. Strong and calloused. They were that way when I was your age. Now look at yours." He grabbed them, yanked them up as though they were strangers to me, and held them in front of me. "Soft, like a sissy's."

"You know what? I don't want your hands. And I don't want to be a plumber. For your information, I don't like working in shit."

Bull's-eye. I'd renounced a plumber's life, challenging one of Andrew's basic tenets. If you were born a plumber's son, you were lucky and should follow in your father's footsteps.

I thought I saw a tear in his eye, but maybe I was mistaken. Andrew was not an emotional man. He grimaced, turned his back, and returned to the house. The porch lights went off, and the TV droned on.

There was one bright spot that summer of my fourteenth year. In July, my father and I replaced a toilet and added a bidet in the master bathroom of Patrick B. McGinnis's Southampton home. He was a railroad mogul, the former CEO of the New Haven Railroad, and was running the Boston and Maine. McGinnis was around, and we couldn't avoid seeing him and he us.

At lunchtime, my father, as was his habit, went to his hangout for a sandwich and a beer. He never invited me. On the last day of the job, McGinnis spotted me sitting on the ground at the back of the house about to start my brown-bag lunch. "Hey, kid. How come you don't eat with your dad? That is your dad, right?"

"My dad won't eat with the help. You see, master plumbers don't mix with apprentices, even their own sons. At home, my mother insists he eat dinner with me as she refuses to cook separate meals, but he sits far away." I said it with a smile, and McGinnis smiled too.

"Well, I'm not a master plumber, so no law will be broken if you eat with me. A friend cancelled lunch. We got plenty of fried chicken and corn. Toss your lunch in the garbage pail and come with me." He took me to a table just off the kitchen. A black woman brought out a platter of food piled high. McGinnis got two

Cokes from the refrigerator; we drank from the bottles. When I saw him eating with his hands, I did too. The chicken and corn were finger-licking good.

McGinnis talked a lot but didn't toot his own horn. He didn't have to. Just a few weeks earlier, the *Southampton Press*, a weekly, featured McGinnis in its "talks to" column. My father regularly brought home the paper. He didn't read it except to check on his ad and those of his competitors.

Although Southampton was home to many working-class people, the local paper focused on the celebrities. They were achievers, doers, and newsworthy. I read the paper from top to bottom, everything except the classified ads.

The close-up on McGinnis told how he'd started at nineteen as a runner at Lehman Brothers at fifteen dollars per week. By the time he was twenty-five, he was head of the firm's bond desk. He moved from bonds to stock and became the leading railroad analyst and broker. Not content to make piles of money for his clients and himself, he left Lehman to run a small railroad. In 1954, he sought bigger stakes and challenged Frederick "Buck" Dumaine for control of the New York, New Haven, and Hartford Railroad. In the first proxy contest for a railroad empire, Pat McGinnis, an uneducated, street-smart guy, ousted Frederick "Buck" Dumaine Jr., the scion of a New England Brahmin family. The clash was headlined "Pat vs. Buck."

A charismatic person can induce an alcoholic-like state in those around him. McGinnis had me in a semidrunken one, free of inhibitions and ready to expose my secrets. He asked whether I wanted to be plumber. "About as much," I said, "as you wanted to follow in your father's footsteps." My wise-guy comment didn't offend him. He sensed that I respected him. He asked what I wanted to do. "I want to make a lot of money and run a big business, just like you."

"Why not?" he said. "It's a good life. Successful businessmen make money, but only if they are at the top. The second in command earns a lot less, and those below are flunkies—might as well be plumbers. There are risks for the chief. He's prey, a target for every sharpshooter. My railroad had ten cars that produced not a dime in revenue. Why? They were surplus. I found a railroad that needed them and negotiated a fair price. If an employee did what I did, I'd give him a bonus. So I thought it's only fair that I get a bonus. Instead of nagging my directors, I asked the buyer to pay me a commission. The feds called it an illegal kickback. A stinking little thirty-five thousand dollars and the government is out to indict me. I'll win. You know why? It's easy to make a business transaction complicated like the feds are doing. It takes a lot more intelligence to make the deal simple. A kickback is complicated; a bonus is simple. Call it a bonus, and it's not a crime." He was talking at me. No matter. He had my full attention.

"You want to be rich and run your own company? Make sure you cover your ass. You can loot like hell provided you don't conceal what you're doing. The law doesn't much care what you do as long as you disclose it. Aha. I hear your father's truck. Go wash your hands in the sink. I don't want you working in my bathroom with greasy hands."

Late in August, the *Southampton Press* ran a front-page story: McGinnis was indicted for taking a kickback on the sale of ten Boston and Maine cars. He was subsequently convicted and sentenced to two years in prison. He paid my father for the work, but I never saw Pat McGinnis again. Needless to say, I never forgot his advice.

The next summer, I went into business for myself mowing lawns, doing yard work and handyman jobs. I named my company Wojo Services. I prepared a flyer and made two hundred copies on the mimeograph machine in my mother's office. In the spring, I hopped on my bike and distributed them throughout the neighborhood, mainly to homes and to a few small businesses and professionals.

Using the plat maps at the county office, I targeted those most likely to use Wojo's services: old people, too old to work, who had no grown children living with them.

I signed up fifty-two households. I needed workers, kids who had mowers and rakes and were good with their hands. I also wanted my staff to be subservient. McGinnis had said you want to be the boss, and at fifteen, I didn't want any competition. I picked five kids and offered them a salary of one dollar per hour. Why a dollar? In the 1960s, the minimum wage was one dollar. Unlike my father, I observed the law. I didn't want to be indicted as soon as I started in business.

One of my workers complained that I planned to profit from the labors of others. I fired him on the spot, called him a Communist, and urged him to move to the Soviet Union. I didn't want any of the others raising the same objection, so I told them, "My father is a plumber who sometimes works as a subcontractor for a general contractor. He says when he works for a contractor, his pay is less. Why? The contractor takes a cut for getting the business and supervising. That's the American way. If you don't like it, quit now. There are plenty of kids waiting for a job."

There were no more complaints. I had learned an important business lesson, one not taught in business school. When negotiating a deal with labor, it's a good idea not to feel self-conscious about making money from the fruits of another's work. And don't try to conceal the fact.

I was an entrepreneur before I knew what the word meant and damn proud of myself. Only fifteen years old and I had five employees and a lot of nerve. The Jews call it chutzpah, the Irish moxie, but we Poles call it balls, and I had them. I grossed over four thousand dollars in fifteen weeks. My net was a lot less, never mind how much. I worked my ass off. I was all over the place: supervising work, collecting money, paying staff, checking on jobs, fixing half-assed work, and doing jobs when kids played hooky or were sick.

I didn't keep books. I didn't even keep bits and pieces of paper, so I had no way of knowing whether I was under- or overcharging my customers. I also had no means to force payment.

Can you imagine the meanness of some people? Stiffing a kid. I'd go to the door. "Your lawn is mowed, and the grounds are clean. The job took one and a half hours. The fee is three dollars." Fat Polly Malone told me she didn't have the money. She said to come back tomorrow. I let her have it. I threatened to set fire to her house, to punch her beer belly, to dig up her grass. She paid up right then and there. I told her no work next time unless she paid the fee in advance. What do you think happened the next week? She paid the fee in advance.

Another family, of Polish descent, devout churchgoers who confessed every Saturday and prayed Sunday, refused to pay. When I told the priest, he paid me from a church fund and said he would get it back from them. No salvation for those who fail to pay Wojo Services!

I fumed but kept my anger from my parents. I knew my mother would say, "Don't let it worry you. Most people are better than that. Try a little more of that meat loaf. It's good for you." And my father: "You probably did a lousy job. My customers always pay me. But I always do a first-rate job."

I had a lot of aggravation even when I collected. Some tried to Jew me down. "The work wasn't worth the price," they'd say. Or, "I could have done it myself. Take what I'm giving you and be happy. It's still too much." Cheap bastards. Cheat a kid. Lowlifes. I got so angry.

Many years later, when interest rates rose steeply and put the squeeze on home owners with adjustable rate mortgages, I thought back to those days and hoped some of those scumbags who tried to cheat me lost their homes and everything else.

The world is full of cheats: poor folk, rich folk. They're out for themselves. Ethics, morals, are figments of a priest's imagination. I learned this as a kid: In the real world, self-interest rules. To hell with everyone else.

In Wojo's second year, I adopted a new policy. Everybody had to pay before the job started. If they had any complaints, they could speak to me. That solved the collection problem.

I was ambitious. I had made money in Riverhead; why not expand to Southampton? I skipped the Southampton mansions: they didn't have kids mowing lawns the size of football fields, and they had bonded professionals as handymen.

I focused on the lower- and middle-class homes in the north. I knew Polish families from church and local Southampton boys from school. Among them was John Warzelbacher, whose father, like mine, was a plumber.

Warzelbacher became my partner in the Southampton business. We employed the same strategy I'd used in Riverhead: first we got the customers, and then we hired the workers.

Warzelbacher proposed starting a messenger service. He thought of it as a way to tap into the summer people, the Wall Street bankers and lawyers who worked during the week in New York and spent weekends in Southampton.

Warzelbacher had two older brothers. One worked as a caddy at Shinnecock Hills and the other as a lifeguard at the Meadow Club, two exclusive clubs with members who can trace their ancestors back to the Mayflower. No ethnic Americans were admitted to either club, even the rich and well connected.

I had not heard of the clubs as a teenager, but as a successful businessman, I came to know them well and—despised them. Why? They excluded me.

Warzelbacher said his brothers were willing to post signs on the bulletin boards of Shinnecock Hills and the Meadow Club advertising the messenger service. I wrote the ad:

> Need to send or receive an important letter or light package? We provide service seven days per week. To NY? Leave your parcel at the manager's desk by 5:00 p.m. We will deliver it by noon the next day. Parcel from NY to Southampton? Leave a note at the desk with pickup instructions. We will get the parcel to the manager's desk by 5:00 p.m. the next day. The charge either way, Southampton to NY or NY to Southampton, is fifteen dollars including all expenses.

Not a single call. What we did not know was that the New York companies provided their own secure messenger services. They were not about to trust an unknown carrier. I showed I was smart enough at sixteen to want to get into the pockets of the summer folk. It would take a while longer to learn how, and when I did, I became one of them. Some guys have no gratitude. Warzelbacher was one. I had shown him the way, made him my partner, and he was making good money on lawn care. But every time I came to collect my share, he had an excuse. Work was not done for some customers. Others failed to pay. When he did give me something, I was sure it was less than half the profits. Why? His mantra was "I do all the work, and you get half the profits. Not fair."

I asked him why he had agreed to an even split. I looked him in the eye and said, "Honor thy contracts." I thought that came from the Jewish Bible, and Warzelbacher was a religious guy. He had great respect for Hebrews, the ancient Jews.

"You told me my job was a snap. Not true. I'm working twelve-hour days."

"You have a point, but a deal is a deal."

Wojo Services ceased operations at the end of its third year. Most of the workers were unwilling to continue working for me. Some customers made direct hires, cutting out Wojo. Many of the boys, at seventeen, went to work for their fathers or uncles. Some enlisted in the military; others were drafted; the Vietnam War was just starting to heat up.

After three years, there was nothing left of Wojo Services. No customers, no employees. Only me. At seventeen, I was street smart, a veteran businessman, and I was hungry—starved—for more. But business would have to wait. My country came first. In April of 1967, I turned eighteen, and two months later, I enlisted in the marines.

# 3

wice a month, *The Saturday Evening Post,* the all-American magazine, arrived at our door. It had Norman Rockwell covers and wholesome, often patriotic articles. On the surface, my family looked like the families in Rockwell illustrations. The head of the household was tall and broad, clearly a working-class guy. His wife was motherhood serving apple pie. The two teenaged children, a girl and a boy, came from central casting.

I formed this impression at a Sunday dinner on a cold day in late February, 1966. Mom had made a pork roast that sat on the table surrounded by bowls teeming with mashed potatoes, beans, and stuffing. On the cupboard sat a large home-baked peach pie that I couldn't wait to dig into. By late that night, the picture of an all-American family had lost its luster.

Close to bedtime, I lay reading a magazine when my mother barged into my room unannounced. "Don't bother to knock," I snarled. "Just waltz in whenever you want."

"Oh, I'm sorry, Henry; I thought you were keen enough to recognize my footsteps. Next time, I'll call your secretary for an appointment."

She flashed the invitation to a party some of the guys and I had been planning. Clipped to the invitation was a list of the kids we had invited.

The idea for the party originated earlier that month. I was soon to turn eighteen and graduate from high school, and Vietnam was the talk of the country. My friends and I were ready and eager to serve our country as our fathers had in World War

II and wanted a bacchanalia cum orgy as an advance payment for risking our necks to save the world from communism.

We planned to hold the party on a Saturday night in a large Southampton house. The houses were empty in the winter but started to fill up on weekends beginning in April. That meant the party had to be held no later than the end of March and, to be safe, closer to the middle. Not exactly graduation time, but it was the best we could do.

Tom Kowalski had worked that fall with his father on the renovation of an old shingle mansion on First Neck Lane. It was almost complete except for a paint job and new furniture. Everything there was shabby and would be discarded after the interior was painted. The house, on four acres, was secluded and off the main road—the perfect party house. Tom's father, who was also the caretaker, had a set of keys that Tom planned to "borrow." We named the party "the Ides of March Ball," even though the fifteenth fell on a Wednesday, and our party was the following Saturday.

The invitation recited the theme of the party, more than just a graduation party: "Come to the graduation/homage party to be held in a Southampton cottage by the sea. We will honor the men off to defend our way of life against communism. Celebrate your very own brave lads soon to become heroes, dead or alive, wounded or unscarred."

At other parties, we drank beer, smoked pot, and some of the boys claimed they scored. There was lots of heavy petting, but I doubt, even under the influence, the good Catholic girls of Riverhead went all the way. None did with me, and I was captain of the football team. We hoped that an element of sympathy, and a large, impressive house with lots of bedrooms, might make a difference. We wanted the girls to know that this party was special and more was expected of them. One guy even suggested we make the pill available. It was a good idea, but we couldn't get pills, not even one. We were such innocents; the guys thought all a woman had to do was take one or two pills to prevent pregnancy.

My mother's discovery of the party threatened its existence. "Where the hell did you get this?" I snapped at her, but I knew the answer. For my twelfth birthday, my parents gave me a metal box filled with fishing tools. I had enjoyed fishing, but within a few years, I tired of it. It required too much patience and luck. I had little of the former and liked to make my own luck. I exchanged the fishing tools for a basketball but kept the box. I didn't want my parents to know I had traded away their present, so I put the box on a prominent shelf in my closet. I soon found a use for it: my memorabilia. I'd hidden the invitation and the list. My mother had gone snooping.

"Don't you raise your voice to me, young man. What's your gang of hoodlums planning, a break-in of a Southampton house? In case you don't know it, that's a crime."

I said that Tom Kowalski's father was the caretaker and had signed on to paint the house in the spring. Tom planned to borrow the keys from his father. We would clean the house after the party. "It will look the same, maybe better," I said.

"Did young Tom tell his father? Don't bother to answer. What would your father do if he learned that a party was planned at a Southampton house under the care of his friend? That would be the end of it." Mom pointed to the guest list. "You apparently didn't invite your own sister, but you did invite your girlfriend, Peggy. I'll make a deal. You add Mary to the list, and I won't tell your father."

"Mom, you raise a good point. Peggy refused to come. She said, 'I wouldn't come within ten miles of Sodom and Gomorrah.' Peggy was right. This party will be wild. It's not for Peggy, and it's not for Mary."

Elizabeth was not placated. "You put Peggy's name down. If it's no place for her, why did you invite her?"

I said that I'd planned to keep an eye on Peggy and make sure she was not molested. I didn't have to add that the most likely person to attack Peggy was yours truly. Mom was no fool.

"Okay, I have the solution. Mary goes to the party in place of Peggy. Let Mary mingle, but you keep an eye on her. Swear to the infant Jesus you will do just that, or I'll spill the beans."

"It's too late," I protested. "We already invited another girl, Janet Kiviatkovski."

Mom said that Janet's name was not on the list. I said only the names of those originally invited were. "I don't care about Janet. Tell your fellow heroes that Mary's coming. You'll do what I asked you to do?" I nodded and said, "I will."

My mother handed me the invitation, and before putting it back in the box, I examined the remnants of my past. There were the flyers from my lawn-mowing business, my varsity letters, and the letter announcing that I was the captain of the football team. I put the invitation back in the box and put it back on a shelf. No reason to find a new home; there was nothing to hide except what had already been discovered.

I went downstairs and knocked on my sister's door. "It's me, Henry; may I come in?"

"Henry? How disappointing. I was expecting Mr. Darcy. Enter. What can I do for you?" Mary was on her bed with an opened book and motioned to a nearby chair.

"Mary, this is about you, not me." I related my conversation with our mother, even the deal and my oath to Jesus.

"Just as I suspected," she said. "You want me to do something so your friends won't blame you for killing the party. I sometimes wonder about the social life Mom says I'm missing. First, I have a question, and I want an honest answer. A girl who will go nameless showed me the invitation. After we finished laughing, she asked, 'Who do you think thought of "heroes living or dead"?' When we recovered again from a fit of laughter, she guessed it was you. Tell me she was right." I said it was a group effort. Mary shook with laughter. "Not one of you was smart enough to invent that piece of corn."

"What's wrong with a little bit of corn at a time like this?"

"Mom wonders why I show no interest in boys. It's not boys in general; it's the morons around here. I'll go, only because I'm curious, but I'm bringing a book for me and one for you. Once I have satisfied my curiosity, we'll spend the evening reading. In that way, I'll expose you to my social life. When I've seen enough of the party, it will be your job to find a reading room and keep the other jerks away. You've ruined the quiet evening I had planned for myself, so it's only fair that the evening you planned be ruined too. Agreed? You don't have to take an oath."

My deals with Mom and Mary guaranteed that the party would be a bummer for me, hero or not. I had no choice. Kowalski had stuck his neck out. He had to be protected. One hurdle was crossed. Mom wouldn't squeal. And so I learned another trick or two about making deals: you can cover your ass by paying off.

We had to take precautions that no one could see evidence of the party once it began. If we got caught, the break-in would be traced to Kowalski. "My father," he said, "will stick my head in a pail of high gloss paint and keep it there until I'm dead. No question." I knew Tom's father, and his fears were not exaggerated.

The boys had contributed three dollars each to pay for beer, pot, and decorations. Tom held the money. We spent a few bucks on rolls of blackout paper. On the day of the party, after the sun was down, Tom and I drove to the house and covered the windows with the paper, securing it with tape. We put the beer in the fridge and the pot in a kitchen drawer, and placed pretzels, chips, and peanuts in bowls around the living room. Garbage pails were strategically placed to make cleanup easy.

We installed a stereo system in the dining room and stacked records nearby. For some of us, Elvis was still king, and we had plenty of his records dating back to the fifties. But the Beatles, Jefferson Airplane, and the Grateful Dead had dethroned the king in many of our eyes, mine included. You didn't have to be the hippest guy around—and I wasn't—to feel the music belonged to us.

For our transportation, we used four trucks borrowed from our fathers. We met at the high school, piled into the trucks, and parked at a lot that was jammed in the summertime but empty the rest of the year. It was a short walk to the mansion.

Most of the girls wore miniskirts. Some of the guys wore Nehru jackets; others had sharp polyester suits. Mary wore a woolen dress reaching to her knees. She selected a turtleneck and khakis for me.

Inside the music blasted. The air was filled with the smell of pot and booze. Couples danced. As the party heated up, one girl danced in her bra. A guy approached Mary and tried to dance with her. She refused; he persisted. I intervened and politely said, "Fuck off."

"Is this what Mom insists I should join on pain of remaining single? What a waste of time. How crude. How vulgar. There must be a room where we can spend our time reading our books. Let's find it."

"Mary, give it another chance."

"We have a deal. Or we had one."

The bedrooms were on the second and third floors. We picked a large one with bright lights and two big, old leather armchairs. Hanging from the doorknob of each room was a two-sided sign with "Vacant" on one side and "Occupied" on the other. I let people know we were busy.

Mary had selected a Dickens novel for me, *Oliver Twist.* "It's a good introduction to the works of an excellent writer," she said. She had started Trollope's *The Palliser Novels.* "The book I'm reading is so quiet. The contrast between it and the racket below is striking. I'd so much rather live in a Trollope novel than in dumb old Riverhead."

We heard doors open and close all around us and music blare and laughter and hollering and a little drunken hooting. Was I envious? Yes and no. I'm a party boy, not a bookworm, but this guy Dickens was better than I remembered from tenth grade.

The party was to end at midnight. At 11:30, Mary and I left our room. At about the same time, Janet Kiviatkovski was leaving a nearby room. She smiled at me and looked askance when she saw Mary. I held my book up and said, "Mary and I were reading. What were you and Frank doing?"

"That was unnecessary," said Mary. "I'm sure Janet was behaving herself." Then with a grin, she said, "I'm not so sure about Frank."

The few who were sober helped with the cleanup. We warned everyone to be quiet on the walk to the trucks. The troops were dropped off at the high school, except for Mary and me. Tom drove her home, and then he and I returned to the party house. We swept the floors, put the bedrooms back in order, carried the garbage pails to the truck, removed the blackout paper, and inspected the house one more time. I suppose Sherlock Holmes could have found clues of the previous activities, but not mere mortals. We turned off the lights and locked the front door and not long after, Tom dropped me off at my house.

From the porch, I overheard Mom and Mary arguing. "For the eleventh time, Henry was wonderful. It's not his job to introduce me to a group of creeps I already know. Why can't you understand? I'm not you, nor am I anybody else. I'm me. Socializing with the Riverhead clan is a closed chapter. Tonight was my first and last. That doesn't mean I don't want to get married. I do, but to a man whose mind I respect. The man I marry will appreciate my mind even more than my body.

"Education is at the top of my list. I'm eager to go to Stony Brook. Marriage can wait. Despite the fact you don't have the foggiest idea about who I am, perhaps because of a generation gap, I love you."

They said good night. Both doused with holy water and went to their rooms. I didn't understand "generation gap," and I was sure neither did my mother. Whatever it meant, it could not explain the differences between Mary and me. I agreed with Mary when she said our mother didn't understand her and was pleased to hear Mary say she loved Mom. The two of them didn't understand me, yet I loved them.

When the house was still, I climbed down to my bathroom and then up to my bedroom, but I had trouble falling asleep. I opened *Oliver Twist* and read for awhile. I must have fallen asleep, because when I awoke, I found the book open on my chest.

# 4

*I*n the 1960s, it was fashionable for young people to look like bums. Not poor and working-class kids, but just about everyone else's kids, including the very rich. They had long, dirty hair and wore torn jeans, wrinkled shirts with holes, and sandals. You name it, they protested against it, from the Vietnam War to the injustice of women having to wear bras. Cops were pigs. People over thirty were scum. They took drugs that made them hallucinate, and they liked those hallucinations better than real life (including work). They didn't even believe in God. They called themselves hippies, because they were hip, and the rest of us weren't. Al Capp drew a cartoon depicting them and titled it "S.W.I.N.E.," an acronym for "students widely indignant about nearly everything." We smoked a little pot in Riverhead and listened to the Grateful Dead, but I agreed with the cartoonist; *they* were pigs.

One bright spring Sunday, the family paid a visit to Stony Brook, Mary's first choice for college and her soon-to-be new home. The buildings and site were magnificent, much too magnificent for the students. The homeless looked cleaner and better dressed than they did. We were in hippie land. Nothing—not news reels, not TV, not newspaper, not Mary—had prepared us for the sight. It wasn't a handful of students; it was all of them. My family were the only ones normally dressed (or, depending on your perspective, abnormally dressed).

One guy had sewn an American flag to the seat of his jeans. Dad wanted to hit him, but Mary restrained him. "In Hitler's

Germany, the Nazis would have shot a guy mocking the swastika. You risked your life in the war against tyranny. What that idiot is doing stinks, but we are fascists if we prevent him from expressing his views. The popular opinions don't need protection, only the unpopular ones. Please, Dad, practice freedom not tyranny."

"I don't need a speech," Dad said and walked away in case Mary kept on.

There was only one student wearing the flag on his derriere, but many expressed the same sentiment. They applauded posters protesting the Vietnam War, cursed President Johnson, and proclaimed black power. They thought of themselves as nonconformists, but in truth, they conformed to an identical nonconformist position. If I were enrolled at that school, I'd have been the only nonconformist.

A student guide, a girl who looked like all the rest, took us on a tour of the library, classrooms, dining halls, dorms, and cafes. Mary told her the college was more beautiful than it looked in the brochure, and that the students were "her kind of people." As we returned to our car, she whispered to me that Stony Brook, after just a few hours, felt more like home than the place she had lived all her life.

Dad was horrified by the scene. He saw an interracial couple kissing and commented, "I thought mixing of the races was illegal in the US of A." Dad also thought the protestors should be arrested. "Isn't that insubordination? Maybe they're Communist spies?" He suggested Mary look again at Southampton College and live at home. I didn't often agree with Andrew, but this time I did. For Mary's sake, I was silent.

Mom too was disturbed. "Tell me, Mary, is taking a bath, washing your hair, and looking pretty out of fashion? I noticed a chapel but no Catholic church. Is there no room for the true faith in this school? Do you intend to throw away your upbringing and become a hippie?"

Mary was fuming. "Mom and Dad, I'm going to say this as succinctly as I can. I don't accept everything the students say and do, but I'm a lot like them. They dress differently from mainstream America to call attention to policies they hate. Challenging authority helps a society grow. It may also cause a nation to change direction. If you can't accept the right of people to speak out like human beings, not act like sheep, then you will lose me."

I don't know whether my parents fully believed Mary's threat, but they were not taking any chances. They made no more comments about Stony Brook or its students, at least none I heard.

The day before I was to leave for the marines, Mary and I trekked around Riverhead. We stopped at our schools, walked the length and breadth of the downtown area, and ended up at St. Isadore's. Mary suggested we enter the church. It was empty. We sat on a bench. I started to talk, but she motioned to be quiet. She was praying. When she finished, she squeezed my hand and kissed my cheek. It was clear that her prayers were for me. When we got outside, I grew sentimental and dropped my tough-guy veneer. "I hope I see Riverhead again."

"Of course you will," said Mary. "Jesus always looks after the Wojecoskis. Don't take chances. I don't want one part of me to die."

Mary started to cry. As we headed for home, I touched her shoulder and said that I would follow Dad's advice and not volunteer for any missions. When she kept crying, I changed the subject. "Since you introduced me to Dickens, I've become obsessed. Books are among the personal items I'm allowed to bring to boot camp. I'm taking *Bleak House.*"

Mary stopped sobbing and said she noticed I was reading. "Think about college. It opens so many paths."

"Business is my future, not school. I suppose your new soul mates don't have much use for money, but I do. I want all the things the very rich have."

"No," said Mary, "that's mammonism. Don't worship material things. Money comes and goes, but expanding your mind stays with you. You have so much potential. Don't throw it away chasing false gods."

The next morning, my parents and I got into the car. We were off to the depot in Suffolk County where the new recruits were to assemble and board buses for the trip to boot camp at Parris

Island, South Carolina. Mary declined to come. She had told me she dreaded the return trip alone with our parents. "I know what they'll sound off about, and I won't be able to escape."

Andrew backed the car down the driveway. Mary stood on the curb, waved, and held a handkerchief to her eyes. "What's she crying about?" said Andrew. "I don't know much about the little yellow fellas you'll be fighting, but I bet they'll be no match for our American boys."

It took us about an hour to reach the depot where the buses were assembled. Andrew was dressed in his army uniform and marched right over to a marine sergeant, saluted, and said, "I fought in a real war." The sergeant smiled, mumbled something about no two wars being the same, and added that his father saw action in the Pacific. I was so angry with my father's display and ashamed at myself for not realizing what he was up to that I turned away from him, kissed my mother good-bye, and slinked onto the bus. I pulled out *Bleak House* and read for the entire enervating trip. I didn't say much to the boys I'd be living with—but not, I prayed, dying with. These were the last hours I'd have to myself for more than a year.

*Bleak House* is a long and complicated book. What impressed me then was how the young heroine, Esther, whose face was scarred by smallpox, found herself loved, despite the disfigurement, by two men, one old and the other young. She promised herself to the older man, John Jarndyce, but fell in love with the younger man, a doctor. Jarndyce, a gentle and generous man, not only released Esther from her commitment but bought a house for the young lovers. How reassuring that inside beauty can trump outside scars. I wondered whether if I returned wounded, a girl, say Peggy, would find me attractive. I thought not, because I'm not a good person. Esther thinks about others and cares for them. I thought only about myself.

I also thought about the interminable law case of *Jarndyce vs. Jarndyce. How* farcical. How could court and legal fees exhaust the estate so that the beneficiaries got nothing? Years later, I used the case to protect my company against excessive litigation costs. "What the hell do you think this is, Jarndyce and Jarndyce?"

I also brought along *Dombey and Son* to boot camp but never got a chance to read it until many years later.

Boot camp lasted twelve weeks. I was awakened each morning at 6:00 a.m. by a drill sergeant who yelled to our barracks, "Wake up, shitheads, scumbags, weaklings. You're not fit to be marines." The words changed each morning, but the sentiment remained the same. We were beneath contempt and a disgrace to the magnificent fighting force known as the United States Marines.

The harassment continued all day. With the temperatures in the nineties, the sergeants made us run for miles with full battle gear, jump over fences and bushes, climb hills, and simulate combat. Parris Island was also home to flies, mosquitoes, and an assortment of pests that got under your skin, which we called chigoes. Quite a few recruits collapsed from heat exhaustion, and many others flunked out.

By the close of camp, I was fit and believed myself invincible and ready for war. I received the eagle, globe, and anchor, the emblems of the marines, and despite the strain and stress of the previous three months, I was proud to be a member of an elite fighting force.

I was then sent to Marine Corps Recruits Depot San Diego to complete my initial training and then to Camp Pendleton for intensive training in jungle warfare. After a course lasting thirty days, we boarded a jet for the base at Da Nang, Vietnam, with stops at Honolulu and Okinawa.

Our enemies were the Vietcong and the North Vietnamese army, collectively called the NVA; our ally, the South Vietnamese forces. The problem: it was impossible to tell them apart.

Back at the base, I watched TV, read newspapers, and talked to other marines. I couldn't figure out what the war was about, and neither could anybody else. I kept asking why we were fighting the very same people we were protecting. The answer was to keep communism from taking over the world. I would never want to be a Communist. But if those funny-looking Asian people want to be Communists, how the hell was it my business? And why should I risk my life to stop them?

Most of the troops agreed with me. We believed the war should end as quickly as possible, and the troops should get shipped home.

We were constantly told that the enemy was nearly defeated, and the war would wind down. President Johnson and the commander of our forces, General Westmoreland, appeared on national television and delivered that very message.

The Tet Offensive belied Johnson's and Westmoreland's rosy pronouncements. Launched by the NVA on January 31, 1968, it was the major battle of the war. The enemy caught our forces by surprise and showed that it had a lot of fight left.

The NVA was initially successful, almost overran our embassy, and came close to capturing Westmoreland's headquarters. The battle lasted three months.

I fought in the Tet Offensive in the battle of Hue. I served in the Third Platoon, Company A, First Battalion, First Marines, First Marine Division. The NVA initially captured Hue. After a battle raging for more than four weeks, we recaptured the treasury building, the university, the hospital, and the provincial headquarters, and raised the flag over the citadel. Hue was secured. Many marines died; many more were severely injured. My buddy was Sergeant Freddy Gonzalez. He was a star high school football player even though he weighed only 135 pounds. He was all courage and heart. We fought together during his second tour of duty. He died a hero's death and was awarded the Medal of Honor. I think about Freddy a lot and wonder what would have happened to him if he had survived.

The NVA suffered much greater losses than we did. Many of its soldiers were teenagers. Some of the enemy's dead didn't weigh a hundred pounds. We tough marines, trained and well equipped, fought against a children's army. My battalion shot kids. I'll say it once and only once: so did I. Why? I didn't know then, and I don't know today.

I hated Lyndon Johnson, I hated the war, and most of all, I hated myself. Many nights, I awoke sweating. In my dreams, I saw the faces of the boys and girls I had shot. The psychiatrist at our base told us not to blame ourselves; we had no choice. It was our lives or theirs. That was pabulum meant to pacify us and keep us going. In fact, most of the dead kids had been unarmed.

Forty years and hundreds of hours of analysis later, I still have nightmares about what happened in the jungles and villages of Vietnam.

The media made much of the My Lai atrocity. There, an army infantry unit, without provocation, opened fire on the civilian inhabitants, killing three hundred innocent villagers. Lieutenant Calley, the officer in charge, was prosecuted. You know what we thought in my battalion? Thank God we weren't there, because we might have done what they did.

What the press didn't report were the terrorist attacks (a term not yet in vogue) by Vietnamese civilians against our forces. One day, I was in Saigon with marines from my battalion, taking a break. We were standing in the street outside a bar and striptease joint when a local boy no more than ten years old came by on his bike. He dropped a cigar box and rode off. Seconds later, the box exploded, killing one of my buddies and seriously wounding two others.

This incident does not justify attacks on civilians. Terrorist activities, however, made it difficult to draw a clear line between civilians and the enemy.

John Kerry was a Vietnam hero who turned against the war. When he ran for president in 2004, he was accused of being a coward. The electorate did not understand. Only those who were there knew the true extent of the atrocities and the horrors of that war. I'm a Republican, but that year I voted for Kerry.

Nixon was elected president in November, 1968. He began troop withdrawals almost as soon as he assumed office. I declined to reenlist and was discharged in June, 1969. I was awarded the Vietnam Service Medal and the Vietnam Service Medal Ribbon. Did I feel like a hero? No, no, no.

When I returned from Vietnam, I loafed about my parents' house, slept late, and stared into space. I didn't want to socialize, so I only went out late at night when the streets were deserted. I was polite to visitors but made it clear I wanted to be alone. There was one exception: my twin sister.

Mary visited every Sunday. The first few times, she said I wore a "please do not disturb" mask, which she would respect. She hardly talked but held my hand and smiled. She stayed for several hours and promised to return the following Sunday. I liked her company, waited eagerly for Sunday.

On her third visit, I smiled as she entered my room. I asked her to tell me all about paradise—where people who hadn't been to Vietnam dwelled. She was off and running. Her dual majors were nursing and the humanities. Taking a heavy load of courses combined with summer school, she had graduated from the school of nursing. She worked as a nurse in the hospital attached to the college, and in addition, she was taking graduate courses. Her goal was to become a nurse practitioner with a specialty in cardiac surgery. She was also nearing the end of the requirements for an AB in the humanities. "I want to be able to support myself either as a nurse or an English lit teacher or both. I'm never getting married. I must be independent. I don't want to rely on a man. Women are human beings. I refuse to be some man's slave."

Her resolve against marriage weakened as a relationship with a doctor blossomed. Although he was young, she thought he was about the best cardiac surgeon in the hospital. The very next week, he rose from the best in the hospital to the best in all of New York. "He is," she said, "like us in one respect. His ancestors emigrated from Lvov, an ancient city founded in the thirteenth century in Poland." She told me that when Poland was conquered by neighboring countries, Lvov became, depending on the conqueror, part of Austria, Russia, the Ukraine, and the Soviet Union. After World War I, Poland emerged as a nation, and Lvov became part of it. David's distant relative, who remained in Lvov until 1940, wrote a book titled *Why I Speak Four Languages*, reflecting on his life under different rulers. "David is fascinating," my sister said, beaming. I had never seen her so happy, and I was startled and a little uncomfortable because I was so miserable, but I didn't want to dampen her pleasure.

I asked what she meant when she implied he was different from us. "I'll tell you if it becomes relevant, but we are as different as the Lodges and the Kellys. Oh, there's another way we are not different. Half the books in his library were also in mine, and the other half are books I want to read."

I asked how she got to inspect his library. "Mind your own business," she said and then added, "He's a perfect gentleman, Goddamn it!"

Mary's mentions of David trailed off in later visits. When I asked what was new on the David front, she said he had abandoned Stony Brook for the greener pastures of Columbia Presbyterian Hospital and was teaching at Columbia University's medical school. "He does come out to Stony Brook to see me. Not as often as I would want, but he's busy and so important. I tell you this in confidence. I don't see anyone else, and I don't believe he does either. Separation tests the depth of our feelings. I miss him terribly."

Mary's chatter about her doctor affected me. I wanted to talk too and decided to tell her about my years in the marines, which quickly made her cry. When she saw me crying too, she wiped my eyes with her handkerchief and said, "Don't let those fascist pigs ruin your life. Say, 'Fuck you, pigs,' and put that horrible experience behind you."

I didn't say "Fuck you, pigs," right then and there. But I did right after Mary left and many times thereafter. I was not a hippie crying this to anyone who would listen, but I wasn't a warmonger—what they called a hawk. I was a dove who eventually wanted to make a lot of money.

The heart sustains life; the brain controls its quality. In my head, the billions of ions controlling my mood were impaired. I was in a funk. For many months after my return, I just didn't want to do anything.

Even my father recognized that I was depressed. Being a veteran, he knew the symptoms; he'd had them himself after his discharge. He said work sped his recovery. "Come to work with me. It's the best medicine to shake the blues. It did the trick for me. It'll do it for you too."

I told him I respected his work. Plumbing was challenging and the pay was good, but I wanted to do something else. What, I did not yet know. He patted me on the shoulder, said he had confidence I would find my way and that the door was always open to work with him. I thanked him, even gave him a hug. It was one of the very few civil discussions we have had about plumbing.

I kept to myself the fear that if I were to become a plumber, I might turn into my father.

Hard work may have rescued my father; it was Mary's visits that saved me. She and I had started life in the same womb at the same time and grew up in the same household. Her life had purpose and direction. She had launched one career in nursing and would soon embark on a second in literature. I was proud of her and ashamed of myself. I had to make a move.

It didn't happen little by little or even one day at a time; it happened all at once. On a Monday morning, after a delightful Sunday visit with my sister, I vowed to get off my butt and rejoin the human race. I leaped out of bed, raced to the basement, showered, shaved, and announced to the walls, "This is it. I'm on my way."

For starters, I needed a job. My mother said there was an opening for an office boy at Kaplan & Company, the accounting firm where she worked. "You're so good with numbers. You have the stuff to become a top-notch accountant." I applied for the job and got it. My starting salary was seventy-five dollars per week. That sounds like slave wages today, but in 1969, the minimum hourly wage was $1.60; indexed to inflation in 2010 dollars, it amounted to $10.10. Using the same index, my salary then was the equivalent today of about $750.

What I learned at Kaplan was that I didn't want to be an accountant but that I had a knack for what to do with money. I was still a lad, but I had come a long way since I started mowing lawns.

# 5

This happens many times. Two young lovers separated by circumstances remain apart for twenty years. They marry others. Then, by chance, they meet. The years vanish, and the love that once was is rekindled. The force is so strong that it overcomes their will. They abandon their families and start a new life together.

It was the Wednesday before I was to start work at Kaplan. I went downtown to get a haircut. As I left the barbershop, who should I meet but Peggy Woijek. With a broad smile, I said, "Have we met before?"

She didn't miss a beat. "I think it was the ides of March party in a Southampton mansion." Peggy, of course, had refused to attend despite my passionate entreaties. I had not seen her in several years, and she was prettier than I had remembered. I laughed and did something crazy that took even me by surprise: I lifted her into the air and twirled her around until she begged to be put down.

Peggy was enrolled at Southampton College, majoring in art history, and working at the Parrish Art Museum. I told her I was starting a career in business. I blurted out that I was determined to be successful so that I could afford to marry her. Peggy appeared to be shocked. "Henry Josef Wojecoski, I have no intention of marrying you." But her fluttering eyes and her body language told a different story. As soon as she issued her declaration, she took a step toward me and tilted her head up, and I did what any sane man would do. Right there at noon on Main Street in Riverhead, we sealed the bargain with a kiss.

I am eternally glad we met again after only a short separation. I hate to think of the damage we might have done if our meeting had been delayed for twenty years.

I now had the strongest of incentives to succeed.

At Kaplan & Co., I threw myself into the assigned tasks. As I performed them, new ones were added. I soon became the office factotum. I answered the telephone, ran errands, filed papers, and learned rudimentary double-entry accounting. The office opened at 9:00 a.m. I arrived at 8:30. The office closed at 5:00; I stayed many days until 6:00. During the work day, I asked to help those who were overloaded. My willingness to work made me popular with the staff; it also attracted the attention of Morris Kaplan, the owner of the company and its senior CPA.

Kaplan took the time to teach me accounting. I became so good that Kaplan sometimes took me along on calls to clients.

One of the firm's most important clients was a branch office of Amalgamated Loan and Finance Company, a company operating throughout the country that was engaged in making small loans. I went there with Kaplan to assist him and later, on a few occasions, worked there alone. I met the operating personnel and called loan officers. Once, I had lunch with several young officers. I must have made a good impression, because I was invited to Amalgamated's Christmas party. I would have been invited to Kaplan & Co.'s party, but there wasn't one. Old man Kaplan was Jewish. Although he was the only Jewish person at the firm, he was the boss. Companies are not democratic institutions; they are dictatorships.

I liked Kaplan. He was kind, patient, and a good teacher. He was my first business mentor. Working at his side, I formed a lasting impression that accountants performed an essential function, without which a business cannot operate. I thought about Wojo Services. Abysmally run. Not a single record. Many years later, I ran Amalgamated and then a hedge fund. I always had accountants close by.

I considered going to school and becoming an accountant. Kaplan encouraged me and even offered to help with tuition. I was flattered, and I almost said yes on the spot, but I held back and thought about it overnight. Accountants provided a service not unlike plumbers or carpenters. They helped others. True, accountants were a big step up on the ladder. They dressed well, kept clean, and were solidly middle class. I recognized the interdependence of accounting and business. Of the two, I preferred business. What I wanted was to run a business. I wanted to be Mr. Kaplan's client, not Kaplan himself.

Lending money is a sound business. It has no inventory problems, no going out of business sales—in fact, no markdowns at all. Its inventory is currency, money, nice and clean, stored at a bank. The company makes loans to customers whose savings are insufficient to meet a pressing need: a wedding, a medical emergency, home additions, repairs, and general improvements.

When the lender has exhausted its own capital, it borrows money from a bank at wholesale rates. It then lends out the borrowed money at retail, i.e., higher rates. Of course, there is risk. Some loans will default. Volume makes up for that. It spreads the risk among many borrowers. It also makes for hefty profits.

Shakespeare gave the business a bad name. He lived mostly in the sixteenth century, before the Industrial Revolution. Financing was not thought of then as the fuel that runs industry. In October 2008, when the credit markets went dry, business came to a halt. That's how important credit is.

Amalgamated didn't finance major corporations, but on a lower level, it provided the means for consumer purchases, which, in turn, made businesses hum. The image of Shylock, a greedy, weeping old man, was outdated centuries ago.

After working at Kaplan & Co. for a year, I applied for a job at Amalgamated. Kaplan gave me a wonderful letter of recommendation. Ed Dominico, the head of the office, hired me. I started as a collection agent. The job came with a perk, my first ever—the use of a company car. A collection agent has to travel all over the county. I didn't abuse the privilege, but I did like showing off. Many times, I took a shortcut through my neighborhood, tooted the horn, and waved at people I knew. Very few guys my age drove a company car.

I had had plenty of experience collecting at Wojo Services. I used the same technique. I embarrassed borrowers at work by announcing in a loud voice, "Don't you feel lousy failing to pay your loan? Let's arrange now with your boss to pay your debt. He can deduct each week from your wages until the loan is repaid."

Would you believe some of these deadbeats claimed not to owe a cent! I'd pull out the loan agreement and issue a threat: "If you don't arrange to pay, the next guy you hear from will be the sheriff. He'll come with handcuffs."

I didn't know if that was true, but neither did the borrower. And I was big and mean looking. Most times, I convinced the debtor to have a fixed amount deducted from his salary and sent to Amalgamated.

Deadbeats out of work presented a more difficult problem. I went to their homes. If they had a TV or a car, I asked for collateral. I promised to return the collateral when the debt was paid. Most times, it wasn't, and Amalgamated sold the collateral. Life is tough. My motto is this: don't borrow if you can't repay.

A collection agent got paid as much as a junior loan broker. But I didn't want to be a collection agent all my life. A year later, I became a loan broker.

The Riverhead branch was Amalgamated's only office in Suffolk County. The county is vast and sprawling, occupying two thirds of Long Island. It includes 142 towns and villages and half a million people. Although there are small enclaves of wealthy families (mainly in the Hamptons and the town of Huntington), most of the residents are working or lower middle class, the very people served nationally by Amalgamated.

I regarded borrowers with a healthy amount of suspicion. Incurring debt was appropriate if the funds were invested productively or needed to meet an unexpected event. I deemed it morally wrong to use loan proceeds for a self-indulgent purpose. Rather than borrow, I urged some to seek a second job or part-time work for a stay-at-home spouse.

I was different from loan officers who made loans based on the borrowers' employment record. Their only concern was whether the borrower's salary covered his living expenses and monthly repayments. I applied a homespun philosophy in deciding whether to make a loan. Was it necessary? How would the proceeds be used? Could money be obtained through taking a second job? And even after the loan passed my personal smell test, I investigated to determine whether the borrower had gotten the best price. I was one of the few loan officers who looked behind the data to external circumstances. My insight into a borrower's needs gained the respect and trust of my customers. They recommended me to their family members and friends. In a business in which loyalty is rare, I developed a book of devoted customers.

My salary was one hundred dollars a week including a Christmas bonus. I gave my mother ten dollars weekly for room and board and spent about ten dollars on dates with Peggy, whom I saw almost every weekend. My salary was not enough to get married on, but Peggy was patient. "We're young. I can wait. I have a lot left to do before I tie myself down to babies."

My time at Amalgamated was a happy change from my Vietnam years. I had a girl, a job, and a chance for a future.

There was a change too for Mary. David returned to Stony Brook. He was named chief of cardiac surgery, the youngest head in a major hospital in the country. Mary moved into David's apartment and said with a big smirk, "It was the only way I could get access to his library."

There was a problem: he was Jewish. Before I had met David, Mary told me how they had solved the problem with his parents.

In orthodox Jewish families, children who marry out of the faith are considered dead. The family recites the kaddish, the prayer for the deceased, and observes a week of mourning. The Markowitzes were not orthodox. David was their only child, and no matter what he did, the parents would never abandon him. David knew that. With tongue in cheek, he proposed a solution to the dilemma: he and his parents would convert to Catholicism. "The Jews of Portugal and Spain did," he said, "and they were observant Jews. The converts continued in secret to observe Jewish rituals and gave lip service to the rites of Catholicism. We can do the same. We'll go to temple on Yom Kippur and eat matzos on Passover. In fact, Mary will go with us. That's all the religious holidays we observe. In the same spirit, we'll all go to church on Christmas and Easter Sunday. In that way, we'll be one happy, ecumenical family."

David had deftly shifted the focus from whether he should marry a shiksa to whether he and his parents should convert to Catholicism.

When David brought Mary to meet his parents, she preempted the subject of conversion. "For twenty-five years, I've lived in an observant Catholic home. We use more holy water than drinking water. We have framed prints of Jesus and Mary in every room and crosses over every bed. The pope himself could live in our house and not find it lacking any rite or ritual. If Catholicism is the one true faith, salvation is my right. I've paid my dues. Your son told me the Markowitz family observes one fast day a year and eats matzos instead of bread for two days. I'm converting to Judaism."

Benjamin Markowitz was so happy, he kissed her on the cheek and spent the next hour teaching her the hora. Carole took Mary shopping. They bought the ingredients for chicken and matzo ball soup. After they made the soup, Carole said, "Now that you know how to dance the hora and make chicken soup, I declare you a Jew. You don't have to formally convert. Our eyes tell us you are the most beautiful of Jews. David tells us you are the smartest."

The happy couple turned their attention to winning over the Wojecoskis.

Mary invited David to the house on a Saturday morning. Before he arrived, she told the family, "This is the man I love. He's the most marvelous man in the world. If you are so bigoted and blinded by prejudice and cannot accept him, make no mistake: I will reject you."

Elizabeth rubbed her eyes and crossed herself.

Andrew bowed his head and left the room.

I wanted to dance for joy. "Mary, since you love David, I love David."

Moments later, there was a knock at the door. It was David. Mary didn't have to introduce him; he took care of that. "Andrew, you and I are both plumbers. When pipes are plugged, you unplug or bypass them. I do the same with arteries that are blocked. The heart has four valves. They allow blood to flow in and out of the heart's chambers. Plumbing valves control the flow of water. When they leak, you replace them; when heart valves leak, I replace them. We're in the same line of work."

"How do you like that?" said Andrew. "From now on, call me Dr. Wojecoski." In ten minutes, David had won over Andrew, a feat I had not accomplished in a lifetime.

David then turned his charm on Elizabeth. "You and me are going to make a million dollars. Tell me where you find the rare herbs you brew into your body cream. We'll package it and with your face on the bottle sell it as the elixir of beauty."

Elizabeth rushed into his opened arms and said, "I see why Mary loves you so much."

David was dressed casually in a blue sweater and pressed tan slacks. In a flash, he removed his sweater and slacks, revealing a blue satin workout outfit. He opened a gym bag, kicked off his shoes, and put on a pair of signature Kareem Abdul-Jabbar basketball sneakers. He was as tall as I was, about six foot two, but his arms were longer. His wingspan was equivalent to that of a guy four inches taller. His hair was dark and wavy; his eyebrows, thick. His ears were large and stuck out from his head. He was not handsome, but he was athletic. He bolted out of the house and returned with a basketball. "Well, big brother, do you know what this is? It's a basketball. Your baby sister said you were a star in high school." He then head-faked, I fell for it, and he darted around me and tossed the ball at the ceiling. "Put on your sneakers, and let's go."

We played half-court pickup basketball for over an hour in the playground down the street from our house. We were unselfish, passing the ball to each other rather than hogging it. We rebounded and defended aggressively. Nobody could beat us. For two guys who had just met, we played as though we had been on the same team for years.

We were both soaking wet when we got home. I took David to the basement, where we showered. He changed back into his sweater and slacks. I loaned him a shirt. When we returned to the living room, we looked very much like the brothers we had become.

They had a civil wedding. I was the best man. Andrew and Elizabeth hosted a lunch at the Perkins. I invited Peggy. The newlyweds left for a two-week honeymoon in France and Italy. Before leaving, Mary kissed Peggy and whispered in her ear. Peggy blushed slightly and glanced at me. There was, of course, no need to tell me what Mary had said.

When Mary and David returned from Europe, they moved into a home in Stony Brook overlooking Long Island Sound. It was a wedding present from David's parents.

Stony Brook is less than an hour from Riverhead and about the same distance from the Markowitz home in Roslyn. David and Mary were comfortable with both sets of parents. The in-laws were not so comfortable with each other. Benjamin Markowitz was a stockbroker on Wall Street. His wife was an avid gardener and a concert bassoonist. The two sets of parents had nothing in common except their children and, later on, their grandchildren. They were polite but distant. It was different between David and me. We were brothers from the outset.

# 6

*Y*oung office workers are happy to see the work week end, and many celebrate with a drink or five in a nearby watering hole. In the 1960s, the ritual was named "thank God it's Friday" (TGIF). At our office, it was part of our religion. We held services every Friday beginning at 5:00 p.m. at the bar at the Perkins, drank tap beer, and gossiped about work, sex, and sports.

One Friday in mid-February of 1974, Ed Dominico, an Amalgamated assistant vice president and the manager of our office, was seated at our traditional table. We knew something special was in the air because he rarely came to our Friday sessions. "Hey," he said, "don't I know you jerks from somewhere?" We laughed, pulled up chairs, and sat down.

Joe Keegan brought up business. He was the top producer and wanted to make sure Dominico knew: "Low man on number of loans closed buys a round. No bullshitting. We'll go around the table. State your numbers. Ed's here, and he'll know if you're lying."

I was the last to speak. I had closed the fewest. Let them boast about quantity; I'd brag about quality. "I've closed the fewest loans, three," I said, "but my loans don't go to the crapper. They don't even fart."

"So what? You buy," said Paul Toski.

Dominico signaled for quiet and said, "No, I'm buying. Wojecoski's loans have all been solid. In three years, not a single default. That's unique. This year, the company is honoring the outstanding broker from each state. I've nominated Henry for loan broker of the year from New York. I've canvassed other managers, and when I told them of Henry's perfect record, they agreed to his selection. My Rochester counterpart called Henry a 'fuckin' miracle' and claimed he must walk on water. The Albany chief said he wished just one of his brokers could close a loan that stayed performing for at least a month. Another asked to borrow Henry for a year. Now, let's drink to Wojecoski. Salute, Henry! I gotta run. You shitheads pump him for his tricks and see if you can figure out how to keep your customers paying their goddamn loans. Maybe next year I can nominate the entire office for an award."

Our Friday sessions generally lasted about two hours, long enough to down three beers. That day's session ended with one round. After Dominico departed, our usually raucous table became quiet. Then, one by one, the guys peeled off. Some made excuses; others left without saying anything. Only Keegan and I were left.

"Congratulations," he said as he got up to leave. He added, "It's easy to be perfect if you make only a few pissy loans. Rainmakers like me have big balls. We take chances. This shitty outfit doesn't appreciate me. Don't tell anyone, but I've got some pretty important irons in the fire."

I gave Keegan the finger and said, "What's the big job? Collecting garbage?"

The others were jealous; my work received recognition. Did I feel triumphant? Did I want to pound my chest? Did I want to celebrate? Did I even want to tell Peggy or my folks? No. Athletes get excited when they win. Victory for me meant a transfer to New York City. Why New York? Peggy loved New York. To her, the city was the art capital of the world. Home to hundreds of museums and art galleries. She cried with happiness every time she left for New York and cried with sadness when she returned. She said she would be happier in a tiny apartment there than in a spacious home in Riverhead.

I shared her dream. New York was the major leagues of the business world. That's where the princes of finance lived and worked, and I wanted to be one of them in my daydream of daydreams. I also wanted to marry Peggy and make her happy. In my present state, anything seemed possible.

On Monday, the Amalgamated package alluded to by Dominico arrived. Inside was a letter from Richard E. Hargrave, the president and chairman of the board; the company's annual report; a schedule of activities for the convention; a tag with my name and the designation "Loan Broker of the Year—New York State"; and a check for two hundred dollars.

The letter called loan brokers "the heart and soul" of the company. "Every year beginning with 1974, on the second weekend in April, the outstanding broker from each state will be celebrated at a convention in New York. The winners will receive a check for two hundred dollars plus travel and out-of-pocket expenses."

On the back of my letter was a handwritten note initialed R. E. H. "Henry: What an achievement! Three years of perfect loans! You hold the company record. No good deed goes unpunished. I'd like you to lead a workshop and teach this year's best brokers your techniques on how to weed out the bad and promote the good. If you're willing, we've got time on Saturday afternoon. Beverly Ryan, my secretary, will help you."

The convention was two months away. I had a lot of work to do. But on that Monday, my heart was filled with hope. I had an opening: run the workshop and score a touchdown.

I worked every night and all day on the weekends preparing for the convention. I wrote scripts for mock interviews with customers, which closely followed my actual sessions. I called Hargrave's secretary and told her I planned to put on a play and needed three couples to act as husbands and wives. I asked whether she could find suitable actors within the company's ranks. "If possible," I said, "make them young and attractive." She laughed and quipped, "I'll call central casting." I said the scripts were handwritten. Before I could make a request, she offered to send a messenger to pick them up, type them, and return the original and one copy to me. It was my first taste of corporate life.

There was nothing scheduled for the Friday afternoon of the convention except check-in at the New York Hilton, at Rockefeller

Center, a few blocks from Amalgamated's offices. I asked Beverly if I could meet the actors at about 2:00 p.m. on Friday and suggested she pick the place. She said she would reserve a conference room near Hargrave's office for the rehearsal. She also suggested that she line up five couples and I choose the best three.

The workshop gave me an opportunity to shine. The annual report contained a clue as to a second and even bigger opportunity for me.

At home, my reading room was the bathroom installed for me by my father in the basement when I was eight. It was private, quiet, and had good light, and the toilet seat was comfortable (later, I dubbed the seat the best ergonomic design of all time). The company's annual report was in my crosshairs, and I placed it on top of the toilet tank, which served as my book rack.

On the first page was a photograph of Hargrave alongside a heading, "President's Letter." It discussed Amalgamated's financial performance for 1973. The company was profitable for the year, as it had been for the past thirty-five years. Hargrave noted, however, that results overall were lower for the third year in a row. "Management," he said, "is determined to reverse the trend. A task force of senior executives advised by investment bankers has been formed to find and develop a new line of business related to the company's core activity. I hope to report next year that 1974 was a banner one."

I thought about joining the search for a new business but then despaired. How could I, an uneducated, inexperienced loan officer, perform a task daunting for professionals? I remembered a passage from a book I had read as a child. It was about a track star in high school so certain of defeat that he refused to try out for the US Olympic team. The coach encouraged the boy to compete. "No one ever won a race by not entering." The book ended with the young runner winning a gold medal.

If I came up with an idea, I might have an opportunity at the convention to present it to Hargrave. Even if he didn't accept it, it would give me another chance to put myself in front of him. I'd suggest that I work on the new business out of headquarters. I imagined Peggy's face as I told her the news: "Peggy, I'm moving to New York. Will you come with me?" Just before going to sleep, I resolved, like the runner in the book, to go for the gold.

The idea for a new business would not descend from the heavens to my brain. I would have to do a lot of research. Southampton College's library was open to the public. On weekends, I went there and read articles on financing, many involving real estate.

Real estate prices on the east end of Long Island were on the rise. In Riverhead, comparable houses to those sold a few years earlier were on the market at hefty increases. The market there could not compare with the red-hot market in the Hamptons. Oceanfront properties were selling for over one million dollars. Year-round houses owned by locals were being snapped up by New Yorkers at high prices. The housing market was a hot topic of conversation even at our house.

"Did you hear," said my father, "the Bevandoskis sold their house for fifty thousand dollars? Our house is better located, larger, and in better condition. I'll bet I could get sixty-five thousand dollars if I were willing to sell. I'm not. Nice to know we're rich."

The escalation in home prices was not confined to eastern Long Island. Other areas were also experiencing a boom. Some days, I just stared into space and thought, *How the hell can a consumer loan company capitalize on the booming housing market?* Then it came to me, but it was complicated and difficult to explain, even for me, the originator of the idea. I remembered Pat McGinnis's comment about making a deal simple when I was a kid eating lunch with him in Southampton. I needed practice.

On Friday, I took Peggy to dinner and said I would treat. Peggy looked surprised, as we usually split the bill. When she raised her eyebrows and teasingly asked what I wanted in return, I said, "Only your ear."

After we were served beers and ordered our dinners, I jumped right in. "Peggy, real estate prices are on the rise. It's the talk of the town."

"You're the first person to mention it. Why do you bring it up? What difference does it make? I don't own a house, and neither do you."

Sidney B. Silverman

"Our parents do," I said. Peggy blew that off. "My parents aren't ever going to sell, and neither are yours. See that big oak? There is as much chance of our parents moving as that tree. I know about the art market. You can sell a painting by a well-known artist, buy lots of paintings by unknown artists, and hope they gain recognition. That has nothing to do with our home sweet home. We're not going to sell our house and buy six shacks."

"I agree. Forget sell. Suppose you were heavily in debt and paying a high interest rate? Suppose you needed lots of cash to buy a business? Suppose the only way you could borrow a big chunk of dough was to take out a new mortgage on your home? Would you do it?"

"Wait a minute. We have a mortgage on our house. How can we put a new one on?"

"The old mortgage has priority over the new one. Until the old is paid, the new gets nothing. So what? When Andrew and Elizabeth bought their house, they paid fifteen thousand dollars. They paid five thousand in cash and borrowed the rest from the bank. As security for the loan, the bank put a mortgage on the house. The bank's loan was safe because the house was worth fifteen thousand dollars—five thousand dollars more than the loan. If my parents failed to meet their mortgage payments, the bank would kick them out, take over the house, and sell it. The bank keeps ten thousand dollars and forks over the balance to my poor parents, who are out on the street.

"Today, my parents' home is worth sixty-five thousand dollars—that's what similar homes in the neighborhood are selling for. Over the years, the mortgage has been paid down to five thousand dollars. A new loan of forty thousand dollars, secured by a second mortgage, would give the bank collateral of sixty thousand dollars. Since a mortgage is already on the property, the new mortgage is a second mortgage. A company in the business of making loans should jump at making second mortgages. Borrowers needing money and owning homes that have shot up should seize the opportunity."

"I get it," said Peggy. "The loans made by Amalgamated are small loans and are not secured. Large loans require security. If people like our parents need a large loan, their only security is their homes. Since real estate has appreciated, so has their security. Will banks make second mortgages?"

"Peggy, give up art and come into business. You're a natural. Banks are too stodgy to make second mortgages, but Amalgamated might. It's looking for a new business. Second mortgages might just be it. But here comes our dinner."

We gossiped over dinner, but I was thinking about business. So was Peggy. As I was paying the bill, she said loans are used to buy paintings. "Would you believe the collateral for the loan is the painting? A house is much better security. You like the accountant Kaplan. Why not test your idea on him? I'll bet you won't even have to buy him dinner."

On the way home, Peggy asked if Amalgamated needed a new business. When I said yes, she asked, "What's wrong with its old business?"

"You mentioned Kaplan. He taught me how to read a financial statement. Reading between the lines, Amalgamated is doing lousy. I'll discuss that with Kaplan, along with second mortgages."

"Henry, I take it back. If you have to, buy Mr. Kaplan dinner."

Five years before, when I had started work at Kaplan & Co., he and I carried lunch boxes. I'd asked my mother, "I know why I bring lunch to work, but why does the boss?"

"Mr. Kaplan is kosher," she said. "That means he can eat only special food prepared in a special way and served on special plates. There are no kosher restaurants in Riverhead. I respect him for observing his religion's rituals."

Depending on the weather, he ate in the office or in a park a short walk away. During the year I worked at Kaplan & Co., I often ate lunch in the park, saw Kaplan, but sat at a separate bench. I thought it might violate his religion if I sat at the same table eating, say, a ham and cheese sandwich.

All this time later, on a clear but chilly day in March, I found Mr. Kaplan at a table in the park. I greeted him and asked if I could sit down. When he smiled and nodded yes, I took the seat across from him. When I told him about my three-year record of no loans defaulting, my selection as New York state broker of the year, and the Amalgamated celebration to honor one broker from each state, he beamed. "Henry," he said, "you've got the right stuff. Keep it up."

Encouraged by Kaplan's warmth, I said Amalgamated was pumping up earnings by including interest on nonperforming loans even though the company received not one red cent. A footnote explained that Amalgamated recorded such phantom income as long as efforts were being made to collect. When the branch manager declared further efforts would be futile, the loan was declared "defaulted," and no further income was reported.

Kaplan said general accepted accounting principles, referred to as GAAP, permitted the practice. He did not like the accounting convention; he thought it distorted performance. When I said I'd spotted the practice through the discrepancy between cash flow and earnings, he reached over and said, "I see you remember what I taught you—trust cash flow. No wonder your company places a high value on your record of perfect loans."

Only then did I turn to the real purpose, my new business plan.

"Small loans default," I said, "because they are not secured. I've thought of a new business for Amalgamated—loans secured by second mortgages. What do you think?"

"If the property has appreciated in excess of the first mortgage, and the housing market remains stable or moves up, it might turn out to be a better business than small loans. But you have to be careful. The market swings widely. You should test market value against a property's intrinsic value—i.e., the cost to reproduce the house less depreciation. Intrinsic value is to market what cash flow is to earnings. Intrinsic and market should be close; so should cash flow and earnings."

I had one more question. I asked Kaplan how I should dress for the convention. "Wear a dark blue suit, a button-down white shirt, and a conservative striped tie. Make sure your shoes are black and polished. Bring along a sport coat, slacks, casual shirt, and loafers in case you have free time. At the convention and at meetings at Amalgamated's office, always wear your blue suit. It's a business uniform."

I asked where I could buy the clothes. Kaplan suggested Shep Miller's in Southampton. "They carry a classic line of men's clothes. What you buy there will be correct."

I gained confidence from my lunch with Kaplan. Hargrave might not accept it, but I would not look like a fool. When I returned to the office, I called Hargrave's secretary, Beverly, and asked if his schedule permitted a meeting on the Friday of the convention. She gave me an appointment at 10:30.

I revised the script for the workshop and mailed it to her. When I called to make sure it had arrived, she said she would leave the original and one copy with the front desk of the Hilton to hold for my arrival. "Don't worry," she said. "I'm keeping a copy. If the Hilton slips up, I'll make copies." She added, "I'm interested in meeting the new star from the east." *It's time*, I thought, *for the "new star" to buy his new clothes.*

I went to Shep Miller's on the Saturday before the convention. The store screamed, "We cater to quiet old money." I felt lost, out of place, until a man, definitely gay, with a full head of gray hair, dressed in a suit and tie, greeted me, called me "sir," and in a decidedly English accent asked how he could "assist" me. I told him I worked for Amalgamated, had been designated loan broker of the year from New York State, and on Friday would be off to a company convention in New York. There would be several business meetings, and as the representative from New York, I wanted to be dressed properly. He congratulated me, shook my hand, and motioned me to follow him. He picked out the clothes. All I did was try them on and pay.

The bill was a month's salary. I wondered whether I could charge my purchases to out-of-pocket costs as mentioned in Hargrave's letter. Just in case, I saved the receipt.

Years later, when I was rich and owned a summer home in Southampton, I shopped at Shep Miller's. I always sought out the same salesman who had helped when I was a raw kid. He remembered the young Henry and said I was a confident young man.

On the Friday of the convention, I arose at dawn, dressed in my new clothes, and dashed to the railroad station as I had seen commuters do in cartoons. I boarded the early morning train and arrived at the Hilton at nine o'clock.

I'm not particularly religious, but in times of great need, I pray to Jesus. I prayed every day in Vietnam. Now it was my business future, not my life, at stake. Was it proper to turn to Jesus? Would He think I was wheedling Him? I took a chance.

# 7

*O*nce I checked in and spent some time admiring my twentieth-floor room, I headed out to my appointment with Hargrave. I took no notice of the large towers lining both sides of the Avenue of the Americas or of the throngs rushing by me. I entered Amalgamated's building and pressed ten on the elevator board. The door opened to a reception area where an elderly woman greeted me. A few minutes later, a much younger woman appeared, walked directly toward me, smiled, and reached for my hand. "I'm Beverly Ryan, and you must be Henry Wojecoski. Mr. Hargrave is expecting you."

Beverly was an attractive woman who just missed being beautiful. Her features were too pronounced, her figure too plump. As we approached Hargrave's office, she said in a low whisper, "Don't be intimidated. Mr. Hargrave may seem like a god, but he's a mere mortal."

Her advice did not cure the yips. I was frightened, so frightened that when Hargrave greeted me and we shook hands, his appearance did not register. I did see him look at his watch and heard him say, "Well, young man, you have a business plan. Let's hear it."

I had practiced my speech so many times that I knew it by heart—except for the very moment I was to deliver it. In a flash, it came back, and I had to remind myself to go slowly:

"Middle-class people owe money to loan companies and to credit card companies. They owe on cars, taxes. They pay very high interest rates, plus they have the burden of making different payments. They'd be better off converting all their debts into a jumbo loan at a lower interest rate. If Amalgamated provides the loan, the company wins and so does the customer—but how can we do this?"

For the first time, my eyes focused on Hargrave. He seemed very old, but at that stage of my life, everyone over forty-five seemed ancient. Everything about him was large. His head, belly, eyeglasses. He was bald except for a wisp of gray hair atop his head. His nose dominated his face. It was thin, sharp, and resembled the beak of a hawk. He wore a brown suit, blue shirt, and a loud tie. What would Shep Miller think of his outfit?

Hargrave was enthroned in a high swivel chair surrounded by oversized furniture, including a mahogany desk. In front of the desk were two chairs. I sat in one. A couch, coffee table, and two chairs were set against the rear wall. Off to the side were a conference table and six more chairs. It felt more like a cluttered museum than an office. Dominico didn't have an office. He sat in the same room with all of us, only off in a corner. Mr. Kaplan's office was about a quarter the size.

I paused to make sure Hargrave was following me. He looked annoyed by the brief silence and turned his chair around so that the back of his head faced me. "Is that it?" he said.

Hargrave's action and tone of voice were insulting. I had worked hard and put so much stock in my presentation, only to find that Hargrave didn't want to hear it. I wanted to say, "You discourteous old bastard. Turn around and listen to me." Instead, I said, "There is a lot more to my plan, but since you have turned your back to me, I take it you have heard enough." He turned his chair around, saying he was under stress, and asked me to continue. That was the entire apology I was going to get.

"Home values are on the rise. Most have appreciated above existing mortgages. Also, the first mortgages have been reduced through years of monthly payments. If we were to give people a second mortgage, there would be very little risk attached to it. Even less risk than there was for the first."

Hargrave's eyes seemed to be closing. I feared he would soon be asleep. I discarded the rest of my presentation and put on my salesman's hat. "I know how I would sell this new product to our clients: 'Take out a second mortgage and receive in cash what is yours, a part of the equity you own. Apply the cash to pay all your outstanding debts. Use the balance for that vacation you always wanted but thought you could not afford. Buy a new car. Do both. After all, the money belongs to you. You aren't borrowing money; you're unlocking an asset that is your very own: the appreciation in your home that you were wise enough to buy many years ago.'"

Hargrave seemed to be listening now but without much interest. "I know our loan brokers could sell thousands of second mortgages at interest rates equal to those charged on small loans. And since the second mortgage is secured by the borrower's own home, defaults will be rare. Defaults on home mortgages run only about 1 percent. Amalgamated wouldn't have to bother with phantom income, since 99 percent of our loans would be performing."

His eyes opened wide at the mention of phantom income. My gamble paid off. I had his attention. He got out of his chair and strode briskly toward his office's open door, which he closed. Back in his chair, he glared at me. Now to make the plan become his.

"Mr. Hargrave, as you can plainly see, if we move ahead, we have a head start over the competition—a built-in customer list, our family of borrowers. From among our existing customers, how do we find those with debts and untapped equity in their homes?"

Hargrave held up his hands as a signal that I should stop. "A question on every loan application asks whether the applicant owns a home and the amount of any mortgage placed on it. Our credit agency can tell us if the borrower has other debts. The office managers at each of our branches prepare a prescreened list of candidates. Then the loan brokers take over. They meet with the candidates. Using company criteria, they offer the loan you mentioned."

I had filled out hundreds of loan applications. My question was designed to bait the trap. Hargrave swallowed it, hook, line, and sinker.

"Brilliant, Mr. Hargrave," I said. "You have supplied the missing pieces and much more. In a matter of minutes, you have brought the project to life. There are two more details. How do we determine that houses have appreciated? How do we motivate loan brokers?"

"Easy," said Hargrave, "we hire a local real estate appraiser. He gives a horseback opinion on the value of our borrowers' homes. We motivate the loan brokers the good old American way: pay a bonus on each loan. We can start with fifty basis points per loan. That's half of 1 percent of the loan."

"No wonder you're CEO of Amalgamated."

I had never heard the word "sycophant." In Riverhead, all we knew was "ass-kisser." Although it was contrary to my nature to kiss anyone's ass, I was a pragmatist. I wouldn't get anywhere unless I flattered the hell out of Hargrave. He smiled, exuding pride and pleasure, but I wasn't fooled. I knew with whom he was pleased: himself. The plan was now Hargrave's. This vain man would not discard an idea he thought he conceived.

Hargrave said he had a lunch meeting with senior staff and outside investment bankers to discuss buying a business, and that he would bring up "our" proposal. "The company saves a lot of money developing its own business. Beginning at two, Ms. Ryan told me, you'll be in the conference room down the hall holding a rehearsal for the workshop I asked you to run on Saturday. I'll stop by and give you a heads-up on my meeting. You may have a lot more work to do at the convention."

Hargrave walked with me to the door, put his arm on my shoulder, and said, "Our company needs young blood. Not just any old young man but one with ideas. I'll see you later."

As I walked to the elevator, Beverly caught up with me. "The rehearsal is in two hours. I can find an empty office and some magazines to read. There's one near my room. "

I was exhausted from my meeting. Also, the night before, I hadn't slept well. I needed to rest but didn't want to admit it. I said I was headed to my room at the Hilton. There were things I had to do.

Beverly was a sensuous woman, and I knew even then that there was something special about such women. They do not turn their charm on for everyone, but when they do, it hits with blinding force. That's what happened to me when Beverly moved close, took a deep breath, and said with mock innocence, "Not much fun alone in a hotel room."

I pretended not to understand. I was curious why a sophisticated New York woman would deign to flirt with a rube from Riverhead. I wanted to ask her but realized the question would rub her the wrong way. I didn't want to take the chance of alienating Hargrave's secretary. Instead, I said, "True, it's not much fun, but I have a busy weekend and need time to prepare and think."

I tried to sleep but could not. I was too excited. I showered, stretched out on my bed, and daydreamed.

At about one, I changed into my casual clothes: a maroon corduroy jacket, dark gray flannel pants, a white La Crosse tennis shirt, and loafers. I felt confident in my dress. I thanked God for Shep Miller's and that nice salesman.

I entered the conference room a few minutes late. The actors were already there. So was Beverly. She introduced me and said, "Break a leg," which stunned me until she added, "That's show biz speak for good luck," and left me to my own devices.

I handed a script to the couple nearest to me, a tall skinny guy and his short, fat partner. We completed the first run. The woman, Judy Tabacco, was sharp; the man, dull. I got the idea to mix and match partners, taking the three best of each sex and making my own pairs.

I started on the second couple. We were smack in the middle when Hargrave opened the door and stuck his big head in. He beamed at me. "Excuse me," he said, "I need Henry for about an hour." Looking from one to the other of my cast of characters, he said, "I wouldn't do this to you fine actors and actresses if it weren't urgent. Take a coffee break and come back at three-thirty. All right with you, Henry?"

I did not change outwardly, but deep in the recesses of my soul, I inflated. The effect on the actors was almost audible. They had regarded me as a joker and the rehearsal and play as a waste of time. All that changed once Hargrave intervened. As they filed out of the room, several looked at me with a mixture of wonder and dread.

Hargrave locked my arm in his, and we strode to his office. He motioned to me to sit on the couch instead of the chair in front of his desk and took a chair near the couch. He leaned back and stared at the ceiling for what seemed like five minutes but was probably less. Then he looked directly at me. "I pushed our idea," he said in a confidential tone. "It was preferable in some ways to buying any of the businesses they were proposing. Buying a business is expensive, but it comes with a track record. Our business is a startup and costs nothing, but success is a gamble. I stressed our own brokers would sell the new product to our existing customers. When all agreed to give it a shot, I said we were missing one piece, an officer to run the new business. I profiled the new officer: one drawn from among the loan brokers, one of the gang but better. The brokers will identify with him, and he'll be able to motivate them.

"Henry, I would like you to be that new officer. You will have the title of assistant vice president, division of second mortgages. You'll have an office here at headquarters. No staff, but you may tap all the resources of the company, legal, accounting, business, secretarial, etc. Your job will be guaranteed for a year. If you don't produce ... well, you will."

My heart beat rapidly. I was so happy, I wanted to kiss the messenger. The day had started in despair and was now an unmitigated success. I controlled my feelings and neither said a word nor showed any emotion. Hargrave had more to say.

"Your salary will be fifteen thousand dollars per year plus benefits. Human resources, our employment office, will find you a one-bedroom apartment close enough to walk to the office. I expect you to start in two weeks."

"Thank you, Mr. Hargrave. I'm pleased you have faith in me. I can certainly start in two weeks, but I'm eager to put our plan in operation. If it's all right with you, I'll start in a week. I'd like Amalgamated to furnish the apartment. I doubt I'll have time to buy furniture. I'm like you. I don't like to waste time. I plan to discuss your plan over this weekend with the loan brokers. I'll need a list of the brokers attending the meeting and background information on each. "

Hargrave said yes to everything. He called Beverly and asked her to provide "Mr. Wojecoski" with the list of attendees and all information she had on them. He then called the head of human resources into his office: "I want you to find an apartment for a new employee, Henry Wojecoski. A one-bedroom apartment on the West Side will be fine. Furnish it at company expense. He will be moving in next week. Make sure it's comfortable for a young bachelor"—here, Hargrave smiled conspiratorially at me.

He endorsed my idea of sounding out the brokers present, "the company's best," on Saturday after the workshop and also at the farewell dinner in the ballroom at the Hilton. He asked me to describe the new business to them. "It's a good idea for them to get used to hearing you in control. They'll spread the word to the others when they get home."

I thanked Hargrave for his confidence. The juices were running, the adrenalin surging. My tank was filled with high octane as I left his office. The struggle wasn't over, but the first and most important stage was. And I'd won. Hands down.

My spirits were soaring when I entered the conference room down the hall. Two men rose from their seats. I motioned to them to sit. Beverly was there with a cup of coffee for me, a package of sugar, and two small plastic containers, one filled with milk, the other cream. She asked how I took my coffee. When I said, "Milk, no sugar," she prepared and handed it to me. I thought she whispered, "Now I know how to serve your breakfast coffee," but maybe she said something else.

The rehearsal for the workshop lasted another hour. We were as ready as we ever would be for opening night or rather opening matinee the next day. I asked all to attend the workshop as I anticipated a need for extras. I invited the cast, including extras, to the dinner following the workshop and added, "Senior officers will be present, so those interested in mingling with the brass will have a golden opportunity. Suits for men and dresses for women."

On the short walk back to the hotel, I thought about Neil Armstrong, his flight to the moon, and his historic words: "one small step for man, one giant leap for mankind." The moon is close. Hell, I want to land on a planet. Maybe even the largest, Jupiter.

Scheduled for Friday night was an informal welcome reception and light dinner in a ballroom at the Hilton followed by a showing of *American Graffiti.* I had already seen the movie in Southampton, but it was the kind of movie you don't mind seeing again—about teenagers coming of age in the '60s. It was relevant to a lot of us.

I hadn't planned to work the reception, but I was supercharged. I introduced myself as a loan broker from the Riverhead office who would soon move to headquarters and run the second mortgage division, a new line of business for us brokers. I told the loan brokers essentially the same thing. "I know how hard we work and that we're undercompensated and underutilized. We can do a lot more than make small loans. Soon, we'll have a chance to show our stuff. The company is embarking on a new business activity that'll establish our company as an innovative and leading financial institution and, by the way, make a lot of money for us. You'll hear more tomorrow night from Hargrave and me."

I talked to practically every broker there. One summed up the sentiment: "Small loans are a thing of the past. Business is off and will slide even lower. We need a new line."

Real estate excited them, but they knew very little about second mortgages, except for what a broker from California named Epstein said: "In my state, mortgage loans are regulated. Lots of paperwork. Mortgages have to be filed. Need lawyers. We may need a license."

"Don't worry," I assured him. "Amalgamated stands behind you. Everything will be kosher."

That night, in my room, I smiled with satisfaction as I surveyed my surroundings. The carpeting was thick, the sheets were soft, the towels were plush. There was room to whisk Peggy around the floor in a ball gown, but she was nowhere nearby. As I drifted off, I thought about the billions of stars and planets forming the galaxy. They were shining and so was my personal star.

New York is a great city. It has hundreds of movie theaters, restaurants, bars, stadiums, and arenas. You can find anything there. A girl in high boots and short skirt, standing in front of the Hilton, asked me if I wanted to party. Why insult the poor thing? She was trying to earn a living. "No, thanks," I said and smiled. When some gay guys waved at me, one dressed in drag, I told them where to go. "Fuck off, queers." Riverhead shuts down at nine, even on Saturday night. New York goes to bed but not to sleep.

The schedule left Saturday free for us to explore until the workshop at five. Some of the guys planned to tour the porn shops and movies along Eighth Avenue, others to see a ballgame at Yankee Stadium. Not me. My day was booked. First, the Museum of Modern Art, which Peggy referred to as MoMA, and then the Whitney, the Metropolitan Museum of Art, and finally, the Guggenheim. When I rejected joining the others and told them my plans, they laughed. None accepted my offer to join me. One guy even questioned my manhood. He asked why I wanted to spend my day in dead museums instead of going out on the town. I said, "The girl I'm planning to marry loves art. She said, 'Don't miss the museums.' I wouldn't do it for anyone else."

I set out by foot at 9:00 and returned by foot at 3:30. I made an effort to study the paintings and the artwork that made each museum distinctive. It didn't work. The museums and the paintings merged. By the end of the day, I couldn't remember a single painting and could barely recall the different palaces housing the artwork. I was an ignoramus. How lucky I was to have a cultured woman like Peggy who understood art. I missed her more than ever because I was alone, a stranger in her world.

How was I to explain my indifference in viewing Peggy's temples? Perhaps I could hide behind the free handouts I collected at each museum and two purchased calendars, one from MoMA featuring modern art and the other from the Met filled with the classics. I stashed my cache in my suitcase and rested my weary body. Just before five, I took the elevator to the third-floor ballroom, the site of the workshop and dinner.

I sat at a large table surrounded by the cast of ten, five men and five women. In front of us, in folding chairs, sat the brokers.

On the side, in tall straight-backed chairs, sat Hargrave and three other old men. Hargrave introduced me to the brokers. "Henry has been appointed to a new office, director of a new line of business, second mortgages. At the farewell dinner, you will learn more. On with the workshop. Henry, it's your show."

I said that the folks around the table—all Amalgamated employees—would act out three mock interviews, each demonstrating a way to make a loan default-proof. "Did you know," I continued, "each defaulted loan wipes out the profit on six performing ones? I want anyone who wants, at anytime, to shout out a comment. Don't bother to raise your hand. I'm sure we'll all learn more from your comments than from the play."

The first couple, Joyce and Robert Jones, wanted a loan to enlarge their house. "Too many kids, too few bedrooms." I made the loan but required that the proceeds go directly to the contractor. With their permission, I called the contractor, played by one of the extras. He was happy to learn he would be paid by Amalgamated but unhappy about the condition imposed. "My father's a plumber," I said. "I know that if payment on a job is assured or paid in advance, he lowers the price. I want you to reduce your price by 10 percent."

The Jones were thrilled and thanked me. I told them a better way to thank me was to repay the loan. I then discussed with the contractor a way to make the loan default-proof.

The law protects workers by giving them a "mechanic's lien" on the unpaid balance. The contractor had no need for a lien as Amalgamated was paying him directly. It was easy to persuade him to assign the lien to Amalgamated. He made the assignment conditioned on the Joneses' consent. I told the contractor I would call him back and put both Joneses on the phone.

The Joneses, who feigned love for me when I got the price reduced, now looked at me with hatred. The wife was the first to speak: "You mean if we miss a monthly payment, you can throw us out of our house?"

I explained that they had thirty days to cure a default. If it were not corrected, Amalgamated would surely foreclose. "It's a tough world. If you don't meet your monthly installments, you may lose your house. One with too few bedrooms is better than no house at all. Why don't you step outside and discuss it? I want you to know that if you don't agree, Amalgamated will not make the loan."

The Joneses stepped a few feet away. In a voice audible to all in the room, the husband said, "This guy is tough. Let's tell the bastard to go fuck himself."

"Not so fast," said the wife. "We'll never get a better deal. He knocked off 10 percent. Let's make repayment our first priority. We can delay other payments."

They resumed their seats. The husband spoke: "Okay, Shylock, you win."

"Me, Shylock? I'll bet you've never read *The Merchant of Venice*. Shylock is a villain because he asked for a pound of flesh. Amalgamated doesn't want your flesh or your blood, just our money back, plus interest. The interest is our profit. The profit motive is part of capitalism. I'm sure you'll agree with me it's the best economic system in the world."

Mr. Jones apologized, said like all patriotic Americans, he loved capitalism and hated communism. He asked if Amalgamated would please make the loan. They signed the agreement. I gave them a second agreement for the contractor and added, "When he signs and returns it to me, he'll get a third of the loan. The balance will be paid when the job is completed. In case of dispute, you and the contractor go to binding arbitration. The loser pays the cost of arbitration."

I asked those who had been called Shylocks to raise their hands. A sea of hands went up. One broker, a black guy named John Hughes from New Jersey, said he had been called "a Shylock and a Jew bastard." There was scattered laughter. I asked how he responded. "I said, 'Antonio was a deadbeat. I have zero tolerance for deadbeats. My company serves a good purpose. It helps people realize their dreams. If you intend to beat me the way Antonio beat Shylock, you should leave right now.' The customer apologized. He was a good credit risk, so I made the loan."

I put a mark next to Hughes's name and thought if I ever need help, Hughes would be a good one to call on.

The second couple wanted a loan to take a cruise to celebrate their first anniversary. The husband said his wife's parents were rich. "He owns a machine shop in Smithtown. Her parents paid for our honeymoon. We've had a great year. I want to pay for a cruise to the Bahamas, but we have no savings and have to pay for the full trip in advance." I looked at the budget I had asked them to prepare. They had a surplus but essential expenses were missing. "I see no item for food. Did you fast the whole month?"

I would have turned them down, but I got an idea. I asked the wife if her parents would guarantee the loan. I then asked the husband if he would be comfortable if his in-laws did that. We made an appointment for the next day. I used extras to play the in-laws. They signed, Amalgamated made the loan, and a lucky couple set sail for the islands.

One broker asked if I thought it was okay to lend money for a "fun purpose." I said no, but the parents' guarantee made it all right. A second asked why the guy didn't borrow directly from his in-laws. "After all, that's what he's doing, only he's paying interest to us." Before I could answer, another did: "It all has to do with his manhood and you know what. It will rise faster and stay there longer if he pays."

The brokers howled. I checked Hargrave. He too was laughing. I said, "On that note, we'll go on to the third case."

Mary and Philip Johnson had good income. Phil, judging from his salary (supported by W-2s), was a skilled auto mechanic. The problem was that their monthly expenses almost equaled his income. The wife was pregnant and due within six months. They wanted to add a nursery and convert an unfinished basement into a playroom. The purpose was a good one, but as we went over their recent purchases, I doubted if they had the self-discipline to make room for another payment. I suggested the husband's employer deduct the monthly payment from his earnings and remit it to us. As long as the husband stayed employed, Amalgamated's loan would be repaid.

Phil called his boss, James O'Reilly (played by another extra), and put me on the phone. O'Reilly said Johnson was hardworking, honest, and the "best damned mechanic in the shop." He asked how he could help. I explained the need for the loan and that Amalgamated was prepared to advance the full amount, provided

O'Reilly agreed to deduct the monthly payment and remit it to Amalgamated. He agreed.

I gave the Johnsons the forms—a loan agreement and an assignment of wages—and when Mary Johnson returned with signed papers, I handed her a check and wished her good luck.

There were hands raised and shouts throughout the room. One broker questioned the relevance of a good purpose. "Suppose Mary was not pregnant, and the Johnsons wanted to use the proceeds to gamble in Las Vegas or support a drug habit." Before I could answer, another asked, "Suppose a guy wanted to buy his mistress a diamond ring. Would you say no?"

Many thought we should not impose our sense of morals. A loan should turn on the creditworthiness of the borrower. One broker summed up the sentiments of the group: "Who the hell are we to tell people what they should or shouldn't do? We're not the pope. As far as I can see, none of us are even priests."

There was a second school. Good purpose shows good character. In the final analysis, honest people will pay their debts.

I said the leader of our company was here, and I wanted to hear his views.

Hargrave stood and introduced his three cronies: Robert Barrett, Amalgamated's chief financial officer; Russell Clark, the company's general counsel; John Rooney, a director of the company.

Hargrave said Amalgamated was a family company that had built its reputation on helping its customers. "I hope we never intentionally make a loan supporting an illegal or immoral purpose. That should give you plenty of room to maneuver."

Hargrave asked the three visitors if they cared to comment. Rooney said he wanted to say a few words. "I'm not part of the company. I'm called an independent outside director. I look at forecasts, financial statements, and the like. Tonight, for the first time, I glimpsed the actual operations. I like what I see. You're going to make a success out of second mortgages. I own only one hundred shares of stock. On Monday, I'm telling my broker to get me ten thousand more."

I thanked Rooney for his confidence. I said we would work hard to justify it. I then thanked everybody for their participation and declared the workshop over.

As we adjourned to a nearby room for the farewell dinner, people came up to me, shook my hand, and said, "Good going, good job. Do you have a card?" I knew I had hit it out of the park, but I had to restrain my excitement. I wanted everyone to think my performance had been effortless.

After the dinner tables were cleared, Hargrave spoke. He said he had learned a lot from the workshop and from meeting and talking to us. He wished he had started the brokers' convention years ago, and he hoped one day to bring all the brokers, not just the best, to New York for a giant convention. He concluded by mentioning the new activity, stating his "110 percent support."

I then described the business much as I had to Hargrave, whom I called a forward-looking, enthusiastic, and first-rate leader. When I concluded, several brokers stood and clapped. It must have been contagious because the whole room erupted in applause. Even Hargrave, Barrett, Clark, and Rooney stood and clapped. What did I do? I raised my hands like a prize fighter and bowed.

The brokers stayed in the dining hall and talked and talked. Several Vietnam veterans wanted to discuss the war, but I deflected their questions. We talked shop, sports, and sex. I got to know everybody, and I promised to stay in touch. Just before midnight, I returned to my luxurious room and collapsed into bed and the soundest sleep of my life.

The next morning, I said aloud, "I didn't reach Jupiter, but I made it to Mercury."

When I returned to planet Earth, I called Peggy. It was Sunday. She was almost out the door, on her way to church with her parents, when she picked up the phone. I sensed she was in a hurry, so I blurted out the news in *Daily News* headline fashion. "A new job in New York. Salary fifteen thousand dollars. A one-bedroom apartment paid for by the company. Walking distance to MoMA." I heard Peggy tell her parents she was not going to church. "Henry's on the phone. I'm too excited. Maybe I'll attend the second service. Please go." I told her of the ominous beginning when Hargrave turned his back and the glorious end when he offered me the job and the apartment. We said we loved each other so many times that I lost count. We ended the call agreeing to meet that night.

My second call was to Mary and David. He picked up the phone and insisted on a play-by-play recount of the weekend. When I finished, he told Mary to pick up the extension and, forgetting that the phone amplified voices, he shouted, "Your brother climbed Mt. Everest. Never in the history of business has a kid without an MBA gone so far so fast. All in one weekend. Henry, can you lend me some money? Mary and I have good news too. Let's celebrate—the whole family. You're still at the Hilton, right? Hop on a train to Mineola. My parents will pick you up and take you to this great restaurant specializing in Sunday brunch. We'll call Elizabeth and Andrew. Things are looking up for the Wojecoski-Markowitz clan."

When we were gathered at the restaurant, David insisted I retell the events of the weekend. I tried, but I couldn't, because he kept interrupting and embellishing the story. By the time he finished, you would have thought I had replaced Hargrave. Then Mary told their news.

David had been named an associate professor at Columbia's medical school and was going to join a crack team of cardiac surgeons at Columbia Presbyterian. "Hold it, Mary, that's not our big news. Mary's pregnant. The prenatal test shows the baby is fine and a boy! We plan to name him Henry. Then my dear brother will owe me one. When he has a son, he must name him David. Oh, and guess who's been named an associate professor at Columbia's nursing school—our very own Mary. So that there's no confusion, her offer came first. There was real competition for Mary. Stony Brook offered her more money to stay as head of nursing and to teach. Mary turned down the better offer to be with me. I'm the happiest tagalong that ever flew behind a kite."

David's father, Benjamin, ordered a bottle of champagne. He toasted "three marvelous children, soon to be joined by a fourth." He then asked if the baby Henry would be circumcised. "You bet the kid's foreskin he will," said David. "He will also have a bar mitzvah," added Mary. "We want our son to be a Jew not only in name but in spirit."

"Andrew and I don't care what he is," my mother said. "If he's your son, we will love him to pieces." After years of living with Andrew, Elizabeth had developed a talent to defuse. In this case, it reached new heights before controversy had a chance.

David leaned over, kissed Elizabeth, and said, "If we have a daughter, I promise you she will be baptized even if I have to drown the hellion with my own two hands."

"David, don't you dare call my granddaughter a hellion. She's an angel." Elizabeth looked at the ceiling and crossed herself.

Out of the blue, David said, "When, Mr. J. P. Morgan, are you going to marry the exquisite Raquel Welch, also known as Peggy Woijek? Mary and I are busy, and we'll be even busier after little Henry arrives. If you want us to attend, you've got to give us plenty of notice. Like right now!"

"Leave Henry alone," said Mary. "He knows a good thing. I'm sure when they're ready, we'll be among the first to know. Henry needs time to catch his breath."

Mary was right. My job was guaranteed for only a year. Job security came before marriage. I was ready to assume risk but wanted Peggy to have a sure thing. I was twenty-five and she was twenty-four. We could wait, though not much longer.

# 8

*F*or as long as I can remember, birds built nests in the eaves of our house. They did not bother us, and we did not bother them. That harmony ended in the spring of 1974. My mother hung a wicker basket near our front door, intending to fill it with a pot of begonias, but a mother robin beat her to the punch. She deposited two eggs in the basket. The mother and the father, who took turns sitting on the eggs, screeched every time we went in or out of the house. We took to using the back door and, when we had to, sneaking out the front. On one of my last days at home, I saw a fledgling fly from the nest. When I checked, the nest was empty.

When my parents offered to take me to my new apartment, I thought of the baby robin. If she could leave her nest unaided, I, a twenty-five-year-old man, would also fly the coop alone.

On Sunday, April 21, 1974, I rented a car, packed my belongings, and drove to New York. My new home was a five-story remodeled tenement on the corner of Sixty-Eighth Street and Columbus Avenue. The building had been converted from a single-room-only fleabag occupied mainly by drug addicts and prostitutes to modern studio and one-bedroom apartments designed for a rising group of young urban professionals. But it took more than ten years for the group to get a name—yuppies.

The front door was locked. I followed instructions provided by human resources and pushed the button on the intercom system box marked "super." A gruff bass voice answered, "Yes?" I shouted back my name. "Not so loud. I can hear you without the intercom. Open the door when the buzzer rings. I'll meet you in the lobby."

Minutes later, a big black man, the super, gave me the key to my apartment. "Take the elevator to five. Your apartment is 5-C. The key will also open the front door. Write your name on this card, and I'll add it to the names appearing on the intercom. When you have visitors, they'll ring your bell. Make sure you know who they are before letting them in. Security is a top priority in this building."

After living almost all my life in a tiny attic room and racing to the basement every time I had to go to the bathroom, my one-bedroom apartment seemed as grand as Versailles. More important, I was free from the confines of my parents' home—just like our front-door bird.

In furnishing the apartment, human resources had thought of everything, including a television set, telephone, and a refrigerator crammed with food. I made dinner, pasta with marinara sauce and a salad with Kraft's blue cheese dressing. My mother had fed me a big lunch, so all I needed was a light supper. I watched TV and went to sleep.

The next day, I strolled to Amalgamated's building, which I now thought of as mine. I was full of confidence and, yes, a touch of conceit. I saw myself as the company's great white hope. I nodded to the receptionist and sauntered to my office. It was a small inside room within shouting distance of Hargrave's and adjoining the space of his secretary, Beverly Ryan. She asked me to call her by her last name. "Everybody does. I hate the name Beverly. It's too proper, not me at all."

My first task was to call the branch managers, outline the criteria for a second mortgage, and ask them to scout out prospects. Ryan handed me a list of names and suggested, when I was ready, that she initiate the calls and tell the managers she was calling from Hargrave's office on behalf of Mr. Wojecoski. "They'll pay more attention if I drop the boss's name."

She also handed me a big red folder. "In the file, you'll find loan contracts, mortgage forms, and a memo discussing the ins and outs of second mortgages, all the material you'll need for your meeting at ten with Hargrave and the lawyers." She turned and sashayed away, shaking her behind. Was it deliberate? How could it not be?

Ryan was probably in her early thirties. I wondered whether I ever thought a woman that old was attractive. I could not remember any except for my present company. I fantasized over what she would look like naked and got slightly aroused before settling down to read the file.

At ten, I entered an empty conference room, determined to learn the rules that would get my new business off to a flying start. The critical issues were these: what is a second mortgage and what are the steps necessary to create one? Our small loans failed so often because, other than a lawsuit, there was no penalty attached to default. The new loans would be tough on deadbeats.

At 10:30, I was still alone. By 11:00, I was boiling with rage, in no condition for a seminal meeting. Hargrave had done it again. When we first met, he had insulted me by turning his back. Now, he was a no-show. This was worse.

A few minutes later, I was at the door, ready to leave, when Hargrave arrived with three lawyers: Russell Clark, whom I had met at the workshop, and two younger men holding yellow legal pads and pens. The lawyers wore similar uniforms, three-piece dark suits and highly polished black shoes. Clark introduced Robert Stultz, calling him a rising star at the firm of Bissell, Wright & Clark. The third lawyer, Michael Sachs, was an employee of Amalgamated who had started as an attorney with the Bissell firm.

Hargrave offered a weak apology. "Sorry, Henry, I was discussing strategy about a pending stockholders action brought against the board. I forgot about our meeting until Russell reminded me."

If you have ever sat in a room for an hour waiting for others to appear and then, when they appear, they excuse their tardiness by saying that they were busy with other matters, you will know how I felt: worthless. What a lousy way to start a new job. To hell with the consequences, I was ready to strike back. I looked at Clark and said, "I wish you had reminded the boss earlier that all of you were to meet with me at ten." Then, turning to Hargrave,

I unleashed my anger. "If the new business is to save our failing company, I need help, not neglect. If you had gotten word to me that you were going to be late, there were a lot of things for me to do. Cooling my heels in this room was not one."

Hargrave was stunned, turned red, but said not a word. Years later, he told me he wanted to fire me on the spot. He didn't because he had hyped the new business and me to the board in an effort to save his own job. He feared that if he fired me the first morning, he'd have been sacked too. He also had to consider the other brokers, whom I had bonded with at the convention. Morale would have fallen when they heard I had been canned.

The lawyers took their cue from Hargrave and said nothing. Stultz gave me a discreet thumbs-up.

Having obtained some measure of payback for the damage done to my ego, I turned to the subject of the meeting. "The new business, defined by Mr. Hargrave and me, is the same as our old business, small loans, with a twist. Our new loans will be secured by mortgages on the borrowers' homes. The threat of foreclosure should make them think twice before defaulting. I want our brokers to make sure all the documents are in order so that a technicality doesn't wipe out our security. Before I instruct our brokers, I want to make sure I know what we marines call 'the firing procedure.'" It didn't hurt to let these guys know I was a battle-hardened ex-marine.

Clark spoke first. He urged that the second mortgages should be filed as soon as all terms were agreed to. "The key to the new venture is to tie the loan to the borrower's house. A less than prompt filing puts the security in jeopardy."

Clark's advice contradicted his firm's memo. How could that be? I was still angry. "You must be mistaken. Filing triggers payment to the borrower. Is that right?" When Clark nodded, I went on. "The memo says that before paying, we should make sure the first mortgage permits a second (many do not), and make sure there are no liens other than the first mortgage or any unpaid judgments. What's right, Mr. Clark? Pay the money and then do our homework or the reverse?"

Clark stammered. His field was finance, not real estate. Stultz, the real estate expert, had written the memo. Clark said I should rely on the memo and not his off-the-cuff remark.

I had other technical questions, which I directed to Stultz. He looked to be in his mid-thirties. He was short, no more than five foot eight. His blond hair was thinning; in a few years, he would be bald. I thought that when I needed outside counsel, I would call him. I liked him. He was not, like Clark, a bullshit artist.

After the meeting, Stultz asked me where I lived. He too lived on the West Side, on Central Park West. He said he worked out at the McBurney YMCA on Sixty-Third Street off the park. "It's a good place. If you join and work out early in the morning as I do, we can sometimes have breakfast together."

I joined the Y. We breakfasted together many times. We also bonded, a tie that would last all my life.

After the meeting, I returned to my office. Ryan initiated the calls to the branch managers. The longest and most satisfying one was to Dominico, the branch manager of the Riverhead office. During my last days in the office, I'd told Dominico about the new business. He jumped the gun and, while I was still in the office, searched for likely candidates. He said there was real interest.

I knew Dominico came from a fishing family and fished in his spare time. I ended the call by thanking him for the quick feedback and added, "It seems the fish on land are biting. How about the ones in the bay?"

"Henry," Dominico said, "it's a lot harder to catch a fish in the water and a lot more satisfying."

My first day at headquarters was over. I assessed the events. I'd made one friend, Stultz, and two enemies, Hargrave and Clark. I stretched out on my bed, mentally and physically exhausted. If every day was like this one, I'd soon die of a heart attack. I had no appetite. I opened *Our Mutual Friend*, Dickens's last novel. I'd become a Dickens addict.

Later, at a pizzeria in the neighborhood, I called Peggy. I skipped the drama and said everything was fine. She must have had suspicions because she kept asking me what was wrong. Finally, I said business was tough, but I survived. "If I've learned anything from the first day, you're going to have to put up with a grumpy husband." I told her I loved her and missed her. What I didn't tell her was that I was glad we were not yet married. Things were too uncertain.

Over the next several weeks, I was in and out of Ryan's office, and she popped in and out of mine. Although I liked looking at her, my stops were all business; hers had a decidedly different slant. She touched my hand for no reason other than to make contact. She ran her hand through my hair, suggested I needed a haircut, and offered to do the job herself. She admired my abs and said, "I just love strong men; they have big muscles in the most interesting places."

One day, I asked the obvious question: "I know why I like you, but what the hell do you see in me?"

"You remind me of my first love. As a young girl, I fantasized about my first time. It would happen in a five-star hotel in Paris on a canopied bed after a champagne dinner. Instead, we were in a drive-in movie theater, eating popcorn and drinking Coke, when we climbed into the backseat of his VW. I was sixteen; he was seventeen. There have been others. I won't tell you how many, but none as sweet as my first. Your voice, your androgynous looks, your brooding Marlon Brando stance remind me of him. I'm not sixteen anymore. I've been married and recently divorced. I think quite often of my first love and wonder what would happen if we were to meet again."

Ryan's confession inspired me. I said I was almost engaged and told her a little bit about Peggy: her interest in art and her determination to remain a virgin until our wedding night. "It's hard on both of us, but I respect her decision." She gave me a sexless kiss on the cheek, and we parted.

The flirting ended, until late on a Friday afternoon. I thought I was the only one in the office when Ryan showed up. The top two buttons of her blouse were open, revealing her ample breasts. "Henry, it's six-thirty, time for dinner. All work and no play. How about a dinner date? Dutch treat. I'm celebrating the first year of my divorce. I need company, and you, dear Henry, need a break."

I suggested a small Italian restaurant I had passed on my way to work. We were shown to a booth. I selected a ten-dollar bottle of wine and asked Ryan if it was all right. She put her mouth against my ear and murmured, "Whatever you want." During dinner, she paid more attention to my knee and thigh than to her food. I must confess: I too was distracted. I kept gazing at Ryan's breasts. As we were about to leave, Ryan said, "In the week before you arrived, there was so much talk about your apartment. I'd like to see it. Don't tell me it's a mess. I don't care. I also know it's nearby. Henry, you bad boy, is that why you picked this restaurant?"

I recognized the best thing to say at certain times was nothing at all. I thought if only Peggy had not been so rigid, I would have the will power to resist. Instead, I offered Ryan my arm, and off we went.

When we entered, Ryan, ignoring the couch and four chairs in the living-dining room, exclaimed, "Oh, just what I feared. No place to sit down but on your bed." She kicked off her shoes, took off her blouse and skirt, stretched out on the bed, and motioned to me to join her.

We kissed and kissed and hugged and kissed. One thing led to another. Afterward, Ryan held me and massaged my chest and stomach. "Henry, you were wonderful. You lasted so long. Did you sense I had two groans? That's my term for an orgasm. Oh, Henry, I never thought I could get drunk on sex. But I am. I'm also addicted. Very little to drink and nothing to sniff, and I'm drunk and stoned. It's been so long since I've made love to a man. I was horny all day today. Let's take a cleansing shower. There's something more I want to do."

In the shower, Ryan concentrated on my genitals. She washed them slowly and thoroughly. When she saw I was aroused, she turned off the water, kneeled on the floor, and gave me a world-class blow job.

While Ryan was soaping me, she touched my forehead. Soap got in my eyes. It was irritating until she began to fellate me. Then the annoyance ceased. From the experience, I developed a way to rid myself of petty annoyances. I call it soap in my eyes. Then I think about Ryan, the shower, and the blow job. The annoyance, just like the soap, disappears.

While she was getting dressed, Ryan revealed a secret. "When I first took the job as Hargrave's secretary, he stared at me, his eyes moving up and down my body. Then he started to touch me at odd times. At first, I thought it was accidental, but it happened too frequently. I didn't know what to do. I needed the job, and the pay was good. If I complained, he might fire me. One day, he was out of the office at a meeting. He called and asked me to bring a file to him. He said the material in the file was confidential, and only I should deliver it. When he told me he was in room 1005 at the Hilton, I was suspicious, so suspicious that I took his silver letter opener with me for self-defense. When I arrived, he was dressed (if you can call it that) in a silk robe, black with large red lapels. The robe ended a few inches above his bony knees. His skinny, hairy legs stood out. On his feet, he wore velvet slippers. He reeked of aftershave lotion. God, how I hated the man! No, that's not true. I didn't hate him. I found him physically repulsive. He's old. Sixty years old and married. I speak almost daily to his poor wife, Betty. What's wrong with old, married men? Why don't they exercise their libidos on their poor, needy wives?

"I handed him the file and turned quickly to leave. He grabbed my arm. 'It's you I want, not the file.' He threw me down on the bed. I resisted, but then I shut my eyes and gave in. When he was finished, I cried and told him he had raped me. He claimed I consented. I voluntarily came to his hotel room. 'What did you think you were going to do, take dictation?'

"I was in the process of getting a divorce. I cried as I told my divorce lawyer what had happened. He gave me good advice. You should have seen Hargrave's face when I told him, 'Mr. Hargrave, if you so much as touch me again, I will sue both you and Amalgamated for sexual harassment.' Then, on my own, I added, 'Also, I will tell Betty.' He was contrite, apologized profusely, twice said never again.

"The only reason I'm telling you this is that I want you to be careful. If Hargrave ever found out about tonight or even had a hint that we were intimate, I'm sure he would fire both of us. Did you know it's a violation of Amalgamated's code of conduct for employees to be sexually intimate? The rule says something like this: 'Employees, at all times, shall conduct their personal life in a dignified and proper manner. Sexual relations between unmarried employees shall be deemed a violation of the rule.' Believe me, it is strictly enforced. At last year's Christmas party, a cute guy from the mail room and a file-room clerk were discovered almost naked in a closet. Both were fired. So please, be careful."

I was frightened. What if we were found out? And why had she pursued me, knowing what the policy was? Had I known, would I have taken her to my apartment? We had left the office together, kissed in the restaurant, walked arm in arm to my apartment. What if we were observed? The affair had to end right now. "Ryan, I find you irresistible, but, jerk that I am, I'm consumed with guilt."

"I understand, Henry. I've met a man I like. He's old but wants to marry me. I wanted one more fling. Don't worry about finding a cab for me. And, Henry, I'll always cherish this evening, right up there with the backseat of the VW."

I was happy to be relieved of hailing Ryan a cab. It posed another opportunity for us to be seen. It was late. There were scary people out on the street. The neighborhood was still very much in transition. I feared for Ryan's safety, so I got dressed and saw her into a cab.

I had been in New York for about a month. I was popular in the office except with the one who really mattered, Hargrave. He gave me the silent treatment except when he couldn't possibly ignore me. Then, between gritted teeth, he said good morning or good night. I was safe as long as the new business was headed north. If it fell apart, Hargrave would delight in firing me.

Ryan was a different matter. I wasn't married, so technically, I'd done nothing wrong. Who am I kidding? If Peggy had an affair or if she even kissed another man, I'd have shot them both and turned the gun on myself. I'm jealous and proprietary. No double standard. No more fooling around. One transgression may be excused, but two represents a course of conduct.

The next day was Saturday. I went to confession. I made the sign of the cross and said, "Bless me, Father, for I have sinned." The priest asked for details. I told him I had made love to one woman even though I was practically engaged to another. The priest asked for details. I described everything, including the oral sex. The priest seemed most interested in that aspect. "Did it occur before or after you had intercourse?" He even asked where it occurred. When I told him the shower, he appeared to smile. Or maybe I'm imagining the smile, because he was so damn curious!

I recalled his prurient questions some twenty years later when scandal erupted and the church had to pay millions to the victims of pederast priests. By then, I was a rich, prominent man and got a call from a certain cardinal: "God wants you to help His church survive these tumultuous times." I told that cardinal off. "God wants you to teach the priests to keep their hands off kids. You'll get not another nickel from me until the priests observe what God wants."

One day in my office with the door closed, I told Ryan I confessed my sin in order to gain additional strength to resist her. "Nah," she said, "you never wanted me. I filled in for Peggy."

"That's not true," I said. "I lusted after you from day one. I still do, but there's nothing good that can happen between us and a lot that's bad. To be honest, I'm sorry it's over, but it's over. My will is strong."

There were many times I wanted her, especially over the next few months before I married Peggy, but I stayed far away.

# 9

*A*ccording to the book of Genesis, God created man, the Garden of Eden, and animals. Adam was lonely. He needed a mate, and none of the animals would do. God came to Adam's rescue and created Eve from Adam's rib. Adam called her "woman" and delighted in her company. The chapter ends, "On account of this a man leaves his father and his mother and clings to his woman."

I was ahead of the biblical story. I had left my father and mother but had no woman to cling to. I can never know how lonely Adam was in the Garden of Eden, but I'll bet two fig leaves and a serpent that in my one-bedroom apartment on the Upper West Side of New York, I was lonelier.

I pleaded with Peggy to move in. She said no. She also rejected overnight visits. She was a good Catholic girl and making love prior to marriage was prohibited. I protested. "Times have changed. I read in *Playboy*, women who don't want to have sex with a guy turn down a second date. Why? They know what's expected. We've had dozen of dates. We're engaged, for God's sake. The church is out of step. And so are you."

"I know jumping into bed is usual behavior. It's not my style. I choose to treat my marriage as a sacrament and consecrate my wedding night by my first act of love. But if you find my outlook intolerable, I'll change. I don't want to live with my principles and without my Henry."

Peggy refused to attend the ides of March party because she had suspected it might turn into an orgy. Peggy was a good girl then and a good girl now, and I didn't want her to change. I waited. Eight months after I moved to New York, we were married.

She wanted a big wedding party, but I didn't. I told her parents, "Why waste the money? Everyone comes to the church but only family and friends to your house for a light lunch. Marriage is a serious affair. The service will be dignified and so should the party." Her parents agreed. They saved a lot of money.

The wedding lunch ended at 4:00 p.m. We left for the airport and our flight to Bermuda. The travel desk at Amalgamated got us a package deal at a hotel on a beach that was full of honeymoon suites. As we checked in, Peggy said, "After we unpack, let's come back down, drink, dance, and make friends."

I looked at her as though she was crazy. "Once we get to our room, we ain't ever going to leave." Peggy realized then why I wanted the wedding party to be short; I was in a hurry to get to our room.

After unpacking, Peggy changed to a silk nightgown, part of her wedding trousseau. I took off my shirt and pants and popped into bed in my undershorts. We made love for the first time. It was, in a way, anticlimactic; we had come so close on other occasions. We made love two more times. I was ready for a fourth round when Peggy raised a pillow and, facing me, said, "If you come near me, no, if you even look at me, I will hold this pillow over your head until you suffocate." I laughed, and we went to sleep.

The next morning, we woke at about the same time. I made a move. She jumped out of bed, ran to the bathroom, and locked the door. I pleaded with her to open the door. I said I had to urinate really badly and promised not to touch her.

We showered, got dressed, and went down to the dining room for breakfast.

The faces on the newlyweds told the story of the night. Some sat silent. One man looked dour. A few exchanged loving looks. I wore a Cheshire cat grin. I told the waiter in a voice loud enough for the whole room to hear, "I would like a double order of pancakes and bacon. Man can't live on love alone." Some of the men laughed. Peggy kicked me, but gently, with a smile on her face.

After breakfast, Peggy suggested we spend the day on the beach, swimming and sunning. I stared at her in disbelief. "C'mon, Peggy, the hotel charges a bloody fortune for the room. Let's get our money's worth and spend the day in bed."

"No. I'm going to our room," she said, "locking the door, and changing into my bathing suit. When I'm finished, I'll return to the lobby. It will then be your turn. I won't enter our room with you." Right in front of the elevator, we reached an agreement. There was a time and place for sexual intercourse and a time for all the other pleasures of life. Peggy designated the time for sex after we brushed our teeth and hopped into bed for the night. She called it the "right time rule." I agreed. What else could I do? We kissed. We went to our room, changed into bathing suits, and spent the day frolicking in the sea.

We followed the "right time rule" all our lives. It made good sense, so much so that I wondered why couples carried on in public. Why didn't they save their passion for when they had brushed their teeth and hopped into bed?

Back in New York, Peggy searched for work. A patron of the Parrish Museum was on the board of MoMA and wrote a letter of recommendation, which led to Peggy's part-time job assisting in setting up exhibitions and preparing catalogues. She also enrolled in the Parsons School of Design at Thirteenth Street and Fifth Avenue in the heart of Greenwich Village.

Peggy and I were Riverhead kids, but her interest in art made her a touch bohemian as well. Peggy didn't want me to change but felt that a few rough edges could be rounded. She chose a classmate, a gay guy named Joe Bernstein, to assist her. He was bone thin and had brown hair as long as a woman's. Joe's uniform was jeans and a long-sleeved shirt with a worn collar and cuffs. When it was cold, he added a sweater and a scarf.

Fridays after work, I met them outside Parsons. The other four nights, I was at my desk until eight or nine o'clock. The three of us made an odd trio. Peggy dressed to accentuate her figure. If I have already said so, too bad, I'm saying it again. She had a great figure. The one universal reaction to Peggy's looks was to say wow. I dressed like the square I was.

Through Peggy and Joe, when I wasn't selling second mortgages, I met artists, writers, and poets. The older ones were beatniks; the younger, leftover hippies. They thought Johnson and Nixon and their buddies were arch villains, patriotism was a venereal disease, and the Vietnam War was an international crime. None had served. Although I now agreed with their views, I didn't like the way they expressed them. I let them know I'd seen active duty as a marine. "War," I said, "is always atrocious, but man must observe his duty. Otherwise, anarchy will replace democracy."

If I were not a big, tough-looking guy, I'm sure they would have mocked me. Instead, one said he had nothing against the troops, only the leaders who presided over the slaughter. I blanched when he added "of little kids."

Over time, with help from Joe, I lowered my voice and learned to listen a lot more than I talked. Nixon was still president but would soon be forced to resign. I was happy to see the last of him.

We yakked away at Julius, White Horse Tavern, Cedar Tavern, Minetta Tavern, and our favorite, Barrow Street. It had no sign either inside or out. You could walk by it a hundred times and not know that behind the shuttered windows was a bar. It was the closest thing we had to a private club. We ate Italian in Minetta Tavern and listened to jazz at Nick's. A lot of gay guys and lesbians, friends of Joe, frequented these hangouts. Peggy and I were accepted by them. What did I think about homosexuality? As long as you observe the right time rule, it was okay by me.

We got to know the Village. It was a heady time for both of us. The more you absorb new experiences, the more you're able to grow. Looking back, the days in the Village helped me to lose my country bumpkin outlook and manners. I acquired a degree of sophistication, learned to mix with different types, and, yes, became a better businessman. More important, Peggy liked me better. "What's the sense of living in this great, diverse city," said Peggy, "if you don't imbibe?"

I recognized the transformation when we spent time in Riverhead. It wasn't our clothes that made us different but our outlook. We were broader, more accepting of new ideas, and tolerant of ideas held by others. How did we show our new personas? We avoided confrontation until we were alone. Then we skewered the right-wing views of our friends. We weren't exactly strangers in our old home town, but we were different, natives who straddled two worlds. As the years passed and our fortunes changed and we had a daughter and a son—Regina and David—we grew further from them in every way except our affections.

# 10

"*M*oney isn't everything—health is 10 percent."
Twenty-five years later, the author of that quip lay
dying, and the relative value of money and health had flipped.
Was there such a thing as a health addict? Is it worthwhile
to spend one's life keeping fit? If you do, is there a guarantee
that you'll live longer? It was too late for me. I was hooked on
money.

It all started with my measly salary of fifteen thousand
dollars, which was 50 percent more than I had been paid as a
loan broker. It whetted my appetite. I wanted my new business
to go through the roof and my salary to go with it.

I refused to leave success in the hands of others. I took
to the road, working all day with loan brokers from Maine to
California. The work week was seven days, and many of those
days, I worked fifteen hours. The effort paid off. At the end of
the first year, Amalgamated revenues from second mortgages
was $25 million; in the next year, it was $35 million; and by the
fifth, it was a whopping $150 million, as much as other company
businesses generated altogether.

The stock market pundits had classified us as stodgy, no
growth, and no pizzazz. Our stock price languished. As second
mortgages increased our earnings, Amalgamated gained
recognition. In 1975, the year I came aboard, Amalgamated had
traded in an inactive market at about ten dollars. Five years
later, trading had picked up, and the stock hit fifteen dollars. Its

present performance was better than its past, but the company was far from superstardom.

John Rooney, the independent director who had attended the workshop and thereafter purchased ten thousand shares, took me under his wing. Near the end of my first year, we had lunch in the company cafeteria. "I told the board," he said, "that the company's increased business was due to two factors: Hargrave's brilliant decision to hire you *and* your hard work. I serve as chair of the compensation committee. My committee passes on the salary of senior management. Although you're not there yet, I'm adding you to my list. Your new salary is twenty-five thousand dollars plus one thousand stock options. And you're moving to a new office with a window. Unless you have any objections."

"I have one. Next year, if business continues to be good, do you think you could spring for lunch at the 21 Club?" I meant it as a joke. Rooney took it as one, but played it back on me. The following year, he discussed my compensation over lunch at 21. "Your raise," he said, "would have been more, but I deducted the cost of our meal. Do you still want lunch at 21?"

"Next year," I replied, "let's skip lunch." To my joy, we never did.

Rooney made his bundle building, owning, and managing parking garages in high-traffic areas. His garages were unheated and open to the air. Some rose as high as fifteen stories. Rooney believed walls and heat were unnecessary—"Cars don't catch colds." His competitors' garages were mainly on one level and had walls and heat. They also had far less capacity and cost more per parked car to operate. Rooney's design eventually became standard, but not before he had built garages in the best areas.

At our yearly lunches, always at 21, he urged me to find ways to increase Amalgamated's earnings. "The big players are conglomerates," he said. "They operate many different businesses. One feeds off the other. It's called synergy. Amalgamated could achieve synergy if it used lending to fuel a new business and the new business to increase its lending operations."

At our annual lunch in 1978, I floated an idea that had been running through my head. It grew out of my many meetings throughout the country with real estate appraisers. I thought their reports were too highly influenced by subjective factors, principally location. They appraised a house south of the railroad tracks higher than one on the north simply because it was south. It wasn't that the southern house faced a park and the other a billboard. That I could accept. What I questioned was the assignment of a huge premium based solely on location. I believed it was time to wake up home buyers to the bargains on the wrong side of town.

Rooney disagreed. "There's no room for Christopher Columbus in the real estate business. Buyers are like sheep. They follow the flock and for good reason. A home represents their biggest investment. Playing it safe is to buy where everyone else is. They're against gambling on their homes."

"Rooney, listen to me," I said. "Make it worthwhile, and people will take a chance. Suppose Amalgamated purchases fifty homes all in lousy condition and located in the same rundown neighborhood. We sell them for no money down."

Rooney shook his head no, raised both hands, and interrupted me. "Our stockholders will shoot us. That's not business; that's charity."

"No. Amalgamated sells them for more than it paid but not for cash. Let me finish. Amalgamated buys a house for fifty thousand dollars and sells it for sixty-five thousand dollars. At the closing, the buyer doesn't pay any part of the purchase price in cash. Instead, he signs a mortgage agreeing to pay sixty-five thousand dollars in monthly installments over twenty years. I call this mortgage *subprime*, because it differs from the traditional mortgage, which requires the buyer to make a down payment of 25 percent. The subprime finances the entire purchase price."

"You call it subprime; I call it shit. The buyer gets a house by promising to pay the purchase price over twenty years. A great deal for him. What's in it for Amalgamated? It parted with fifty thousand dollars in coin of the realm and gets back a piece of paper. What's to stop the home owner from walking away whenever he finds a better deal and sticking us with his shitty house?"

"Amalgamated doesn't use its own funds to buy the house. It borrows the purchase price of fifty thousand dollars by drawing down on its line of credit. It pays interest of 5 percent to its banks but charges 9 percent on the subprime mortgage. The difference is $3,450. That's our profit on one house. Now multiply that by the ten thousand houses we purchase and resell . . . well, I'll let you do the arithmetic. You call the business insane; I call it a first-class synergistic, new business.

"The houses start out being wrecks, handyman specials, rusty and rundown in downtrodden neighborhoods. The combination of these circumstances allows Amalgamated to buy them at a small fraction of what they'd have been worth in good condition and in good neighborhoods. We require the buyer to invest his hard labor in specific areas of remodeling, repairing, and renovating. If the buyer lives up to his commitment, his sweat equity has raised the value of his home from fifty thousand dollars to at least sixty-five thousand dollars. Now, if he walks, Amalgamated, which owes fifty thousand dollars to its banks, forecloses on a sixty-five thousand-dollar piece of property. If you knew anything about working-class guys, you would know that they love their homes made beautiful by their sweat. They are not likely to take a walk."

Rooney was quiet for a time. He appeared to be concentrating on his lunch, the famous 21 hamburger. I knew he was not, because ketchup and bits of an onion dripped down his mouth, and he was a fastidious eater. With ketchup still oozing, he asked, "Where are you going to get the inventory? A handful of houses ain't a business. You'll need tens of thousands of homes to make the project viable."

"I've seen several New Jersey neighborhoods choc-a-bloc full of distressed houses, all located within blocks of each other. Nearby are homes with fresh faces, selling for much higher prices. How about touring these places with me?"

Rooney deflected my offer. "Where are you going to find the buyers?"

"Amalgamated has thousands of clients in New Jersey. Their loan applications state whether they own homes. We'll screen for family types who meet their payments, work in the trades, and rent. We'll offer them the American dream—home ownership—and make it possible by eliminating the down payment."

Rooney ate and thought, and I let him digest the idea. "The directors know I favor you," he said. "But Alfred Lewis isn't your fan. He's also a straitlaced banker. Let's bring him along. If he supports the plan, it will sail through the board. I'll give you a week's notice so you'll have time to get everything set."

I didn't wait for notice. Right after lunch, I called John Hughes, the loan officer who'd talked about Shakespeare three years ago at the convention. I thought he was sharp then, and our frequent contacts reinforced my impression. I outlined the plan and told him two directors, Rooney and Lewis, might want to see a pilot area. Before showing them one, I suggested that we, along with a skilled appraiser, tour some depressed neighborhoods. We agreed to meet several days later at Hughes's office in Newark.

That night, over martinis, I told Peggy of the new plan. She asked about demands on my time. "It will be crazy. I'll be travelling a lot and working long hours. I'll miss you and Regina and David. It will take about two years out of my life."

"Regina is three. Kids don't develop long-term memories until they're five. In later life, she won't remember her father was never home—that is, provided you're not chasing another new business when she's six. David is a baby who barely knows *me*. So you're safe for now as far as the kids are concerned. Henry, I'm worried about me. I learned today I'm pregnant. I don't know if I can manage three kids, one an infant, all by myself."

I assured Peggy that she, Regina, David, and the new baby were all that mattered. "The creation of another child is far more important than the birth of a new business. The timing is an omen, a sign from Jesus that I must reject gold."

Peggy laughed, hugged me, and kissed me and switched to business lingo: "You've told me the downside; what's the upside? How much gold is involved? And while you're counting the bars, make me another martini." Those were the days before pregnant women were teetotalers.

Before dinner was over, two happy, tipsy people had struck a deal. We agreed to hire a sleep-in maid and, when the new baby arrived, a nurse for the first two months of the baby's life. Peggy would have more free time than if I were around.

I met with Hughes and the appraiser over a three-day period. We toured neighborhoods in the Oranges, Montclair, and surrounding towns. One district stood out, across the railroad tracks from an upbeat neighborhood. The market prices of the wrong-side houses were half of the others.

The meeting with Rooney and Lewis was like pushing against an open door—all the work had been done prior to their inspection. Lewis did raise a slightly hostile question. He said his bank required a mortgagor to pay cash equal to 30 percent of the purchase price before it would grant a loan for the balance. He called his bank's mortgages "prime" and questioned whether "100 percent financing or what you call 'subprime' is too risky."

"Risk," I said, "can be managed. We select customers who'll improve their houses with their own labor. Sweat equity is what we called it in my hometown. In my opinion, a home owner is less likely to default on a house in which his urine is the mortar securing the blocks."

Lewis only looked like a stuffed shirt. "Cash equity is the norm," he said with a big smile. "Sweat equity might open a whole new world."

Rooney and Lewis jointly called for a special meeting of the board. I made the presentation, and with Rooney and Lewis as cheerleaders, the board approved five million dollars for a pilot program—one million dollars more than I had requested. I was instructed to report back within six months. I floated out of that meeting room, higher than a kite.

When I got home, I took one look at my harried wife and said, "Where the hell is the sleep-in maid? The new business starts tomorrow."

Over the next two months, Hughes and I purchased seventy-five distressed homes (for Amalgamated) at depressed prices. The cost was $3.75 million. We hired a cleaning service to remove the trash—abandoned cars, tires, hundreds of bottles, cans, cartons, and about a ton of garbage.

We culled our list of small-loan customers, choosing as potential buyers those who did not already own houses, who were paying their loans on time, and who were working as carpenters, mechanics, electricians, plumbers.

It was easy to sell the homes because of the inducement—no down payment. We bound our customers by terms in the subprime mortgages to restore the houses. Hughes and I regularly checked on the progress of their improvements. They were on target, and many were ahead of schedule. I wasn't surprised. The owners took pride in their new homes. The improvements increased both the value of the property and the neighborhood. It was a win for the buyers and for Amalgamated.

I took before-and-after photos of the houses. When the pilot was completed, I showed the pictures to the directors and presented the financial results. Our average profit per house was fifteen thousand dollars. Our overall profit on an investment of $3.75 million was $1.125 million. "Is it likely," I asked, "that our mortgagors will walk away from their spiffy new homes?"

The board answered my question by authorizing five more programs. And it approved my request to move Hughes to headquarters. He was the only black executive at Amalgamated.

I wanted to protect Hughes from company bigots. He was important, and I wanted his workplace to be a happy one. With the board's approval, I took preemptive action and called a staff meeting, and introduced Hughes with a warning: "The board has authorized me to state that Amalgamated is an equal-opportunity employer. Anyone who doesn't like that should walk out the door right now and never come back. If anyone thinks racial slurs are amusing, think again. They will be reported to me and to the board with my recommendation that the comedian be fired."

Hughes worked with me on our next five programs, in Illinois, Florida, Ohio, California, and Virginia. All were home runs. When the profits were tallied—and the projections calculated—we got the green light to go nationwide.

Thirteen years later, our subprime mortgages were in every state, and the company was involved in every aspect of real estate. We owned property and were real estate brokers, mortgage brokers, and financiers. We owned a title insurance company and an appraisal company. Amalgamated was transformed from a small loan company to the first countrywide, integrated real estate company.

I thought the company name was too stodgy and no longer described our activities. I thought, *Why not ask my kids? They're with it.* Regina said, "The stock exchange symbol is AMG. Why not call the company AMG?" The kids went on to discuss things of importance to them.

I raised the issue with the board, which formed a committee and hired a PR firm. It took a month and a fee of twenty-five thousand dollars for the firm to suggest AMG. I raised a stink: "My daughter came up with the same name in two minutes. Pay the money to her." Too late—the fee was paid in advance as a retainer.

Boards are cumbersome and ineffective, and waste money. If I could impose one reform on corporate America, I'd abolish the board of directors.

I began my climb because none of my small loans defaulted. The record in subprime mortgages was also excellent. There were some mortgagors who, because of changed circumstances, could not meet their monthly payments. Instead of defaulting and turning the house over to us, they sold their homes at a profit. Why? Throughout the 1980s, the market was on the rise, the improvements increased value, and that intangible "location" moved in our direction. No bank holding a portfolio of triple-A prime mortgages could match our record.

Stock analysts took notice of the dynamic change. The price of our stock soared. Eighteen years after I started with Amalgamated, adjusting for stock splits (there were five), a share was selling at over $350. Our company was hailed as one of the ten best performing stocks. In 1998, my stock options were worth twenty million dollars.

AMG rewarded my efforts with intangible and tangible benefits. In my tenth year, I was named to the board and the position of executive vice president of real estate. Although Hargrave held the title of CEO, my department drove the company, which was reflected in my salary of five hundred thousand dollars, my matching bonus, and options on fifty thousand shares of stock. I was the highest paid officer in the company. My office was on the southwest corner and every inch as large as Hargrave's.

When he retired in 1985, I was named CEO and given two seats on the board to fill. I named my lawyer, Robert Stultz, and my brother-in-law, David Markowitz.

AMG not only made money hand over fist but was regarded as an exemplary corporate citizen. County leaders praised us for improving their towns and cities. We were awarded good-citizen medals and keys to city halls. The greatest honor came in 1987, when I was awarded the Presidential Medal of Freedom. President Reagan made the presentation in the Rose Garden, and the ceremony was covered on national TV. The president said my work "made it possible for working-class Americans to realize the dream of home ownership without government assistance. Mr. Wojecoski's achievement underscores the efficacy of private enterprise and its superiority over big government."

My AMG family was represented at the ceremony by several directors and some senior officers. Of course, my own family was there. My mother cried, Peggy beamed, and our four children fidgeted. My father said he was too busy fixing toilets and couldn't come—another slap in the face.

After the presentation, Reagan took my arm and escorted me to his office. He invited me to join the Council of Economic Advisers. I accepted and asked how he found enough hours in the day to run the biggest enterprise in the world.

"Simple," he said. "I delegate responsibility to experts. They report back either in writing or orally. I glance quickly through written reports. If a report seems important, I ask a staff member to read it and tell me the problem and the solution, in a few words. Oral presentations pose a more difficult problem. I have to fight to stay awake. As Nancy knows, when I can't sleep at night, I think about an oral report, sip a glass of warm milk, and drop off. The trick to running the country is to pick excellent advisers and give them their heads."

I had only disdain for Reagan's management style. I'm a hands-on guy. I couldn't sleep if my responsibilities were discharged by others. As we chatted, a vision appeared. Our positions in the Oval Office were reversed. I was sitting in Reagan's chair expounding upon a Wojecoski approach to the presidency, and he was seated in a chair in front of my desk, fast asleep.

That was the first time I let my ambition run free—the first time I realized that I might have all the money I could possibly want and that my next goal might be to become president.

# 11

*B*us drivers spend their vacations on the road. My lawyer, Robert Stultz, traveled throughout the country photographing old courthouses. Mary and David visited hospitals. I was the exception to the busman's holiday syndrome. I worked all day in real estate promoting home ownership but had no interest in owning a home. To me, a home meant a private house with a front lawn and a backyard in the suburbs.

Our dream abode was an apartment in the heart of the city. Neither the size of the rooms nor the furniture was of importance. What had mattered was that our one-bedroom flat, selected and furnished by someone else, was in the art and business capital of the western world. I lived there alone for eight months. After Peggy and I were married, she moved in. Almost immediately, all hell broke loose.

Essential services failed, one after the other. First, the elevator—out for a month. When it was fixed, it coughed, wheezed, held its breath, and stalled. We prayed to God every time. Peggy and I took to the stairs, all five flights. The frequent climbs, she said, made it unnecessary for her to work out at the McBurney Y.

Then the hot water stopped. When that got fixed, rust was added to the water. Peggy joined the Y, not to exercise but to take a shower.

A tenant's gas stove exploded, barely sparing her life. We were too terrified to cook.

The electricity was dicey: on one day, off the next.

Talk about heat. We got it only on sizzling summer days.

We named the building "the house that Murphy built," after the man who decreed that anything that can go wrong will go wrong.

Adversity builds character. It also brings people together. The tenants formed action groups and protest groups, and declared a rent strike. We cried, complained, and also laughed. In a generally anonymous city, the tenants bonded.

On weekends, Peggy and I looked at vacant apartments in the neighborhood and asked, "When was the last time the elevator failed? How about hot water and heat?" We were skeptical about the upbeat answers. How could everything work in other buildings and nothing in ours?

We stayed put. Even if the utilities didn't work, it's hard to beat free. There was another reason: we were happy, very happy in Murphy's one-bedroom apartment with a view on the fifth floor.

When we learned in November 1975 that Peggy was pregnant, I asked Amalgamated's human resource department to find us a two-bedroom apartment in a building that worked. The company found a five-room apartment on Central Park West. Our apartment didn't face the park, but we were on a high floor, and our bedroom had a partial view of the Hudson. There were doormen, spiffy elevators, a modern kitchen, and rooms that were outsized. Did our grand apartment change our lives? Only in one respect. On the day we moved in, we varied the "right time rule" and made love while the sun was setting.

Regina, our first baby, was born on June 6, 1976. We named her after Peggy's great-great-grandmother. She was a big baby, seven pounds at birth. She was followed by David, her sister Gabryel, and her brother Antone. After the birth of Antone, Peggy said, "This is it. Our family is complete. We have two girls and two boys. I don't want to go through another pregnancy. Child-bearing is a closed chapter." As the family grew, we moved to larger apartments in our building, but after Antone's birth, even our three-bedroom apartment was too tight.

In 1987, both the real estate and stock market took a tumble. Peggy thought the time was ripe for the Wojecoskis to buy a home, not in the suburbs but right here in town. She focused on brownstones because she liked a relaxed style of life where one is free to come and go without elevators and doormen. The houses were mostly narrow, dark, converted into small apartments. Extensive renovation would be required to turn them back into single-family homes. One stood out: it was a Georgian-style, red brick, double-wide, forty-foot mansion on 104th Street and Riverside Drive. The facade was ornate, with large window ledges, small stone balconies, and front and rear gargoyles on the upper floors. It had views of Riverside Park and the Hudson River.

Built as a one-family home for a beer baron, it had fifteen bedrooms and ten bathrooms. In the early 1960s, a brother and a sister, both doctors, each with large families, had bought it and used the building for medical offices and living.

Now retired, the doctors had put the house on the market. The building had drawbacks. The East Side was fashionable, not the west. Although parts of the West Side were considered chic, 104th Street was beyond the pale. And the house was too large for one family. The sellers knew that home owners don't much like being a landlord in their own houses, so all the drawbacks were reflected in the price—a terrific bargain.

West 104th Street was all right for the Wojecoskis. We're reverse snobs.

Although we were a large family and liked extra space, the problem of the house being too big remained. Peggy loved the townhouse, dubbed it "Hudson House," and wrestled with ideas on how to make it ours. A chance conversation at a Thanksgiving Day dinner showed the way.

Mary's in-laws, Carole and Benjamin Markowitz, hosted the dinner. My parents, Peggy and I and our four children, and David, Mary, and their five children, were guests.

David and Mary lived in a penthouse in Washington Heights overlooking the Hudson, an easy stroll to the Columbia University Medical Center. David was chief of the Center for Advanced Cardiac Care within the highly regarded Division of Cardiology. Mary was dean of the nursing school. Our Regina and Mary's son Henry, the eldest in each family, attended the same school,

Trinity School on West Ninety-First Street. The others would enroll there too.

David and Mary liked living near the medical center. Their hours were long and irregular. Being able to walk home was a great advantage. They also loved the view from their penthouse and the wraparound terrace, but the apartment was too crowded. At dinner, Michael, the second Markowitz son, complained about his older brother, Henry. "He stays up late reading. I have trouble sleeping." Actor that he was, he yawned and, in a loud voice, said, "Yawn." Michael is handsome, bright, a favorite among the cousins. His vocal yawn drew smiles and a guffaw from Regina.

Peggy's eyes were on fire. She tugged me and said, "Come with me right now."

When we were out of earshot, Peggy said, "Let's share Hudson House with David and Mary."

She started to sell me on it, but I said, "I'd like nothing better. Sell them."

On Sunday, the four of us spent the day inspecting the house. David, bursting with enthusiasm, wanted to build a squash court in the basement. We played together at the Yale Club, where David was a member, and at the New York Athletic Club, where I played host. He won most of the time, but I was competitive. "Now we can play," he said, "whenever we want to on our own court. We can teach the kids. There's plenty of room for a pool table and a small theater. The basement is perfect as a joint family center."

The ground floor housed the original kitchen, wine cellar, pantry, and servants' rooms. David envisioned a library running the width and depth of the floor. It too would be shared. The rest of the house would be evenly divided. "Our families," David said, "will partition the third, fourth, and fifth floors into two private apartments. It's impossible to imagine a more perfect solution to our housing dilemma."

A back door off the ground floor led to a scruffy backyard. Located high above Riverside Park and the Hudson, it had lots of potential. Peggy saw large modern sculptures set in a Japanese rock garden. David countered with a playful suggestion: convert it into a family cemetery. "I not only want to live here during my lifetime but for eternity."

The asking price was $990,000. I advised offering the full sum so we'd be sure to get the property. "We can try chiseling, but it makes no sense. The price is a bargain, the property unique; let's grab it. I know a bank that will give us a mortgage for the full purchase price. We'll spend our money on improvements."

We bought the house, made all the improvements, and, within a year, moved in. Sometimes, dreams turn into nightmares. Not Hudson House. The kids ran happily through both apartments. The parents, following an unwritten rule, waited for an invitation. I hired a cook and a butler. Most nights, all thirteen of us ate together. It was an ideal mix of communal and private living.

The children loved the house but none better than Michael. "It was my yawn that planted the seed in Aunt Peggy's brain."

Hudson House was featured in *Architectural Digest* and the garden in *House and Garden*. In 1989, the *New York Times* did a feature story in the "Home" section titled, "How Two Families Embrace Communal Living."

David and I played squash regularly, sometimes early in the morning. There were nine carrels in the library, one for each child. They studied alone and tutored each other. My favorite time came when I sat in a red leather armchair reading, but in truth, I was watching all the children hard at their studies.

I loved my children, and I'm sure they loved me, but our relationship was strained, and it was my fault. I was distracted when I was with them. I thought about work when I should have been concentrating on them. I was bored with the playground, swings, slides, monkey bars, and particularly the filthy sandbox. My father never spent time with me, except when I worked for him. Why was I having to do what Peggy called "parenting"? When the children were reluctant to spend a weekend day with me, I knew I needed help. I turned to Irwin Diamond, a psychiatrist, recommended by David.

"When you're doing childlike activities with your children," the psychiatrist said, "your thoughts turn to business. Kids have sharp antennae. They sense you are not with them. Try practicing the art of humanitarian selfishness. Take your children to activities you enjoy. You won't be bored and, I bet, neither will they."

I started by taking my two oldest to a matinee of the New York Ballet Company and to an early dinner at Rumplemeyer's. On other occasions, I took all four to Leonard Bernstein's young people's concerts. I also took them to ball games, tennis matches, and shows. We took long walks exploring ethnic neighborhoods in and around the city followed by meals at local restaurants. The only place that was off limits was the playground. It worked. My children invited their friends along. They enjoyed the outings, but not as much as I did.

There were other problems I encountered over the years, ones I had difficulty understanding. I maintained contact with Dr. Diamond and consulted with him from time to time.

I don't know whether it was the society of Hudson House, my secure feeling at work, my excellent family relationship, or all of the above—I was a happy man. Then shit happened.

In 1995, our sainted Mary, our love, our joy, our happiness, developed ovarian cancer. She fought hard and got the best treatment, but there was no beating the disease. Within a year, she died.

At David's insistence, Mary was cremated, her ashes spread under a Camperdown elm near their wing of the house. David bought a concrete bench and placed it near the tree. He spent hours sitting on the bench. He grieved so long and hard that he lost interest in reading, sports, life, even his children. Some days, he stayed in bed all day; others, he stayed up all night. Peggy took a leave of absence from the museum and cared for the rudderless family.

For about a year, David saw no one and barely talked. He refused treatment for his deep depression.

I let him grieve for a year. Then I cornered him in his family's kitchen one day after the children had left for school. "You stupid, self-indulgent bastard. Do you think Mary would want you to resign from life? Neglect your children? Abandon your career? There's medication. There's psychoanalysis. You've been in mourning for a year. Get over it. Rejoin the human race."

My entreaties didn't work. Neither did Peggy's. But when all five of his children dropped down on their knees and begged him, "Come back to us, Daddy. We lost Mom. It's not fair that we lose you too," he promised to make a new start.

We played squash again, but his heart wasn't in it. He failed to score a point and—worst of all—didn't seem to care.

"The house is haunted. I see her everywhere. Maybe a change of scenery would help."

I suggested we sell the house and buy another white elephant. "You can get away from the house but not the Wojecoskis. You're tethered to me. I have no sister, only one brother. I'm not letting you go."

"I don't want to leave Hudson House. Mary's ashes are here. My analyst suggests I take a trip, hike in the Alps, spend a month in London and Paris. Anywhere, just get away. "

I met with Dr. Diamond about how I might help David, whose depression was so severe. I feared he was suicidal. My analyst arranged for me to meet with David's. "Mary," David's analyst said, "was the glue. She bound you to David and David to you. She moved gracefully and easily between her different worlds. The Jewish origin of her husband, the mixed heritage of her immediate family, and the Polish American culture of her twin brother's family. David mourns the loss of his wife. He is unlikely to take his own life but more than likely to end his close relationship with you. He must do so if he is to get on with his life. David knows and fears this. I have probably told you more than the code of ethics allows."

A few days later, David said he wished to discuss a personal matter. I was prepared for him to say that he was moving. Instead, he said he would soon be off on a two-week cruise. "I know it's unnecessary to add, but please look after my children."

David called every night. He spoke to his children and to Peggy and me. I couldn't tell much, but I learned a lot on his return.

David introduced Peggy and me to his new friend, Joan Barclay, a blonde who was strikingly attractive—and a cold-blooded WASP. She worked in public relations, specializing in high-end furniture and design. Although she was adept at dissembling, we felt her tone of voice and emphasis on superficial concerns reflected instant dislike.

"Oh, David talks about you all the time, but he failed to prepare me for how attractive both of you are. Peggy, where did you get that dress and the shoes? Henry, promise me you will take David shopping with you." She was unctuous. She was as unlike Mary as seltzer water is to champagne, but I was prepared to accept her for David's sake and that of my nieces and nephews.

I never got a chance. They got married, and she took David over completely. Although she moved into Hudson House, we rarely socialized. In the past, we had gone on family ski trips, tramped through Europe, chartered buses to wilderness areas. All that ended. David and Joan lived separate lives from us.

When my secretary informed me one afternoon that Dr. Markowitz was in the reception area waiting to see me, I took it as an ominous sign. We lived in the same house. Anything David had to say he could say there. Why come to my office? I was anxious and went to reception. When we were in my office, I asked if everything was all right.

"Everything's fine," he said. "It's simply an issue of identity. You've been my brother since we met in 1973. I'm married to Joan. For the sake of my marriage, I must get over Mary. That's hard enough, and it's made harder being so closely associated with you. I've a letter resigning from AMG's board of directors. I've sold my stock worth, would you believe, for five million dollars, all because of you. I plan to turn the money over to Joan's brother, a money manager. Please understand, Henry, if Mary had lived, we'd have stayed brothers until we died. But that was not to be."

His resignation and sale of stock made no sense. As the company prospered, the board held meetings in famous resorts and exotic locations. The directors enjoyed the surroundings, none more than David. Why give up a perk? He had discussed with me whether too much of his wealth was in AMG's stock. "Do you think I should diversify?" He accepted my view that diversification was a euphemism for an uninformed investment plan.

"AMG has plenty of room for growth," I had said. "When it's time to exit, we'll go together."

I knew David did not want to resign his directorship nor sell his stock. He knew that I knew he did not want to take these actions. What did two middle-aged men do? We cried.

Our nieces and nephews spent time with us when they were young, but as they grew older, they had more important things to do then say hello to Uncle Henry and Aunt Peggy. We understood.

On the plus side, David returned to work and reclaimed his former position as New York's top cardiac surgeon. We thought he had forgotten Mary until one day, Peggy called me over to a window, and we both witnessed David sitting on the concrete bench under the Camperdown Elm with his hands over his eyes, trying desperately to hide his weeping.

Nothing, not David's remarriage, not his resignation, not his sale of stock, not even Mary's death, could separate us. David, Mary, Peggy, and I were inextricably bound together. All four of us were family.

# 12

*E* cumenical life is an acquired taste; heritage is etched in your soul.

Mary's death and the appearance of David's new wife stirred a yearning to return to our Polish American roots. Peggy was the first to raise it. "We've ignored our own kind for much too long. We should buy a summer house in Riverhead. Our parents live there, and so do a lot of our people." Seeing me gasp in horror, she modified her position. "What would you say to Southampton? We could spend summers at the beach and spend time with our parents and old-time friends. I'll bet your relationship with your father would improve. It couldn't get any worse. Maybe we could recreate Hudson House by the sea."

My secretary called a Southampton realtor and made an appointment. When we arrived at her office, the anorexic blonde claimed to have had no record of the call. She asked for our price range. "Show us only oceanfront property," I said. "We'll discuss price when we find what we want." She did a double take. I guess the broker was accustomed to people with names like Ford, Murray, and Lehman buying beachfront houses, not a pair of Poles.

"Are you sure you can afford it, Mr. Wojecoski? They are very expensive—"

I interrupted her. "We're poor, but we have lots of money."

She smiled between clenched teeth. "There's not much available, and what there is you may not like. There's one that's been on the market for several years. It has charm but nothing else."

The house was old-guard Southampton, what they called a cottage—eighteen rooms—on three acres, with about three hundred running feet on the ocean. "The same family," she said, "has owned it for maybe three generations. They have spent almost no money on upkeep. It was once so grand. Years of neglect have turned it into a teardown: a perfect site for one of those new mansions. That's what you'll want. "

If Peggy had heard her, she made no sign. She walked through the house once and then again and a third time before she said a word. "My husband and I were born and raised in Riverhead. We believe in gutting fish, not houses. We're going to get something to eat. We'd like to come back this afternoon with a contractor."

"It's Sunday," the startled broker said. "Only real estate brokers work on the weekend. No one will come out on a Sunday, not even for an emergency."

"I have in mind John Warzelbacher. Do you know him?"

"Of course. His company is the busiest contractor on the East End. People wait a month for him."

"My wife and I grew up with John," I said. "He'll come. What I want to be sure about is that we can get into the house."

The broker said she was stuck in the office all day. "If you want to see the house again with or without Mr. Warzelbacher, call me."

She drove us back to her office. I called Warzelbacher. "For a chance to glimpse the magnificent Peggy," he said, "of course I'll be there. I know the property. What's the asking price?" I covered the phone and asked the broker.

"Three million, but they're eager to sell. You can get it for less."

I relayed the information to John. "Henry," he said, "it's a steal. The land alone is worth a lot more. The house is a disaster, a negative, but we'll discuss that later. Hey, buddy boy, you sure have come a long way since we were cutting lawns. See ya at three."

I hadn't seen John for twenty years, but when we met, it was as though we had never been apart. We hugged, he and Peggy kissed, and all three of us laughed. The broker unlocked the front door and deferentially asked if someone from the Warzelbacher firm could stop by her house on Monday. John brushed her off, telling her to call the office. "I've been calling your office every day this week. I have a plumbing problem. Promises but no action. How come they get you immediately?"

"Henry and I were business partners when we were sixteen. We were marines together in Vietnam. I've had a crush on Peggy since I was eleven, when we sang together in the children's choir at St. Isadore's. You see this?" He held up his right arm. "If they wanted it, I'd cut it off and give it to them. We're part of the Riverhead Polish American clan. Because you're with the Wojecoskis, I'll break a company rule, override the dispatcher, and send a plumber tomorrow to you. Maybe—no promises—I'll come myself. Now leave us alone so we can assess the house."

Warzelbacher pointed out that the lead pipes needed to be replaced with copper. The wiring, dangerously flawed, could cause an electrical fire. The kitchens and bathrooms were from the Stone Age. The roof leaked. New gutters and leaders were needed five years ago. The porch sagged, plainly in need of support. "To fix the house," he said, "would cost more than tearing it down and starting from scratch."

I didn't need my old buddy to tell me that. I needed an impartial voice to convince Peggy. Instead, he inadvertently provided a green light. "John," Peggy said, "you can hire artists to duplicate the Mona Lisa. The paint will be fresh and the strokes will show not a single crack. The remake won't fool anyone but a fool. To me, this house is a classic. I don't want a reproduction. You said it can be restored. How much?"

Warzelbacher gave us a ballpark figure—one million dollars. I took one look at Peggy, who was staring at me, and I thought, *She's mine; she's alive; I'm hers, and I'm alive. For a stinking four million dollars, I can make her happy.* "John, I'll buy the house and restore it on one condition. You agree to be the general contractor." We didn't shake hands. We just looked at each and smiled.

We bought the house, and Warzelbacher restored it.

Peggy was right. The house was the Mona Lisa. Had we replaced it, no matter the cost, the new house would have been a fake.

The house had only one drawback, a social one. It's no more than a quarter of a mile stroll on the beach to the fancy Meadow Club. Some of my business "friends" who made money off me were members. They invited Peggy and me to drinks and dinner. We wanted to join and said so to one of the members, who just happened to be the president of the club. He tossed off my request. "Membership is a waste of time and money. Any time you want to come here, call me. Glad to have you as a guest."

I said to Peggy, "We're good white Christians who happen to be Polish Americans. Being Polish disqualifies us. Just like being Jewish or black. Then why cozy up to me in business? I'm good enough to make money for you but not to club around with."

I was glad when those guys lost fortunes during the Great Recession. Poles are not good enough to join the Meadow Club? Take that multimillion-dollar loss.

I'd like to hire terrorists to blow the place up.

The contrast between the Meadow Club and Warzelbacher Contractors was stark. We couldn't get in the door of the club. Warzelbacher worked for a year on our house without a contract. Why were we unwelcome in one and embraced in the other? The answer was family.

To call someone family is to begin, not end, the analysis. Most families function normally. The parents love the children, and the children love the parents. Our family was dysfunctional. I loved my mother always, and she loved me. Andrew was a different case. As soon as I reached the age of discretion, I disliked him. As time passed, he faded into the background. I forgot to dislike him. He never forgot to loathe me.

Elizabeth, a regular visitor at Hudson House, rarely came with Andrew. He stayed in Riverhead, claiming to despise New York: "Too big. I get lost crossing the street." There was another reason: he didn't want to see me.

Dr. Diamond discussed, as possible motives, envy and jealousy. He advised me to praise my father's hard work as a plumber and sympathize over the injustice that his important work was not properly rewarded.

At a rare family dinner at Hudson House when Andrew was present, I talked about the hard work of the men who built the cities and towns. Then instead of praising him, I inadvertently patted myself on the back. "In my mortgage business, I value sweat equity over cash equity."

Andrew's eyes flashed. "Yeah, sure. Money is all that matters to you."

"Not true," I said. "My subprimes are supported by labor, not cash."

"As a kid, you had no stomach for hard work. Now that you're a big-shot money lender, you sit on your ass and suck money at rates even a Jew wouldn't charge. You claim you want to extend the American dream of home ownership to working-class families. You're not interested in their welfare, only in picking their pockets. Thinking about your slick practices is the only time I'm in favor of communism."

His words stung me. I gasped for breath. I looked at my mother. She signaled for me to be quiet. I pretended to ignore his attack by engaging in a diversion. "You know, Dad, I almost lost my life fighting communism." Andrew respected my military service, the only thing about me he respected. He made no reply, and the conversation continued as though there had been no outburst.

My psychiatrist asked me to arrange a joint session with Andrew. The doctor thought with his help, I could be drawn into praising my father. Andrew rejected meeting my doctor: "I have no problem with you. It's just that you put on airs. Think you're better than the rest of us. All you do is push paper. The world would be a better place without paper pushers."

Visits to my parents' house were strained. We were crowded in their small home—sometimes all nine grandchildren showed up at once. It was also clear that the kids wanted to be on the beach. To relieve stress, Peggy and I came alone. "Where are my grandchildren?" said Andrew. "Whaddya do? Teach them to hate me?"

Peggy persisted. She invited my parents to dinner parties peopled by rich and famous friends. Andrew remained mostly silent. One night, I overheard a friend ask if he was proud of me—what a softball question to any parent but him. I dreaded the answer, because his harshness would startle my friend. "My boy pulled himself up by his bootstraps," Andrew said. "He was born a plumber's son, too poor to go to college. Look where he is today. You bet I'm proud of him. His twin sister too. Before she died, she was the dean of the school of nursing at Columbia University Medical Center. My wife and I must have passed some good genes on to our kids."

My friend turned to me, beckoning me toward him. "Lucky you," he said. "Your father is proud of you. Mine looks down on me. I'm a failure because I'll never reach his heights."

Maybe there's a touch of dysfunction in every family.

My analyst lectured me on causation. "Your father's hostility may be based on your conduct toward him. As you heard, he's proud of you. It's not your success that's troubling him. It's something else. Let's dig to find the cause. The way you present the early years, he was a destructive force and you a good son. Speak to a contemporary of your father and get an objective view."

Roman Warzelbacher, John's father, worked jobs together with Andrew. On some, I worked along with Roman's three sons. He was an obvious candidate. When I told Roman I wanted to meet with him and why, he invited me to the traditional Warzelbacher Sunday feast. "We'll eat, but then you, John, and I will slip away for a talk."

Roman Warzelbacher and his wife, Anna, lived in a contemporary ranch-style house in Shinnecock Hills, a section of Southampton inhabited mainly by year-round residents. The house, like its neighbors, sat on a quarter-acre plot. Roman had put up a large addition, so the house towered over its site. On Sundays, pickup trucks with the logo of Warzelbacher & Sons Plumbing, Heating, Air Conditioning lined the driveway and small backyard.

Their open front door led straight into the addition, which was even larger than it looked from the outside and packed with family, at least thirty people ranging from babies to grandparents. The children jumped, skipped, sang, and played with toys. Teenagers took turns strumming a guitar. In the center of the room was a large table. Stacks of plates, utensils, glasses, and napkins lined the sides. Roast turkey, ham, vegetables, salads, steamed potatoes, gravy, sauces, cakes, and pies occupied the middle.

This, I thought, was a blue-collar family gathering. It was informal, casual. At the Warzelbachers', the family helped themselves to food prepared by the family. In family dinners at Hudson House, we had a cook and a maid. In other respects, the gatherings were the same. The children, parents, and grandparents bore a likeness, an attribute of family that cannot be disguised.

Roman greeted me. "Here he is, Riverhead's first citizen," he announced to the room. "We are honored by your presence." He handed me a glass and filled it with wine from a gallon-sized jug. He then took me by the arm and led me to the kitchen. "We always eat together in the great room," he said. "Today, we need privacy. After we get food, you, John, and I will sit around the kitchen table and talk. Okay?"

John thought I looked unhappy and said so. "Hell, Henry, lighten up. Smile, please. You have no right to be unhappy and every right to gloat. Nobody has more than you."

I told father and son about my relationship with Andrew. "He hates me, plain and simple. Want to know why I'm sad? That's the reason. How would you feel if Roman hated you?" I stared at John, who winced at the thought.

"No chance of that," Roman answered. "John and his brothers listened and did what I told them. They always had my love. Over time, they earned my respect as experts in our field."

"Well, I was respectful to my father; it was he who always attacked me. Right?"

"Henry, you are a guest at my house. Do you really want to hear the truth? What purpose will it serve? Nothing can change. What happened, happened."

I told Roman that my relationship with my father was causing unhappiness within the family. "I'm seeking professional help.

My psychiatrist has told me that I must learn the unvarnished facts. I know you don't want to hurt me or Andrew, but maybe you can help."

"You were not the perfect son. Sometimes, you shouted cuss words at your father. Walked off jobs. You were downright nasty. Plumbers are made, not born. A master plumber trains an apprentice the old-fashioned way, by yelling at him. This is especially true when the apprentice is a son. My sons took it; you fought back. You turned out to be a success in life, but as a plumber's son, you were a failure. I'm sorry, Henry. Our Riverhead-Southampton crowd admires you. We hold you out as an example of how far someone can get. Maybe it was your independent spirit that made you a success. You wanted the truth. There it is."

I reported back to my psychiatrist. "Life is a tradeoff. If you had stayed in Riverhead, not rebelled, and become a plumber, you would have had the same loving relationship as Roman and John. Instead, you became a money machine. In an earlier session, you said money can fix problems, and if it doesn't work at first, throw more money. Remember?"

Of course I remembered. It was my mantra. But maybe it wasn't as good a mantra as I'd always believed.

A month later, on Memorial Day, Riverhead held its annual parade. Veterans dressed in their uniforms marched with their brothers-in-arms. In prior years, I was neither invited nor wanted to participate. That year, 1992, I was the sponsor. Andrew and I led the parade. Friends lined the streets. We waived to them. Someone shouted, "Yeah, Andrew and Henry." The crowd took up the chant. I looked at Andrew. Tears were rolling down his cheeks. I too started to cry.

When the parade was over, I invited Andrew to my house for a Memorial Day party. "We'll wear our uniforms."

"Well," said Andrew, "we have a choice. There's bingo and beer at the VFW hall."

That night, there was a big party at my house, but I didn't go. I played bingo, drank beer, and kibitzed with old friends and my father. Before returning home for the night, I kissed my father, and he kissed me. It's the first time I remember us kissing.

At bingo, several guys had discussed Boynton Beach, Florida, the preferred spot in winter for Riverhead's Polish American community. A few owned houses; most rented cabins or stayed in bargain-priced hotels. A few days later, Peggy and I went down to look the place over. We liked a house a short walk to the beach and close to the center of town. It had an attached apartment that the broker said was for grandchildren. I put down a deposit.

The next week, we returned with my parents. "It's yours," Peggy said, "provided you allow us to visit when it becomes impossibly cold in New York. We'll stay in the grandchildren's apartment."

"It's too expensive," said my mother.

"No, Mom, it's too cheap for all you and Dad have done for me. And don't forget, we'll be sharing the house."

"That's the best part of the deal," said Andrew. "We get you all to ourselves."

I've known a lot of dysfunctional families. But some can get over it.

# 13

*P*eople should like themselves. A little narcissism is a good thing. An overdose is bad and can lead to a serious personality disorder. I didn't spend time appreciating me because so many others did.

The directors and employees at AMG worshipped me. I was their king, their god. I became a national figure when President Reagan bestowed a citation on me in the Rose Garden, invited me for a tête-à-tête in the Oval Office, and asked me to join his inner circle of economic advisers. Governors and mayors presented me with awards for my work improving their cities and towns.

I confess. I was thrilled by recognition. My addiction, however, was not fed by praise but by gold. Rooney was my dealer; Peggy, my enabler. Rooney, in charge of executive salary, set mine beyond the dreams of avarice. Yet I always wanted more. Peggy's role was less obvious but no less important. I could not have continued without her support. It was easier for Peggy than if I had some other addiction.

If my addiction had been alcohol, I might have come home drunk or spent days away on binges, passed out at parties, maybe turned violent, and lost my job. As a money addict, I shared my fortune with my family. Talk about vacations! We went to Aspen every spring and to Caneel Bay for two weeks over Christmas. In the summer, we chartered yachts and sailed the coasts of France, Italy, and Greece. Peggy hired cooks, maids, baby nurses, nannies, and au pairs. Free from household duties, she pursued her career. She rose to senior curator at MoMA and in 2000 was named a trustee. I'm sure she would have gotten there on her own, but my substantial donations didn't hurt.

Peggy had carte blanche to buy clothes and accessories. I bought her jewelry and furs. Her husband was happy; she was fulfilled. Any wonder she never said a word against my addiction?

Now that I was rich and celebrated, did I sit back and enjoy life? No. The superrich own businesses. I wanted my own business.

In 1992, AMG owned subprime mortgages aggregating about one billion dollars. Every day, our real estate operations generated more. The company was overstuffed. At board meetings, I proposed we sell the mortgages. They were profitable, but I believed we could earn a greater return in a new business, owning and operating hotels. The plan was to buy rundown hotels, fix them up, and provide gratis amenities such as shuttle service back and forth to airports, breakfast buffets, beer, wine, and snacks during the cocktail hour. Our bankers projected the annual return from the hotel business at 20 percent, a rate vastly exceeding the return on the subprimes. I even had a name for the new venture, Hotel Amenities Unlimited.

Before Amalgamated could take on the asset-intensive hotel project, it needed to free capital by selling its inventory of subprime mortgages. Generating subprimes was a sound business, but it was bad to hold on to them.

I raised the problem at a board meeting. "We're holding a billion dollars worth of subprimes. The hotel venture will need lots of cash. We can raise it by selling the subprimes, but it will take years if we try a retail approach, and by that time, we'll have another billion dollars worth. The way to do it is to sell them all in one fell swoop."

At our next board meeting, we invited a Wall Street supersalesman, Ace Greenberg, the head of Bear Stearns, to advise us on the most efficient way to sell our mortgages. He drew an analogy between our mortgages and bonds: "Small lots of bonds and leftover bits and pieces of corporate debt are sometimes bundled together and sold as a jumbo bond called a consolidated debt obligation. I never heard of it being done with mortgages, but there's a first time for everything. Why not give my firm a shot? We'll pick a bunch of mortgages, put them in a package, call it a 'consolidated mortgage obligation' and see what it will fetch."

Greenberg's team picked five hundred mortgages worth thirty-five million dollars, paying 9 percent interest, and tested the water.

Since AMG originated subprimes ten years ago, none had defaulted. If mortgagors couldn't meet their monthly payments, they sold the property for more than the mortgage and kept the profit. With a history of a perfect record and a high yield, buyers should have knocked down our doors to buy our model consolidated mortgage obligation. No one even tapped.

Greenberg explained why. "In the eyes of the know-nothing rating agencies, subprimes were classified as junk. Buyers sought a steep discount, and the best and only offer we were able to stir up was twenty-five million dollars. Buyers were spooked. A bond formed by combining mortgages was a novelty. Bond investors lack imagination and want the traditional kind."

I couldn't recommend a sale at a 30 percent discount. Using Stultz as a sounding board, I came up with a new plan.

"Greenberg tells me there are no buyers for a fair price. He found one willing to buy at a discount of 30 percent. I'm not wed to subprimes. I'm a realist. We'll have to take a discount, but not 30 percent, maybe 15. Suppose I agreed to purchase all the subprimes, one billion dollars worth, for $850 million."

"Henry, what have you been drinking or smoking? I know you're rich, but you don't have a free $850 million stashed away somewhere."

"Stultz, old buddy, I propose to use opium, an acronym for other people's money. I'll raise a billion dollars from a newly formed hedge fund. I'll immediately resell the mortgages purchased by me for $850 million to the hedge fund for $1 billion. If things work out, there will be three happy campers: AMG, which sold the mortgages at more than market and will be able to bankroll the hotel venture; me, as I'll make an immediate profit of $150 million on the resale of the subprimes; and the owners of the hedge fund, who will earn 9 percent on their investment."

Stultz looked at me as though I was crazy. He was blunt when a point had to be hammered home and verbose when he was stalling for time. He began by being blunt. "Henry, you know a little bit about lending to working-class families, but you're out of your league when it comes to preparing business plans, spreadsheets, PowerPoint presentations, projections—all the tricks one learns in business school. And you don't have the financial alchemist talent to convert mundane mortgages into highly sophisticated securities."

"I can buy the talent I need."

"Well, in that case, okay. Investment bankers are for sale. But I work on many deals with these guys, and they don't come cheap. You're proposing to start a billion-dollar company. To succeed, you're going to have to pay dearly. I know you're a tight son of a bitch, but it's going to cost you to make this deal fly. You can't do it without a top banker."

"Give me a name," I said. "Give me two names."

"I just got finished doing a deal with a banker," he said. "The stakes were high and the principals unusually obnoxious. Even worse than you. To unwind, we bantered. I said bankers were overpaid, particularly when compared with lawyers. I cited the case of a junior partner who left our firm for Goldman Sachs. In one year, his salary plus bonus was twice that of our senior partner. He wasn't even particularly smart for a lawyer. Brilliant for a banker. Different standards in different professions. Ordinary lawyers become stars when they switch to banking."

"So give me a name," I repeated.

"The guy defended banker's compensation. 'We make deals. You get in the way. Of course a banker is worth more than a lawyer. Would you like to switch? For 10 percent of your bonus, I'll place you.' I laughed and said there isn't enough money in banking to entice me to leave the law."

"'There is,' he said, 'in hedge funds. Talk about big bucks. Those guys make hundreds of millions. Best of all, their take is taxed at 15 percent, the capital gains rate. Make me an offer, hedge fund. I'm yours.'"

Stultz paused, looked me straight in the eye, and then said the candidate's name, James Watson. "Watson," he said, "was a summa cum laude graduate of Harvard and a McNamara scholar at the business school. He's now a managing partner at Morgan Stanley, the whitest of white-shoe investment banking firms. And he is a descendant of the founder of IBM, Thomas J. Watson."

Although I wasn't impressed with background, the rest of the world was. In raising a billion dollars, that pedigree would be an important asset. What did impress me was Watson's academic record and success in the real world.

"Before meeting Watson, there's something we should discuss," I began. "In the summer of 1963, my dad and I worked on the Southampton house of the then reigning king of railroads, Patrick B. McGinnis. Weeks later, he got indicted and sent to the slammer for taking a kickback of thirty-five thousand dollars on the sale of surplus rail cars. He knew the indictment was coming and lamented the way he had handled it. If the payment had been out in the open and described as a bonus, he'd have avoided prosecution. He advised me, 'Let everything hang out, but cover your ass.' Robert, I don't want this deal to backfire."

"That's good advice," said Stultz. "Let's make the record unambiguous. We'll call a special board meeting and have Greenberg and his client repeat their offer. We'll do nothing to advance your proposal until the board acts on the offer."

At the meeting, the board reviewed the need to increase liquidity by selling the subprimes and unanimously approved their sale. Greenberg and his client, an official of the pension fund of the International Brotherhood of Teamsters, joined the meeting. Greenberg repeated the offer. I said it was too low and asked for a higher bid. The teamster representative appeared annoyed: "This is not a Turkish bazaar. Our offer is firm. Ace has told us that after a wide solicitation, we're the only game in town. Take it or leave it. You have a week to decide." The offer was unanimously rejected.

Two weeks later, at the tap room of the University Club, Stultz introduced Watson to me. He was tall, towering over me—and I'm six foot two. His black hair was long but neat, sprinkled with gray. His suit was elegant, a blue pinstripe set off by a light blue shirt with white collar and cuffs. Almost as soon as he sat down at our table, a man waved to him. He nodded back but made it clear when he turned away that he wanted no further contact. His manners, like his dress, were impeccable.

Stultz had previously discussed my plan with Watson, and he had reviewed a ten-year record of our subprimes. Watson liked the concept: a fund holding mortgages rather than stock. Stocks, he said, were a roller coaster: they go up and down. Mortgages generate a constant return. "The pension funds," he said, "are not-for-profit entities. The interest income is tax free. They will stand in line to invest. Henry—may I call you Henry?—you're a genius!"

I thanked him, but with a nod to Stultz that said I was well aware that I was not enough of a genius to run the show alone. I needed a financial wizard and was ready to make the right one my partner. "Stultz says you're tops; I've checked you out. I'm prepared to offer you an interest in the management company."

Watson accepted, provided his interest was 25 percent and he had thirty days to clear the decks at Morgan Stanley. I said okay to the thirty days but said 25 percent was too steep. Stultz interrupted. "Look, Henry, if the deal fails, 25 percent of nothing is nothing. If it succeeds, you won't miss 25 percent. Jimmy is giving up a partnership position in a lucrative firm to take a chance with you. If you're as smart as I think you are, you'll say it's a done deal."

It took only a few seconds for Stultz's logic to sink in. I offered my hand to Watson. "Done," I said. "Welcome, partner."

Once Watson had finished his business at Morgan Stanley, he prepared our business plan and told me the hedge fund would take the form of a limited partnership called Wojo Partners. Partnership interests would be offered to state pension plans at a minimum investment of twenty-five million dollars. The partnership would close once the interests aggregated one billion dollars. I asked Watson how he had picked the name. He said Stultz told him that when I was fifteen, I had founded a lawn cutting business called Wojo Services.

My mind drifted. How far I had come in twenty-seven years: from mowing lawns at three dollars each, to my own billion-dollar business and a chance at a $150 million windfall. I hadn't had a drink but I was drunk, stoned, high as a kite. That's how contemplating real money affects me.

Oliver Twist was a starving orphan boy served a small bowl of gruel. "More, please, sir," he said and got whipped. My plate was full, and I was about to get more. The world is unjust.

In my euphoric state, I barely paid attention to Watson's rambling. He said something about knowing the pension funds, "getting in the door," and that none earned more than 4 percent on their investments. He changed the subject from the pension funds to our vehicle. I woke up.

"The general partner of Wojo Partners," Watson continued, "would be a corporation, 75 percent owned by you and 25 percent owned by me. I propose calling it Wojo Management. It would initially purchase all the subprimes owned by AMG at a 15 percent discount from par or $850 million, and immediately resell the mortgages to Wojo Partners at par or $1 billion. If it works, we'll have an overnight profit of $150 million."

There were two huge hurdles. AMG would have to agree to sell the subprimes at a discount, and the pension funds would have to agree to pay the full price. Watson said, "Partner, you take charge of persuading AMG. I'll assist you. I propose we reverse roles in raising the money. With your permission, I'll take charge of that end, and you'll assist me."

"Sorry," said Stultz. "Henry can't negotiate with AMG directly or indirectly. You'll have to conduct the negotiations. Keep Henry apprised, but he must stay away."

Watson spoke of the need to assure the pension funds that the subprimes, classified by the rating agencies as junk, would not lose even a penny of their value. "What we need is an insurance policy protecting Wojo Partners against loss. If any mortgage loses value, bang! The insurance policy kicks in, and Wojo Partners is made whole. That policy is called a credit default swap.

"AMG's subprimes are equal to or better than primes. I'll never be able to convince the pension managers. Why? They're dumb. What I propose to overcome stupidity is to charge them for a credit default swap guaranteeing them against loss. Since interest on the subprimes is 9 percent, a charge of 2 percent leaves a net of 7 percent, a generous yield when compared to the pension fund's average of 3 percent and high of 4 percent. The logical candidate for insurer is AMG. It has a strong balance sheet and knows how good the subprimes are. We'll agree to split the fee with the company."

Watson negotiated with a committee of AMG's directors and their advisor, Lehman Brothers. The company agreed to sell the subprimes but at a discount of 10 percent, which was $900 million, not the 15 percent we sought ($850 million). It also insisted on keeping the entire fee of twenty million dollars (2 percent of one billion dollars) for issuing the credit default swap. I could have done better with the directors, but Stultz was right; the deal would have smelled bad. Like McGinnis's kickback. This way, it was negotiated at arm's length. The stockholders had no legal beef.

I went with Watson on his first call to the Ohio State Employees Pension Fund. Watson explained the deal, a limited partnership with a 7 percent return guaranteed by Amalgamated. "You're a disgrace to the profession," Watson said. "You earn a stinking 3 percent for your beneficiaries, hard-working Ohioans. I have you slotted for fifty million dollars. If you don't take it, I'm calling the governor and recommending that he order you to have a prefrontal lobotomy." Watson was an imposing figure, self-assured and strong. The Ohio manager was no match. He asked a few meaningless questions and asked for a few days to think it over. He called back the next day, accepting an interest of fifty million dollars.

I saw no reason to accompany Watson on his other calls.

Watson's other meetings were also successful. The only rejection came from a pension fund that found the bar too high. The manager asked for a reduction in the minimum investment from twenty-five million dollars to ten million dollars. A charter provision in his pension plan prohibited a single investment over ten million dollars. Watson told the manager he would consider the request. As it turned out, Wojo Partners was fully subscribed, so there was no need to lower the commitment.

All of the partners except one came from Watson's personal solicitations.

The exception was John Paulsen, an investment banker at Goldman Sachs. He asked for a meeting, saying a representative of his client, an international pension fund, would also be present. The fund was prepared to invest one hundred million dollars. At the meeting, Watson and Paulsen exchanged greetings. Then Watson introduced me. Paulsen did not introduce his companion, a stocky old man wearing a black fedora, which he did not remove, and a dark overcoat, which he did. He was an Italian, an all-Italian from Italy, not an Italian American.

After the presentation, Paulsen said his client had agreed to invest. He handed me a check for one hundred million dollars made out to Wojo Partners and drawn on a bank in Italy.

"We have a form that must be completed before we can accept a partner," I said and handed him the form.

"Of course," said Paulsen. "Give me a few minutes alone with my client. We'll be back in a jiffy."

While they were out of the room, I called Stultz. I told him Paulsen's client seemed unsavory, maybe the mafia itself? "Would we violate the law if we accepted the mafia as a limited partner?"

Stultz said no. "You cannot participate directly or indirectly in the mafia's criminal activities but, for example, I, in my capacity as a lawyer, can defend them. A doctor can administer to them. A bank can open an account for them. A broker can buy and sell stock for them. Similarly, you, an investment adviser, can manage their money. You may not want to accept them, however. That's your decision."

Had we not been in the early stages of raising capital or had the offer been the minimum twenty-five million dollars not the hefty one hundred million dollars, I might have turned it down. Instead, when Paulsen returned with a completed form, I accepted the check for one hundred million dollars.

Paulsen's clients made no effort to hide their identity. The form identified the pension plan as the Cosa Nostra Pension

Plan. The purpose was to provide retirement and death benefits, medical care, and legal representation to the members of the organization. Paulsen was designated as independent financial advisor. All communications and reports were to be sent to him. Distributions were to be wired to an Italian bank.

At the end of the first year, the partners received a 7 percent return. No mortgages defaulted, which enabled AMG to keep the fee of twenty million dollars for the credit default swap. Wojo Partners performed as represented. The company was happy and begged us to purchase new subprimes on the same terms.

The next year, Wojo Management purchased one hundred million dollars of subprimes at ninety million dollars and resold them to Wojo Partners at one hundred million dollars. Wojo borrowed the money to buy the mortgages from a national bank at interest below the return on the mortgages. So it too made a profit. The practice continued for ten years.

I exercised my AMG stock options. I also invested my spare change in AMG's stock and was its largest stockholder.

When I resigned as CEO of Amalgamated, I had recommended John Hughes to replace me. He was the first African American to lead a New York Stock Exchange company. Hughes was a great CEO. The hotel venture revolutionized the industry. Amalgamated became the world's largest owner of hotel rooms. Its earnings doubled and then doubled again—principally because of hotels. The per-share earnings' increase caused the stock price to rise exponentially. I made a bloody fortune from Wojo, but many times more from my stock in Amalgamated.

Success can jade one's appetite, even a money addict's. It can also become boring. People think one makes money through hard work. Not true. The hardest I worked was in 1975. That year, I earned fifteen thousand dollars. From 1992 through 2004, I made many millions. You know what? I hardly worked at all. By far, the biggest increase in my wealth came when I cashed in my chips. That year, I labored not at all.

I spent time serving on presidential committees and advising states, cities, and communities on housing. It was frustrating. My advice was not put into effect and often not even acknowledged. I griped to a fellow advisor, "What's the purpose of working in a vacuum? We have no power." He responded, "If you want power, get elected president."

That was the second time I thought about running for president. True, I had never held public office, but neither had Ross Perot. He made a credible run. If Perot could do it, why couldn't I? The difference between us was that I'd win. It was 2004. We had been running Wojo Partners for ten years. I told Watson it was time to sell our company and AMG as well. I disclosed my ambition. If Watson had laughed, I don't know how hard I would have pursued my dream. Instead, Watson was encouraging. He predicted that I would have great popular appeal, a marine and Vietnam veteran, a self-made man who had devoted himself to the cause of home ownership for ordinary hard-working Americans and a success in business.

Watson sounded two cautionary notes. He knew I was a Republican and urged me to switch my allegiance. Otherwise, he said, I would be "a Jacksonian Democrat running on the Republican ticket." Further, he said, "Bush is unpopular. Although he won reelection in a tight race against Kerry, change is in the air, and next time around, change means the Democrats."

I agreed with Watson that change was in the air but felt a Republican candidate who stayed far away from Bush could lead the charge as effectively as a Democrat. I felt more at home with Republicans. Their leaders were businessmen who celebrated Christmas and Easter.

Watson's second point posed a problem: I had no foreign policy experience.

In our twelve-year relationship, Watson had provided a lot of answers. He did so again. He suggested making a virtue out of necessity. Since I was a Republican and a big party contributor, I should be able to get an ambassadorship to a European country. "It's not uncommon," he said, "to reward a generous contributor with such an appointment. No diplomatic experience is necessary, as embassies are staffed with experienced career officers. Many ambassadors perform only ceremonial functions and leave the hard work to the staff." Watson advised me not to take the easy path. I should involve myself in the work, learn all I could about the trouble spots of the world, meet with heads of state, and write detailed reports. In short, I should distinguish myself as an ambassador and fill the gap in my résumé.

Watson also suggested that I hire a political consultant. "Karl Rove will be available for a run in 2008. He's the best in the business. Personally, I hate him." I had met Rove at several fundraisers. Unlike Watson, I liked the man.

I asked Watson what *he* planned to do. "Study, practice, and play the violin. I have the best time performing as part of a chamber music group. When we quit—and it is about time—I want to fiddle with my fiddle. My hero is a guy named Gilbert Kaplan. He founded a business periodical. He sold it for a fortune. He then embarked on a second career, conducting Mahler symphonies. Nothing else, just Mahler. Now he's sought after to conduct Mahler in the music capitals of the world. I want to perform violin concerti with leading orchestras. I'm as devoted to the violin as Kaplan is to Mahler."

I was stunned by Watson's revelation. He had never mentioned the violin.

I was happy that my partner who had brought so much to the table would soon be free to follow his muse.

# 14

*A*uction fever is a contagious disease that causes victims to overbid. To their affected minds, winning is more important than paying a fair price. A high-profile auction with lots of hype, held in a grand room, spreads the plague.

When we hung a for sale sign on AMG and Wojo Management, we wanted the auction held in a sumptuous setting with lots of ballyhoo. Our goal was an epidemic of monumental proportions.

There's no end of suitable salons in New York, but Federal Hall at 26 Wall Street, directly across from the New York Stock Exchange, is unmatched for historical significance and splendor. George Washington was sworn in there as our first president, and there the Bill of Rights was ratified. In 1842, the original house was replaced by a Greek revival-style building. The new structure served initially as the customs house, later as a subtreasury building, and today as a museum. It is an elegant Doric-columned building. The rotunda, the site of our auction, has a domed, Pantheon-like ceiling. Federal Hall unites three cultures: Greek, Roman, and American.

To create exclusivity and limit attendance to serious buyers, we charged an admission fee of $250,000, the highest ever, which included the right to examine confidential business documents and discuss them with management. By the end of February, 2004, twelve potential bidders had paid for a ticket and spent days inspecting the companies, a process known as due diligence. We wined and dined our guests, heeded their every request, and showered them with affection that rivaled that shown by the ladies of Hamburg's Reeperbahn.

The preauction publicity was substantial but nothing like what accompanied the event itself. The major media photographed the princes of finance as they proceeded along the red carpet, extending from the sidewalk to the rotunda. Television cameras were set up inside the auction room, and the event was shown live and repeated on the nightly news. The main hall was festooned with AMG memorabilia, including citations from governors and mayors and the centerpiece, my award from Reagan and his speech. I stood at the podium with a Sotheby's auctioneer who had been flown in from London. I made the opening remarks, welcoming the bidders to what I dubbed "the auction of the century." I said, "AMG was dedicated to helping hard-working Americans help themselves through their own labor and not to rely on government handouts." I ended with the hope that the new owner would continue AMG's tradition. I then introduced the auctioneer. As I left the stage, I walked up to each bidder, shook his hand, and wished him luck.

The room was supercharged. The adrenalin and testosterone were flowing. I took a seat at the back between Watson and Hughes.

Both companies were sold in less than an hour, at figures more than twice what Watson had estimated.

Lehman and Bear Stearns, bidding jointly, was the high bidder for Wojo Management. They paid five hundred million dollars for a company Watson and I had started twelve years earlier with no capital, not even a copper penny. Merrill Lynch purchased Amalgamated for five billion dollars. I scribbled a note to my seatmates: "$5B + no sense."

Did the buyers suffer "winner's curse," the reaction to auction fever? In this case, the incubation period was four years. When the Great Recession hit, Lehman filed for bankruptcy and Bear Stearns disappeared. Merrill would also have gone belly-up but for the billions of taxpayers' dollars pumped into it.

I was the largest stockholder of AMG and owned 75 percent of Wojo. The sales netted me $1.5 billion. When I got home that day, I picked Peggy up and twirled her around: "I don't give a damn about money anymore," I told her. "I never again want to earn another penny. I'm not going to spit on dividend and interest income, but my addiction to gold is over. Done for. Gone. But not my ambition. I want to be president."

"Put me down right away. I have something important to say. You've won the battle. Who would have thought, those thirty years ago, the office boy at Kaplan & Company would become a billionaire? You've won in business; why isn't that enough? Let's spend the rest of our lives seeking pleasure and avoiding pain."

"A life devoted to fun and self-indulgence sounds good, but without pain, pleasure becomes boring."

"What about public service or starting a foundation to help others? Why do you have to be president?"

"I'm not a do-gooder. My will controls my life. It forces me to strive, to achieve, to seek the highest position in life. If I fail, I'll be sad, depressed, discouraged. But I'll be in worse shape if I don't try."

The AMG-Wojo sale was reported in the *New York Times* and the *Wall Street Journal.* The Associated Press wired the story to its thousands of subscribing newspapers. I was flooded with telephone calls and letters congratulating me. Two were of particular interest. One was from President Bush. "Dear Ouija Board"—that was his nickname for me—"Congratulations on the sale of AMG and Wojo Management! Take a long vacation. You deserve it. Then think public service. The country needs your expertise. Remember, you are one of my constituents."

That was an inside joke. At a private dinner for big donors to the Bush campaign—no reporters—the president dropped his guard and said, "People call you guys fat cats. I think of you as my constituents." The group laughed and clapped. Henceforth, the word "constituents" took on a double meaning.

The second letter was from Karl Rove. He asked me to call for an appointment. "Your knowledge and experience meshes with the administration's policy of private home ownership. We want to do away with all remaining regulations and lower the bar so that more Americans can purchase their own homes.

Our party stands first and foremost for deregulation and private ownership of property."

The next day, I was on a shuttle to Washington to meet with Rove. A ton of money gave me a ton of confidence. I told Rove that housing was a closed chapter for me, but government service wasn't. "I want to serve my country but as its president. I'd be a strong candidate, the strongest the party could run except for one weakness—foreign policy. If I were appointed an ambassador to a major European country, I could devote a few years to foreign affairs. Then I'd have the foreign policy credentials."

"Cheney won't and can't run," Rove said. "Too much baggage and a bad ticker. The 2008 election will be the first since 1952 in which neither an incumbent president nor vice president will be a candidate—a free-for-all on both sides. Mr. Wojecoski, there are a lot of strong candidates from our party: Romney, McCain, Giuliani, Huckabee, Thompson. They've all held elected office and are well known. You've never been elected dogcatcher. You have no name recognition. You'd be a dark horse. The Democrats will probably nominate Hillary. She will be tough. Don't ever underestimate the clout of the Clintons.

"Being an outsider," he continued, "has some advantages. People distrust politicians. You're not tarnished by that brush. You rose to great heights in business without an MBA or even an undergraduate degree. You come from a blue-collar family. Your father was a plumber. Your working-class background will get you votes in swing states like Ohio and Pennsylvania. But you have too many liabilities. They'll sink you before you can get off the ground. First time out of the block, you want the highest office? Run for governor or senator or congressman. A premature start at the top will kill you."

I was prepared for Rove's dismissive comment but, feigning deliberation, sat silent for several minutes. "Ross Perot never held public office before he ran. He was a businessman from Texas. When he withdrew in July 1992, he was leading in the polls. He claimed a dirty campaign tactic was about to be waged against his daughter. He withdrew to protect her. He reentered the race, but his flip-flop cost him the election. He got almost twenty million votes. I'll follow Perot but run not as an independent—as the Republican nominee. If I don't get the nomination, I won't run."

Rove frowned. "Every president has had an American-sounding name," he protested. "Your name ends in 'ski.' Polish. All I can think of is a barely civilized country populated by pig farmers. The only country that's ever elected a Pole to high office is Poland."

"Rove, I thought you were a man of the world. Have you never heard of Fryderyk Chopin? Don't you know in 1978, Karol Josef Wojtla, the archbishop of Krakow, was elected pope? The first non-Italian elected to the papacy since the early sixteenth century! Pope is a much higher office than president. God speaks to the pope, not to presidents, with the possible exception of W. When Bush claimed God and he talk, I laughed out loud. Who does he think he is, the Polish pope?

"Listen hard, Rove. Do you recognize the Constitution as the law of the land? Article II, clause 5 sets forth the requirements for president. You must be born here and be at least thirty-five years old. There's nothing about having a Yankee-sounding name. I'll bet our country will be ready in 2008 for a change to a street-smart Pole from Riverhead, New York. You know something, if Schwarzenegger had been born here, and kept his fly zippered, he'd be a dynamite candidate."

Rove hadn't been prepared for my tough talk. He turned red. He was short, with a large round face that looked bloated. When he regained his composure, he remarked, "You've come a long way from Poland, eh?"

"Are you handing out praise? I'm a second-generation American with only a high school education. On the social scale, I'm an immigrant's grandson. Yes, I've come a long way. And so have you. You weren't born to the purple.

"You could also be taking a slap at Polish Americans. You don't find us very often at the top, except perhaps in labor unions. In this country where all are supposed to be equal, ethnicity makes some more equal than others. When will people like you get it straight? It's the essence of the man, the power of his will, not his background, that determines his fate."

Rove stared at me, his lips tightening, and then he lowered his eyes. "Politics is a dirty business. The media pays big bucks to smear a candidate. Any skeletons you want to stay interred? Don't run."

"Since I've been married, I've been a boy scout. What about things you did as a kid? Is there a statute of limitations?"

"Americans like bad boys. Anything you did before eighteen gets a big yawn."

Rove said primaries were expensive, perhaps as much as fifty million dollars. "You won't be able to raise a cent. The constituency likes to back winners. You're a dark horse. You'll have to finance the primary contest yourself."

Rove also said I would need a savvy campaign manager. "Who knows?" he added slowly. "I may be available. But first, we need to get you an ambassadorship. Are you aware of the price?"

"I know the rules," I said. "Get me the appointment, and I'll wire the money."

Rove said Italy would soon be available. "That's a plum. If I get that for you, I expect a donation to the RNC of two hundred thousand dollars. Pay later, not before. Nothing should come out in the confirmation hearings. If you want to save money, less prestigious embassies cost less."

"It is critical to me to be in the center of Europe. Italy feels right."

Rove asked if I spoke Italian. I told him I would be willing to learn.

"Speaking the country's language," said Rove, "should be a requirement but isn't. The State Department runs an intensive training program including a language tutorial. That and outside instruction should help. A post in Rome may appear glamorous, but it's a difficult assignment.

"Italy is a troubled country rife with corruption. Every project costs more to build because of graft. It starts at the top with Silvio Berlusconi, the prime minister, and works its way down. Berlusconi is openly dishonest. How he got elected is beyond me. The man actually pushed for a general amnesty for criminals (there were then over twenty-four thousand in jail) to keep his personal lawyer, convicted of bribing a judge, out of jail. "Another problem is the mafia. It is a state within a state. It controls 7 percent of Italy's GNP. The country is a hellhole. Would you accept Italy? There is also an opening for an ambassador to the Holy See. You're Catholic. That would be a much easier post."

I wondered if the distractions that went with territory would interfere with my learning curve. Rove was waiting for my answer. "I'm Catholic but not particularly observant. I'd feel hypocritical surrounded by priests and monks. Berlusconi's a businessman. My task, outside my official duties, will be to meet with foreign diplomats posted to Italy from different countries. I want to learn about the problems in their countries. I would be honored to accept the Italian post. Not the pope but the devil, Berlusconi."

"Sit tight. I'll get back to you. The president likes you. You surprise me, Henry. You're frank. You came right out and said what you wanted and why. Who knows, you might make it to the top."

I relayed to Watson the substance of my meeting with Rove and added, "A posting to Rome would be a quick course in foreign affairs. And I'll have access to State Department files on all the hotspots. Peggy said she'll study with me. How can I change my image from a money-grubbing businessman to a savvy foreign diplomat?"

"That's not your job," he said. "Hire a PR firm. The Dorsey Agency is top of the line. I know Dick Hertzel. He's the head of the firm."

Hertzel was pencil thin, nervous, and always in motion. He explained his firm's fee structure: a minimum retainer of one hundred thousand dollars plus expenses. "For achieving a client's goal, we charge a success fee that, depending on the nature of the assignment and degree of success, may be several times the retainer fee. Ambassadors don't hire PR firms. You're no fool. What's up?"

I disclosed my ultimate goal. He made notes, and once he had a full page of them, he looked up and spoke slowly. "There are three trouble spots important to the electorate: Israel, Iraq, and Africa. Jews have a love affair with Israel. So does the Christian right. Pogroms, expulsions, the Holocaust, the Dreyfus Affair provide reason enough for Jews to want a safe haven. Keeping Israel a Jewish state is a key to the religious right's plan for Jews on Judgment Day. Their plan makes Hitler look like Moses." He paused. "Anyone who can find a solution to the Israel-Palestine conflict will get elected God.

"Africa is a forgotten continent, except for millions of African Americans. Programs addressing the misery afflicting Africans will get you support among blacks.

"Each year, opposition to the war in Iraq grows. A strategy to get us out will transform Henry Wojecoski into Henry Kissinger. I can guarantee you extensive media coverage provided your theories are sound, but you, not my firm, must develop the policies."

Shortly after signing on with Hertzel, I received the official presidential appointment as ambassador to Italy, subject to confirmation by the Senate. Although I had had no diplomatic experience, I was well coached by the State Department and quickly confirmed.

Peggy and I enrolled in an intensive course for newly appointed diplomats. I was given access to State Department files on countries throughout the world. I got copies of the files on Israel, Africa, and Iraq.

An instructor said the department encouraged diplomats to spent time in different parts of the world. "A well-travelled diplomat is an asset in his job and to the department. Unfortunately, the costs have to be borne by the diplomat as the budget is tight." The instructor said that entertaining dignitaries was necessary and expensive. "The sum allotted is inadequate. It is understood that ambassadors will bear excess costs. Only rich men should apply to be ambassadors."

Based on information provided by the State Department, my new home was a real palace. A sign outside the embassy could truthfully proclaim, "Julius Caesar slept here!" More recently, the present three-hundred-year-old mansion had been home to Queen Margherita of Savoy, the first queen of Italy.

When I told Peggy about our new accommodations, she said, "I hope hot water, electricity, and heat work better than at the house that Murphy built. Otherwise, Your Royal Highness, we're too old to suffer. I'll find a nice modern apartment in downtown Rome."

On February 5, 2005, we departed for Rome on an official US plane. I felt queasy. I had paid two hundred thousand dollars for a job that I shouldn't really hold. *I'm not a diplomat*, I thought to myself. I didn't get to be ambassador on merit. I'm a fraud. A poor, dumb guy with $1.5 billion who bought himself a title. I became so unsettled that if I'd been in a car, I would have turned around and gone back to Hudson House. Instead, we landed at Leonardo da Vinci Fiumicino and were met by a retinue of Italian officials. They escorted us to a limousine parked about fifty yards from the plane. The car took us to the US embassy on Via Vittorio Veneto.

Peggy was quiet on the flight, but once we were alone in the embassy residence, our splendid royal palace, she looked stricken. "What are we doing here? Where are our children, our relatives, our friends? I hate everything about this frigid palace. I'm homesick already, and it's your fault. Why can't you become president without being an ambassador?"

I too was unhappy, but for different reasons. I'd committed an unethical act to further my ambition. I purchased a government office. That wrong was aggravated by a second. I'd acquired the position not to serve my country but to advance my own interests. I too wanted to head home. "Let's give it a shot. If one of us is still unhappy after six months, we'll leave."

A reception in my honor was held the next evening in the ballroom at the prime minister's residence. There, before diplomats from all over the world, I presented my credentials and conveyed greetings from the president and people of the United States. The prime minister praised Bush as a great leader of the free world and a humanitarian. He then remarked on the strong ties between the two countries, citing the many Italians who emigrated from Italy to America and the flood of tourists from the United States to Italy.

"I refer to the citizens of our respective countries as arrivals and departures," he said.

I was introduced afterward to a number of dignitaries, but one, who was not introduced, stood out. The man from the Cosa Nostra whom I had met in my office more than ten years earlier greeted me. "If you need anything in Italy, just wire Paulsen. I'll take care of it." Mark Daniels, a career diplomat and chief residential assistant at the embassy, overheard the conversation.

"Can you imagine," he said, "inviting the don to a diplomatic reception? Never before has this occurred. How do you know him?" I said we had met once before. He had invested in a hedge fund I had managed.

"Apparently," said Daniels, "the investment turned out well. He's a powerful, ruthless man. He's been known to order the death of those who disappoint him. Do you still have a business relationship with him?" He looked relieved when I answered no.

The local press covered the ceremony. So did *Business Week*. It ran a three-page article discussing my background and my business success, crediting me with inventing subprime mortgages, credit swaps, and consolidated mortgage obligations. The article referred to the presidential medal Reagan awarded me. "Many ambassadors," it said, "have been drawn from the world of business. Henry Josef Wojecoski is the first ambassador to come of and from the people. He is a common man loaded with common sense. We expect his tenure will throw light on the murky world of diplomacy."

We were hardly settled in when the invasion began. Dear friends, casual friends, and people we had met only once called as they were passing through Italy. Peggy turned no one away. In addition, every day, she read the list of arrivals and invited prominent people for cocktails and dinner. She proselytized all guests on my behalf. She stressed the importance of the office of president and alluded to the shortcomings of the incumbent. She said our next president must be smart, worldly, and independent. When asked who that person might be, she unhesitatingly said, "My husband would make a great president. He's brilliant, iconoclastic, and owes nothing to anyone. I'm trying my best to convince him to run."

Peggy wrote down the names of all the visitors. "When you begin your run, they will be invited to serve as charter members of the Wojecoski for President Committee. God help anyone who doesn't join!"

Peggy turned the embassy into an ad hoc campaign headquarters. Our entertainment budget exceeded our government allowance by ten thousand dollars per month.

Peggy's activities kept her busy. Our children and the Markowitz children visited so often that we nicknamed the embassy "Hudson House in Roma." The Metropolitan Museum of Art, through a contact with Peggy, held a benefit and dinner at the embassy highlighting the Vatican museums.

One day before lunch, when we were to eat alone, a rare occasion, Peggy told me about Queen Margherita. "She was a patron of the arts and the founder of Casa di Dante. I've seen photographs of her. She was a great beauty, stylishly groomed with an eclectic collection of pearls. She must have been a gourmet because a pizza, made of mozzarella, tomatoes, and basil, the colors of Italy, was named after her." On cue, the waiter served lunch: pizza Margherita.

"No stay-at-home queen," Peggy continued after lunch, "she was an accomplished mountain climber. In 1893, she reached Punta Gnifetti, a peak in the Alps at an altitude of 4,556 meters. She spent the night in a hut, later named Margherita Cabina. Henry, in July, we're going to spend the night in the queen's hut. When I say 'we,' I mean our children, our five nieces and nephews, and David and Joan. Our guide will be Fred Jacobson, who would have led her had he been alive then."

In July, the residents of Hudson House assembled in Rome. After the kids had turned the embassy upside down and sideways, and David and his wife, Joan Barclay, had recovered from jet lag, we set off for Milan. Our guide, Fred Jacobson, and his two assistants met us at the airport. We chartered a bus for the three-hour trip to Alagna Valsesia, a village in Piedmont in the Pennine Alps and the gateway for our climb to the queen's hut.

I sat with Jacobson. He was tall with a full head of salt and pepper hair and looked very much like Abraham Lincoln without a beard. Upon graduating from Yale, Jacobson embarked on a Wall Street career. At thirty-one, he gave up finance for a life in the Alps where, for the next forty years, he worked as a guide. Jacobson called his addiction "Alpoholism." His Yale classmates called it by a different name. Although the class was full of high achievers, including a president of Yale, a cabinet member, and dozens of leading businessmen and professionals, Jacobson was voted the most successful.

Jacobson was as happy following his addiction as I was following mine. Perhaps the world should leave us addicts alone.

Alagna is a village bursting with mom-and-pop shops. Jacobson advised we spend a few days there acclimating to the altitude. We put the time to good use. We bought hiking gear, practiced basic climbing skills, visited a fifteenth-century church and the Walser Museum. Several days later, we boarded a cable car to Punta Indren and from there began our assent to the Gnifetti hut, a stop on the way to our ultimate destination. We sang and yodeled as we climbed—all of us, that was, except David's wife, Joan. She complained. The bed in the Alagna hotel was lumpy; she couldn't sleep. She had altitude sickness, headaches, and dysentery. Peggy, David, and I took turns diverting her attention by pointing out the scenery and, when that didn't work, trying to engage her in gossip. Nothing helped.

Halfway to the Gnifetti hut, she slipped and twisted her ankle. David checked the ankle and agreed with Jacobson that wrapping it tightly should allow Joan to continue. She tried but claimed she was unsteady and feared if she continued, she would fall again. A stretcher was rigged, and the assistants carried Joan back to the cable car, Alagna, and her lumpy bed. The rest of us continued our climb and reached the Gnifetti hut.

For beds, there were mattresses strewn on the ground with plain covers, no sheets or pillows. Dinner was a thin vegetable soup and a beef stew. I was hungry. The food, which I knew to be bad, tasted good. Exhausted from the climb, we went to bed shortly after dinner.

The final step in our trek was the Margherita hut, the highest refuge in Europe. The climb was steep and difficult, and the altitude was 4,152 meters. We accepted our guide's suggestion that the three adults return to Alagna and the kids complete the climb to the queen's hut.

Four days later, nine confirmed mountain goats appeared at the hotel to cheers and acclamation.

How one handles adversity tells a lot about one's character. Joan was not an outdoors woman; she was also not a good sport. Her constant whining ruined the trip for David and dampened Peggy's and my joy. I never liked her; I now loathed her.

In time, Peggy was as much at home in the palace as her new idol had been in her day. As for me, study and hard work overcame my guilt. Devoting my time to making a contribution to world peace was, I rationalized, an exemplary end. Thinking about my efforts in that way made me feel less guilty about how I had scaled this particular precipice.

# 15

*I*n my previous incarnation, I was not a people person. I was pleasant only to those I deemed worthy—and those who could do what I needed done. When Peggy complained that I had slighted an acquaintance, I fell back on the misanthrope's chant: "I'm friendly toward those with whom I wish to be friendly. Who's benefited by faking friendship?"

Ambassadors represent their countries in foreign states. It's their task to generate good will. An affable attitude is essential. My personality had to change.

There was more to the job than performing superficial tasks in a pleasant manner. A successful diplomat should be an activist, one who analyzes problems and devises solutions. To do my duty, I tackled the hot spots, beginning with Africa.

It is the second largest continent in the world, contains the second largest population, and is the poorest. According to the United Nations, the world's poorest twenty-five nations are all African. Illiteracy, malnutrition, inadequate and impure water supply, and wretched sanitation plague the continent. In East Africa, 70 percent of hospital visits are related to contaminated water. In Zimbabwe, unemployment is 80 percent.

The African governments are, by and large, unstable, corrupt, violent, and authoritarian. Military coups are recurrent. Wars, mass rapes, and genocide add to the people's woes. There are bright spots. The continent is awash in oil, minerals, gold, diamonds, and timber. Agriculture is a big export crop.

The blend of poverty and riches gave rise to my African policy—to create a United States of Africa by transforming a conglomeration of undeveloped, independent states into a united industrialized democratic society. A centralized state could impose taxes on the export of all goods and use the revenue to jumpstart new industry and create jobs.

There are fifty-four sovereign African states. I asked Katherine Nelson, the political liaison officer, to invite to dinner the ambassadors from six representative states: South Africa, Nigeria, Rwanda, Botswanda, Kenya, and Ghana. At the dinner, we discussed the conditions in Africa and my solution, unification. The solution, they thought, might provide an answer. "It's worth a try," one said.

One name came up repeatedly in my conversations—Nelson Mandela. Some thought him the embodiment of Mahatma Gandhi; others, Abraham Lincoln and Martin Luther King. Although he no longer held an official position in his country of South Africa, he was the most influential figure in all of Africa.

I decided to meet with Mandela alone. The ambassador from South Africa arranged a meeting in Pretoria at Mandela's summer home.

Before going to Africa, I returned to New York and then to Washington. In New York, I met with Hertzel, my public relations guru, and discussed my plan for a United States of Africa. I said I had a date set to go to Africa and meet with Mandela. Peggy and Daniels, my chief of staff, would come with me. I also planned to invite John Hughes and his wife. "Hughes, a black man, was a lowly loan officer when I first met him at a company convention in 1974. He succeeded me as CEO of Amalgamated. I was responsible for his march through the company's ranks."

Hertzel liked publicizing my having mentored a black executive but feared Hughes might steal my thunder. "This trip is about Mandela, and you and your plan to transform Africa. Hughes must be instructed to keep a low profile. He should be in the background, politely greet Mandela, but not speak with the press. No more. Hughes is a friend, not a member of your official team. If he has children, bring them along. That will emphasize his presence as part of a family vacation."

Hughes's office at Amalgamated was my second stop—the office that used to be mine, the sprawling space that embodied my power in the company, and now his. He was nonplussed. "You're the ambassador to Italy, and you're going to Africa? I know you. You don't give a shit about Africa or African Americans. What's your Machiavellian scheme? I've heard you mumble about running for president."

I was rattled. If Hughes knew, I wondered how many others knew. "Is my plot to rule the country the office scuttlebutt?"

Hughes interpreted my question as an admission. "You want to use my black ass for your political purposes; it's going to cost you. I'll accept second place on the ticket."

"C'mon, John. It will be tough enough for voters to support me, an uneducated Polish American son of a plumber. You would be an anchor. The country is not ready to elect a black man to national office. It may never be." Hughes was hurt. I didn't want to lose my only asset in the black community, an asset I had earned the right to exploit. I thought for a few minutes before I said, "Lower your sights. Have I forgotten you in the past? In the unlikely event I get nominated and win, think about a cabinet position. Maybe commerce."

Hughes was pacified. "Clinton appointed a black man secretary of commerce. You and I have worked well together. Okay, I'll help with the brothers. Who'd have thought thirty years ago we'd be having this conversation?"

"Me. I knew we were headed for the top. Whether we'll get there is a long shot. CEO of the US of A and CEO of AMG are two very different offices. It's great to have you with me."

"What's the drill?"

"You tell the media you're in Africa with your family as tourists and as guests of your old friend and colleague, Henry Wojecoski. 'If Henry has free time, I expect he'll spend it with us. My family has always cherished our friendship with the Wojecoskis.' At all times, you are to stay in the background. Remember, I'm president and you're secretary of commerce."

"I've had lots of practice playing second fiddle to you. I promise I'll win an Academy Award for best supporting actor."

In Washington, I met with Condoleezza Rice. I told her about my dinner with African diplomats and their offer to arrange a visit with Nelson Mandela and handed her my itinerary.

I said a former business colleague and his family would be traveling with us. "Oh, how nice," she said, smiling. "You're going as a goodwill ambassador to a continent others would like to forget. Our budget is tight. You'll have to pay your own freight."

I asked what she thought about a united Africa. She shrugged. "It would be great for the continent, but the leaders would never endorse it. It would mean a demotion for all but one of them. A head of state won't give up his job, even for a role in a much larger entity."

I mentioned that in January of 2006, I planned to visit Israel, Jordan, Syria, Lebanon, and Iraq. She shook her head. "Iraq is off limits. We can't guarantee your safety." She wanted my itinerary several weeks before I departed for the other countries.

Before returning to Rome, I met again with Hertzel. He said *Time* magazine was salivating to cover my trip. "They believe an article featuring Mandela with a US ambassador will stimulate sales for their magazine within the black community. One of their major circulation goals is to increase black readership. They anticipate the cover will have photos of you and Mandela and announce a United States of Africa: a vision, not yet a reality. This is big. I'd like to go along. I want to make sure nothing goes wrong."

I was new at the PR game and happy to have an old warhorse at my side.

The day before my meeting with Mandela, I met in Pretoria with Hertzel; a senior reporter for *Time,* Anne Holster; her assistant; and a staff photographer, John Whalen. Hughes and his family were there but stayed in the background. Hertzel handed out press packets with charts, graphs, and statistical studies showing how a plan to tax Africa's exports and prudently invest the revenue could transform the continent into an emerging new nation and ultimately into a powerful, developed country. The packet also contained a biography of me, my association with Hughes, and the dramatic highlights in Mandela's life.

Hertzel and his staff had done their job—outlined the story.

The next day, Peggy, Daniels, and I met with Mandela and an official of the South African government, Jacob Tzurba. Mandela was well into his eighties. "I dream of one Africa," he said, "free of corruption. All working together to create a country dedicated to the welfare of all Africans." He agreed to deliver that message to the *Time* reporters and to pose for photographs.

After a photo session and interviews, Peggy, Daniels, and I returned to Rome. Hertzel and his assistant spent an extra day with the staff from *Time*. Hughes and his family went on a tour of Africa.

Three weeks later, the magazine hit the newsstands. There I was on the cover, arms linked with the greatest man in the history of Africa. The story discussed my career and wealth and described me as "mercurial." It told how, based on merit, I had raised Hughes from a loan broker working out of Newark to New York headquarters as the company's first black officer and, when I resigned, picked him to replace me and become the first black CEO of a New York Stock Exchange company. Under the photo of Hughes and me, it read, "Two former businessmen now concerned with the fate of Africa."

I received many comments but none moved me more than that of my brother-in-law, David Markowitz. He e-mailed that he had bought dozens of copies of *Time* and given them to doctors, nurses, and even patients he'd just operated on. David said he had removed from his waiting room every magazine except *Time*, and he urged "Ambassador Wojecoski to take on Israel."

During his marriage to Mary, David and I often intuited what the other was thinking. That sense vanished when Mary died. Was it reborn? I did a double-take when I read the end of the message. "Joan and I have separated. I will always be grateful to her for getting me out of my funk. There was only one woman for me."

Five hundred people sent letters to *Time*; all were favorable. Talk show hosts and news anchors discussed a United States of Africa. None disapproved, though one called it "Pollyannaish." The State Department was silent. It was fortunate that I had tipped off Rice.

Israel was, as David had guessed, next on the agenda. I invited the Israeli ambassador to Italy, Avital Nadish, to dinner. He came casually dressed in a short-sleeved white shirt, open at the collar, and tan slacks. In order to make him feel more at home, in the best diplomatic tradition, I took off my jacket and tie and unfastened the top button of my shirt. "Too bad we can't always do business this way," I said to him as we got underway. Nadish, formerly a general in the Israeli army, was sorely lacking in objectivity. I thought his one-sided opinions, however, might expose weaknesses in Israel's position, which might help me in my search for a solution. I asked him to discuss the Israeli-Palestinian dispute.

When he spoke of the territory acquired after the Six-Day War in 1967, he steered clear of calling it occupied and referred to the land by its biblical names, Judea and Samaria. Later, he used a euphemism for occupied territory: "The conquered territory consisted of the Sinai and Gaza, both Egyptian territories; the west bank of the Jordan River, formerly part of Jordan; and the Golan Heights, Syrian territory. At the conclusion of the war, Israel agreed to return to Egypt, Jordan, and Syria the land that was previously theirs, but only after a peace treaty was signed. Egypt was the first to sign. Israel said, 'Take back Sinai and Gaza.' Egypt said yes to Sinai but no to Gaza. Jordan too signed a peace treaty. Israel offered her the West Bank. Jordan refused. Under principles of international law, Gaza and the West Bank were territories ceded to Israel. Before the war, they did not belong to the Palestinians. Their claim to the territories is untenable. They started a war. They lost. And now they claim the right to territory that was not theirs when the war started or when it ended."

"Hold it," I said. "Why is your government playing games? Israel doesn't want the West Bank or Gaza. You offered the territories to Jordan and Egypt. But to the Palestinians who want it as their homeland, you say no. Instead of peace, Israel has conflict and the enmity of other countries. It makes no sense."

Nadish pointed out that peace was not a one-way street. "Israel, except for the lunatic fringe, is willing to give the Palestinians the conquered territory. All we ask in return is for the Palestinians to recognize Israel as a Jewish state. The stumbling block is not Israel, but the Palestinians. They refuse to recognize Israel's right to exist. The Palestinians openly declare they want not only a homeland in the West Bank and Gaza, but all of Israel. My country is not about to commit suicide.

"Many leaders urge Israel to turn over the territory without preconditions. They find the Palestinian threat unrealistic, as Israel is a military power possessing a powerful air force, navy, and army. The Palestinians have no forces except terrorism.

"Israel doesn't underestimate the effectiveness of terrorism. It is the weapon of the twenty-first century. It's so hard to apprehend a young boy or girl crossing the border, entering a crowded market, and exploding a bomb. The young suicide bomber dies and so do many innocent persons. If the Palestinians forego terrorist attacks and agree to live in peace with Israel, my country will give them the land they want."

I liked Nadish. There was no pretense, no pomp; he was all substance. We talked late into the night. He had read the *Time* article and praised my African proposal. He called it "an innovative approach to a sad situation requiring immediate attention." He further said his government agreed with me and had advocated a similar plan.

I told him of my desire to visit Israel. He offered to make the necessary arrangements for me to meet with Ariel Sharon, the prime minister. He also suggested I meet with Ehud Olmert, the former mayor of Jerusalem, Sharon's likely successor.

I had invited the Palestinian, Lebanese, and Syrian delegates to dinner later in the month and told him so, adding that I planned to visit those states. At the conclusion of my meetings and trips, I intended to report to Washington on a course of action.

As we said good night, he offered a word of advice. "Israel is a warm country," he said. "Rarely do we wear jackets, never ties. Open-collar shirts are our uniform in the Middle East. Although there is a saying, 'When in Rome,' I ignore it—as you can see."

It was beastly hot the night of the dinner with the Arab delegation. I dressed in the appropriate Middle East uniform, open-collar shirt and slacks. I was astonished when they arrived in business suits and silk ties. They seemed equally disconcerted. "Are you Israeli?" asked the Syrian delegate. The Lebanese asked if I was Jewish. Once that got cleared up, I got to the point of the dinner.

"My government wants to be of help. It favors a Palestinian homeland in the occupied territories. We also want to ensure peace in the area, which means acceptance of the right of the two nations to exist in their respective countries: the Jews in Israel, the Palestinians in the West Bank and Gaza."

The group spoke with one voice. Israel should not have been established in Palestine. The wrong was committed in 1947 when Israel was founded. There was only one way to correct the error—force Israel out of the region. I said the UN had granted Jews a state in Palestine, their ancient homeland. Their anger should be directed at the UN and not the Jews. My comment was ignored. They inveighed against punishing conditions imposed by Israel. The only pleasant moment came when I said I planned to visit their capitals. They asked for the date and assured me I would be warmly received. I asked if they had read the *Time* story on Africa. None had.

The dinner meetings provided direct support for my Israeli policy. The country was now united under Israeli rule, with a Palestinian underclass. Given the Palestinians' pledge to annihilate the Jews and Israel's natural response, a two-state solution was pie in the sky. The Palestinians were not willing to live in peace, and the Jews were too smart to permit terrorists free rein in their backyard. The only practical solution was to maintain Israeli control over all the land but give the Palestinians a right to vote. That right, however, would be heavily circumscribed by gerrymandering the Palestinian territory, so that their representation in the Knesset would never be more than nominal. Things could change but only if and when the Palestinians accepted a peaceful solution.

I was prepared to announce my plan during my trip to Israel. I would of course observe protocol and state that my views were my own and did not represent my government's.

In planning my trip, David kept popping into my head. I called him, asked after his parents and children, and issued an invitation. "David, I'm going to Israel. So are you, your parents, your children, my children, Andrew, and Elizabeth. Israel is about family. Our family will hold a reunion there." David sang a few bars of Hatikvah, said "Shalom," and said he would "get everybody on my side of our family on board." The old times were back. We were brothers again.

I told Hertzel about my Israel-Palestinian solution and my entourage. He was enthusiastic about my family: "You lucky fellow. You're every man. Polish, Jewish, a world-class surgeon, nine children, two parents, and two ex-in-laws." He was less thrilled with my political solution. "It's too one-sided. It will offend those self-declared 'humanitarians' whose hearts bleed for the downtrodden, in this case the Palestinians." He paused, and I could almost hear him thinking on the phone halfway around the world. "They're not going to vote for you anyway. The *Times* will be outraged. It has a reputation, well deserved in my opinion, of being anti-Israel." Another pause. "Hey, the *Times*. Let me call one of my buddies there. I'll get back to you."

When he did, he talked fast and excitedly. "Henry, this is bigger than Africa. The *Times* loves the idea of your Polish American family and Jewish relatives meeting in Jerusalem. They're prepared to give your trip top coverage, and get this: Thomas Friedman will write about you in the Sunday magazine. My take is that the *Times* is under pressure to present a more balanced Israel approach. I'm coming along. If you object to the added expense, I won't charge for my time."

Hertzel's bill for the Africa story was $250,000. Have you ever paid a humongous bill gladly? I did. Look what I got! A cover story in *Time* with Mandela's arm entwined with mine. How can a politician running for president put a price on that? Besides, money was unimportant; I had too much. My fortune, $1.5 billion, invested in 5 percent investment-grade bonds returned, each year, too much money. "Your trip is on me, Dick."

The family rendezvoused at the bar of the King David Hotel, with everyone speaking at once. David moderated by age. My father spoke first. He recounted his trip with Elizabeth, Peggy, and me all over Italy. He loved the churches, the beautiful buildings, and the food. "I never thought my wife and I would ever get abroad again, but here we are in Jerusalem." He paused and looked at me before continuing. "Our life without Henry would be so much emptier. There's no better son than Henry. We miss our daughter. Always will, but we see her face not only in our Markowitz grandchildren but in the children of her twin brother, Henry."

David's father, Seymour Markowitz, was next. "I toast our dear Mary's twin brother. He's a national figure. A world leader. Unless I'm way off, he will be the next president of the United States."

Our family is not what you'd call reserved. All shouted, "Wojecoski for president." The nine children paraded around the room continuing the chant. In a public room, in any other country, we would have been told to pipe down. Israel is different. It is accustomed to noise, loud talk, demonstrations. No one paid any attention to us.

The next day, the political business began. I brought the whole family to Ariel Sharon's house. We hit it off from the moment we crossed the threshold. He was a real leader who, as the commanding general of the Israeli forces, had been tested in battle. A man who had smelled smoke and tasted fire. Drawing on his experience, he took our invasion in stride, laughing and joking with everyone who caught his fancy. The photographers had a field day shooting Sharon separately with the grandparents, parents, and children. Candid shots and a group photo followed. Then Sharon and I left the room for a meeting in his home office. While we were gone, an assistant presented a slide show of must-see attractions for our visit in Israel.

Sharon praised my plan. "It makes so much sense that the Palestinians are bound to reject it. They never miss an opportunity to make a mistake. I'm committed to a two-state solution, but I agree with you: it will never happen. The Palestinian leadership will never make the necessary concessions. I will call the *Times* staff into this room. I will describe your plan as an excellent interim solution. A first step on the road to separate states."

He did that and then some. Sharon went out of his way to praise me, calling me an ally and a true friend of Israel, a modern-day Talleyrand. He blessed my family and extolled our living under one roof. "They're diverse, but they love each other. The problem with the Arabs—they're closer to Jews than the Wojecoskis were at the beginning of their relationship with the Markowitzes—but the Arabs' hearts are filled with hate. Under present circumstances, it is unrealistic to share our home the way the Wojecoskis and Markowitzes share Hudson House."

Two days later, on January 6, 2006, Sharon suffered a severe stroke and has remained in a coma ever since.

After the report of Sharon's stroke, I cancelled my visits to Lebanon, Syria, Jordan, and the West Bank. I was sad that I had lost a friend and did not want to dishonor his memory. Instead, I spent the week with my family touring Israel.

Peggy planned our Israeli adventure. "Jerusalem was founded thirteen thousand years ago," she said, "and is described in the Bible. In ancient times, the city was protected by walls, which still stand, as you can see from our breakfast table. Today, thousands live within the walled city, amid open-air markets and shrines sacred to the three major religions. I was so sure that we'd want to explore the ancient city, I've hired a guide. If you don't want to go, you can hang out at the pool.

"Another must is the Israel museum. The anthropological wing has objects a million years old and some new ones that are only two thousand years young. And then there is the Dead Sea Scrolls. I know some of you think museums are deadly, and some probably are. This is a world-class museum. At MoMA, we speak of it with awe.

"Jesus lived and taught in northern Israel around the Sea of Galilee. When we leave Jerusalem, we'll make our base camp at a kibbutz on the Galilee and see the Jesus sites. Our guide today, Sharon Morgenstern, will take us to the Galilee."

I regard visits to historic sites a waste of time. You can't acquire knowledge staring at ruins. If you want to learn, it's better to read books and look at photos—although I confess I've never done that. I went along to be with my family.

After touring the old city for four hours, I changed. The guide's descriptions of the sites sacred to Jews, Christians, and Muslims (the Temple Mount and the Western Wall, the Church of the Holy Sepulchre, and the Dome of the Rock and Al-Aqsa

Mosque) brought them to life. But what made them relevant were the throngs living and worshipping there. I saw dozens of Christians kneeling and weeping at the Church of the Holy Sepulchre and hundreds of Jews praying at the Western Wall. I wondered whether atheists would be impressed seeing people today reciting the same prayers said thousands of years ago.

I missed the trip to the Israel Museum because of a conflict. Avital Nadish, Israel's ambassador to Italy, had arranged for me to meet Ehud Olmert, the former mayor of Jerusalem, whom Nadish predicted would be Israel's next prime minister. When I arrived at Olmert's home, there were two others there—Shimon Peres, a Nobel prize winner and two-time Israeli prime minister, and Shai Agassi, a young Israeli businessman. I was surprised to see Peres and said so. "I'm flattered to meet you, and at the same time, I wonder why you're willing to spend time with me?"

"The United States is Israel's most important ally," said Peres. "Probably my country's only friend. The political scene in your country is very important to Israel. The 2008 presidential election is a toss-up as far as we can see. We think you have a good chance to win. Since you're here, I wanted to welcome you to Israel and extend good wishes."

Peres, an octogenarian, was a brilliant man, but how did he know that I planned to run for president? The Mossad must be as good as its reputation.

Peres deflected talk about the Palestinian question and politely refused to comment on my proposed solution. He asked pointed questions about Hillary Clinton and Barack Obama, but he knew much more about them than I did. His take on the election was that the Democrats would win. But of all the Republican candidates (and he named six), he hoped I would get the nomination and said Israel would be pleased if I were elected.

After more talk about American politics and the virtues of Bush, Peres turned to Shai Agassi, a man of about forty. "Shai," Peres said, "founded a software company when he was twenty-four and sold it fifteen years later to SAP, a German company, for four hundred million dollars. He was on track to become CEO of SAP, the largest software company in the world, when he resigned to form Better Place, a start-up here in Israel. Shai will tell you about Better Place and how it will change the world, but right now, I want to talk about Israeli enterprise."

Peres spoke softly, but the pride he felt in his country's economic success came through. "The number of Israeli companies listed on NASDAQ exceeds all of the European companies put together. Only the US has more listings than us. Israel leads the world in start-ups per capita. We have almost four thousand for every two thousand Israelis. Most of them are high tech. Over 30 percent of the venture capital invested in new enterprises throughout the world flowed last year to Israel. Technology companies are not only big business in Israel, but we export our expertise all over the world. Our scientists have prominent positions in Microsoft, Google, and PayPal.

"We have succeeded in creating a prosperous, growing economy, based on high tech, despite the costs and distractions of defending our country in six wars and many skirmishes.

"Israel is the only highly industrialized nation that has no natural resources—that is, if you don't count the intelligence of our people and the excellence of our universities.

"The Technion, located in Haifa, is referred to by Americans as the MIT of Israel. Here, we refer to MIT as the Technion of the United States.

"What I've just told you and a lot more is discussed in a book soon to be published, titled *Start-Up Nation.* I will send you a copy."

Peres turned to Agassi and said he was the hero of the book. "Only time will tell," said Agassi, "whether I'm a hero or a dupe."

Agassi described Better Place as a project that, if it succeeded, would take Israel off of oil by making electric cars the national car of Israel. "Electric cars," Agassi said, "are not economical and hence not being manufactured because the battery component is too expensive. In my model, the battery will be owned by Better Place. The company will rent batteries to the car's owners. The cost of the car, without the battery, will be less than gas-driven cars. There will, of course, be costs for renting batteries, but they'll be less per mile than the comparable cost for gasoline. The state will help out. It plans to hardwire parking garages where drivers, while at work, can plug in and recharge. Those garages and home outlets should provide enough juice for most driving. If more power is needed, Better Place will operate battery-changing stations where used batteries can be exchanged for newly charged ones. We have a device that can affect the change in less time than it takes to fill a tank with gas.

"Israel is the ideal country for a pilot program. It is small and surrounded by its enemies, thereby requiring Israeli drivers to stay within the confines of their country.

"If one country can run without oil, others will follow. It is ironic that the hostility of the Arab nations toward Israel may someday spell the end of their oil riches."

Agassi said he had made arrangements with an auto company to manufacture, in Israel, one hundred thousand cars per year and had raised two hundred billion dollars to fund the start-up.

What did I think? Israel is a living miracle. If any other country attempted to take out OPEC and Big Oil, I would dismiss it. Israel just might do it.

At dinner with the family, the talk was all about the museum. Regina asked if we could extend the trip so that we could spend another day there. "Dad, you missed it. It's a mistake to come to Israel and not visit the Israel Museum. The modern art compares with MoMA; even Mom agrees. I know you think 'unique' is overused but not in the sense I'm going to use it: the collection of antiquities is unique."

"Schedules are jealous mistresses," I said. "Ours can't be stretched." I pacified the family by promising to return soon.

The next morning, we boarded a chartered bus for Kibbutz Ma'agan, in northern Israel, on the Sea of Galilee. We stayed in private cabins bordering the sea and ate breakfast and dinner in a common dining room, serving ourselves from platters set on large tables. Our bus driver and guide stayed with us.

Each morning, after breakfast, we hopped on our bus, stopping at Capernaum, the Mount of Beatitudes, and the House of St. Peter. These sites had two things in common: Jesus lived and taught there, and they were ruins. We ambled around the uneven paths strewn with rocks and stared at the sites, active two thousand years ago but deserted today.

On the tour and in the bus, I paired off with my brother-in-law, David Markowitz. "When I married Mary," he said, "I knew very little about Jesus. He was important to Mary, so I read about him.

"When Jesus urged his followers to turn the other cheek, he was teaching forgiveness. Compassion was embodied in the phrase 'love thy enemies.' He championed the poor, the downtrodden, the outcasts, the persecuted. He challenged the rich to give away their wealth. Patristic-Christian scholars claim that Jesus would have disdained pilgrimages and placed little value on the observance of rituals and rites. Jesus, they said, preferred the simple life and good deeds over religious compliance.

"Initially, I was frightened by the concept of Jesus, a fear shared by many Jews. As I got to know his philosophy, I overcame my fear."

I agreed with David and said what he was too kind to say—trips to Jesus shrines were contrary to his life, teaching, and philosophy. They were also boring.

On the flight back to Rome, I couldn't get Israel out of my thoughts. This country, founded less than sixty years ago, had a dynamite economy, magnificent museums filled with rare treasures, universities, a symphony orchestra, an opera house, theaters, and concert halls. Why didn't the international media discuss the positive aspects of Israel, rather than dwell on the Palestinian question?

I love my Jewish family, the adults who are 100 percent Jewish and the children who are half Jewish. In general, however, I have reservations about many American Jews. They tend to be liberals, white-collar workers who can't fix even the simplest things. The Israeli Jews are different. They are carpenters, plumbers, elevator operators (have you ever seen a Jewish elevator operator anywhere else?), janitors, and of course scientists, teachers, doctors, and lawyers. I identify with Israelis and love them more than American Jews.

The *Times* had other stories in the magazine that Sunday but none other than Thomas Friedman's mattered to me.

Friedman's comment on my Israeli-Arab policy ran only a few paragraphs. It was muted perhaps by Sharon's illness and the shift in the paper's policy toward Israel. In essence, he said that my solution was nothing more than recognition of the status quo.

Letters poured in from Arab sympathizers criticizing my gerrymandering policy. Hertzel had anticipated the reaction and managed to counter it with several letters from academics and political scientists citing many incidents of gerrymandering in America. One historian pointed out that gerrymandering was often used as a first step toward democracy, replaced over time by redistricting and fair representation.

When Hertzel's bill arrived, I began to wonder whether his computer spit out "$250,000" every time the name "Wojecoski" was entered. I smiled as I wrote out the check, remembering how hard I had labored to make my first fifteen thousand dollars, and how thrilled I had been at my cleverness.

# 16

*I* hid copies of *Time* and the Sunday *Times* magazine in a drawer beneath my underwear and took them out when I was sure I was alone—on the toilet, or in bed early in the morning—and gazed at photographs of myself. Did I have a swelled head? Were my values skewed? Did I spend five hundred thousand dollars to feed my ego? Did I really want to be president, or was I seeking admiration and mass attention?

Peggy knew me when I was nothing and knew me when I was on the threshold of greatness. I put the question to her.

She had discovered the magazines and guessed why they were there—and was not troubled. "You have a big ego, Henry, but also a lot of talent. They've made you the man you are. If you were all ego, I wouldn't love you, nor would I love you if you didn't have some healthy self-esteem. Motives are always mixed, part one thing, part another. You want to be president for many reasons. None of them are evil. Stop analyzing yourself, and let's get on with it. It's going to be tough enough without questioning every step along the way."

Iraq was next on the list. I had hoped to tour the country with a group of fellow Vietnam vets who could talk the language of the boots on the ground and might well have ideas on how we could get the hell out. Rice had quashed the trip, but she couldn't stop me from going public with an Iraq strategy. Can you imagine the headline? "Administration Tries to Muzzle Iraq Critic." I suppose Bush could have fired me, but for what? The marketplace where competing ideas are debated is the hallmark of a democratic society.

My visits to Africa and Israel were not essential to my policymaking. They were developed in Rome. I'd use the same approach with Iraq and trust to that genius Hertzel to find a way to publicize it.

In 2006, Iraq was a hot-button issue among diplomats, some of whom were world-class thinkers. Peggy and I picked out the best minds and invited them to the residence, and it wasn't hard to steer the conversation to that ravaged, blood-soaked country.

The English ambassador was particularly informative. A friend of Tony Blair, Bush's closest ally, he liked nothing better than discussing Iraq—except perhaps for a good bottle of scotch. I made sure his glass was full.

Based on the department's files, domestic and foreign articles, and dinner chitchat, I completed my Iraqi strategy.

I'd discussed my Africa and Israel strategies with Hertzel, who hadn't liked them: "Why don't you give me a written outline so I have something to give to my staff?" This time, I wrote a summary: "Iraq: The Honorable Way Out."

America went to war on false premises. Iraq did not possess weapons of mass destruction, nor did she participate with Al Qaeda in the 9/11 attacks. It was, however, necessary to oust Saddam Hussein, not because he was a tyrant but because *realpolitik* demanded his overthrow. Iraqi's undeveloped oil fields contain the world's largest potential reservoirs. Oil is of strategic importance to the defense and welfare of the United States. It is essential that a government friendly toward the United States control such an important resource. Saddam, a former ally, turned against the United States after the first Gulf War. He claimed that we supported the takeover of Kuwait and that we double-crossed him. America, in Saddam's eyes, was a bitter foe.

The United States had no intention of seizing Iraq's oil fields. Rather, America initiated the war to replace Saddam with a ruler friendly to our interests who could ensure our access to Iraqi oil.

Our troops should be withdrawn and replaced with an international force whose sole duty is to protect the oil fields. A force of fifty thousand troops drawn from volunteers throughout the world should be adequate. Soldiers will volunteer because the pay will be generous. They will wear uniforms similar to the French Legionnaires, who were also mercenaries.

Iraq is too splintered to remain a single nation. Peace will return only when the country is divided into three states, one controlled by Sunnis, another by Shiites, and the third by Kurds.

The net oil royalties, after deducting the cost of the international force, will then be equitably divided among the three states.

Soon after my summary was completed, Peggy and I returned to New York. I noticed a change. Previously, I was an anonymous man in a city of anonymous people. Now, I was a celebrity. Strangers greeted me by name, asked for my autograph, and talked about the *Time* and *New York Times* stories. I was gaining name recognition, the goal of my expensive public relations campaign. In truth, I liked the attention too.

I met with Hertzel and showed him the summary. "Your Africa and Israeli policies were benign. With Iraq, you propose to embarrass the administration by not only making the well-known claim that the war was begun by mistake but also that it is being waged for oil. Thousands of lives have been lost, a hundred thousand young men and women have been wounded, billions spent—all in the name of oil? Henry, you will make enemies in important places. Too big a risk for too little gain."

I protested that all of it was true. "Fuck truth," he sneered.

"But Iraq's exploration property might contain two trillion barrels of oil. We import 85 percent of our oil now. What would happen if we couldn't? That oil is our future."

Hertzel twirled once around in his chair. He picked up his phone. "Get me Larry King." I heard half of the conversation.

"Wojecoski is the hottest prospect on the international scene . . . He found the correct approach to ameliorate conditions in Africa . . . He made it as clear as a fire on a hill at night . . . He dissipated the hypocrisy surrounding a two-state solution to the Israel-Palestinian conflict . . . He's willing to expose the truth about the Iraqi war and how it can be ended . . . You're Wojecoski's first choice, but if you say no, he'll go elsewhere . . . Henry and I like you, but you're not the only game in town . . . Give me several dates . . . He's a busy diplomat . . . Look, we'll try to fit you in but no promises . . . Of course, the usual rules will apply."

"The usual rules" meant King would give me his questions in advance.

I appeared on Larry King Live on a Sunday night in March, 2006. Before the show, I rehearsed with Hertzel and a TV consultant, with Hertzel playing King. I was myself, except when the consultant played me to show me how it should be done. They helped me on substance and on when to raise an eyebrow, how to hold my hands, and when to smile. The consultant came to my house, picked out my clothes, and took me for a haircut, manicure, and, for the hell of it, a pedicure. In the studio, a makeup woman dusted my face with powder.

Introducing me, King reminded his audience that I had been born in Riverhead, the son of a plumber. "Upon graduating from high school," he said, "Henry enlisted in the Marines and saw active duty in Vietnam. When he was discharged, he went to work as a loan broker in a storefront office in his hometown." He traced my business career and the sale of the two companies and only then asked his first question: "After growing up poor, how does it feel to be one of the richest men in America?"

"When I was young and poor, I fell in love with my high school sweetheart, Peggy Woijek. We got married in 1975. Thirty-one years later, I'm rich, still in love with and married to Peggy. Money has not changed my most important relationship. The biggest force in my life has not been money but the power of my will. It has determined who I am and who I will become."

King said he rarely interviewed billionaires. "Surely money has changed your lifestyle?"

I told him all about our travails in our first apartment, "the house that Murphy built." Then I discussed Hudson House and how we shared it with my sister, her husband, their five children, and our four. "It's located north of One Hundredth Street and Riverside Drive—not Fifth or Park or anywhere on the East Side.

In the opinion of our families, it's the grandest house in the City of New York. We've never thought of moving."

King asked about my work as ambassador to Rome. "The job is what you make it. An ambassador must tend to the business of the embassy. I do that. There is also an opportunity through exposure to diplomats from all over the world to gain knowledge of foreign problems. I spend a lot of my free time delving into existing foreign policies and helping to create new ones. Two areas of interest to me, Africa and Israel, received extensive coverage in the national press."

King held up *Time* and the *Times* so the cameras could focus on them. He pitched a few more softball questions, first about Africa and Israel—and then came Iraq.

His questions followed the script. My answers elaborated on the summary. King concluded by saying that he hoped my string of successes was not over. "You have a will that will take you wherever you want to go. I expect to see you again and again."

Peggy was in the studio. When the program was over, she hugged and kissed me. "Your performance was brilliant. You made King's night. I've had a tape made that I plan to hide under your underwear."

My interview got nationwide coverage. It brought home to millions of Americans that young men and women were dying to safeguard America's access to Iraq's oil reserves. I was a hero for unmasking the real reason for the war, but I was vilified by the Bush administration. Rove confided in me what Bush had said. "What the hell is Wojecoski up to?" Informed that I planned to run for president in 2008, the president snapped, "You tell that son of a bitch if he opens his mouth again, I will kill his candidacy by endorsing him. I will tell the American people a vote for Wojecoski is a vote for George W. Bush."

I saluted my president and said, "Mission accomplished."

Back in Rome, Peggy suggested we both get lots of rest. "We're headed for a pressure cooker. Let's take some time off. Travel to other European countries. But let's not forget Poland."

Before I became an ambassador, I was business and she was MoMA. In Rome, Peggy changed course and became an artist. She took painting lessons and rented a studio. I thought her work was great but she disagreed: "I'm not a Helen Frankenthaler or a Lee Krasner; I'm about a shade over rotten. But the lessons help me understand what makes a painting great."

We spent many days in the Sistine Chapel, the Raphael Rooms, and the Gregorian, Egyptian, and Etruscan collections of the Vatican. When we traveled to other capitals, Peggy was my museum guide.

She explained what made a painting a masterpiece. She pointed out lesser works by the same artist and compared them to the famous ones. I was overwhelmed by the vast displays. In self-defense, I devised a "museum strategy." After a quick tour, I picked one or two paintings and studied them at length. Those were the ones I would remember. Peggy claimed she could pick out my choices before I did. "They're always nudes or couples coupling." I countered that nudes were art; otherwise, so many great artists would not have painted them. Erotic art, for the same reason, is also art.

Peggy specialized in landscapes.

In Rome, we were spitting distance from all the centers of European culture. Before embarking on a trip, I'd inform the resident American ambassador of the country we planned to visit, and we invariably were guests at the embassy, especially after we became famous. Excursions were arranged for us to well-known places and those rarely seen by tourists. We were treated like royalty. Of course, we reciprocated when our fellow diplomats came to Rome.

We also took overnight trips around Italy. Our favorite city was Florence; after our second visit there, we discussed buying a villa in Tuscany. "If you don't become president," said Peggy, "that'll be our consolation prize. We'll divide our time between Florence and New York."

We took a trip to Poland late in March 2006, shortly before I resigned. It was a kind of homecoming. We spent days walking through the streets of Warsaw and Krakow, ate in recommended restaurants, and spent an emotional few days in Mala Wies, the birthplace of Peggy's grandparents. There were some families in the village with familiar names, Kuzniewski and Sendlewski. We invited them to a nearby inn for dinner. Peggy took lots of photographs. We kissed and hugged them and gave them the gifts we had brought along: French chocolates, English sweaters, high-quality Polish vodka. Our guests, poor peasants, were overwhelmed. When they learned that I was the US ambassador to Rome, they were thrilled. They found it hard to believe that people from their humble village could be rich and famous.

At the end of the evening, a man about my age remarked wistfully, "Maybe, if my own grandparents had immigrated to America, I too might have become an ambassador, just like my distinguished cousin."

That night in bed, I turned his words around. "If our forefathers hadn't left Poland, we might be poor peasants barely scratching out a living, raising pigs."

Peggy asked whether we would have loved each other as much if we had spent our lives in poverty in Mala Wies. I thought not. "These people have a hard life. Little joy, much misery. Our life has been full of excitement, maybe even more to come. It's a lot easier to love when you live a privileged life."

Peggy disagreed. "Love is etched in your soul. Wealth can't buy it, nor can poverty eradicate it. Your parents lived a hard life, yet they love each other." I'd like to believe that Peggy was right: love doesn't depend on external circumstances. I'm not sure how well we can separate inclinations from motives. I was also not sure that my parents loved each other. I wondered if they stayed together for convenience. I ducked further discussion. "Peggy, what difference does it make why we love? It's enough that we do."

As April approached, I vacillated, for the first time, about running for president. If I won, my private life would end. Whatever we did or said, officially or unofficially, would be fodder for the press. I wondered whether it was worth trading my happy life for a public one full of stress. There was also a chance—let's face it, a good chance—I would lose, and there was nothing I hated more than losing. Even the thought depressed me. I decided to let Peggy decide.

She surprised me, as she so often does. She was all for it. She claimed I knew so much about foreign affairs, and that my business skills, applied to the national economy, might be just the tonic the country needed to get back on track. "You're compassionate, fair, and incorruptible. The country, suffering under Bush, needs a change. It needs you. If you win, and you will, Polish Americans will also win. You owe it to our country and to our compatriots."

If I didn't run, I could retire. Divide my time between Florence and New York. Maybe write my memoirs. Read all the books I've wanted to read. Spend time with my family. The alternative to running was attractive.

On the other hand, I had sought the ambassadorship for the purpose of preparing a run for president. Lots of people knew of my intention. I'm a fighter, not one who runs away. The scales tipped in favor of running. On April Fool's Day, an ominous sign I ignored, I resigned as ambassador to Rome. My duties were assigned to my chief of staff, Daniels, on a temporary basis pending a new appointment.

When word of my resignation reached the Italian press, it praised my service, called me an exemplary ambassador, and expressed the hope that my successor would be as effective. Berlusconi presented me with the Guiseppe Garibaldi Medal for Distinguished Service, the first time it had been awarded to a non-Italian. "I've a feeling we will meet again," the prime minister said in pinning the medal to my lapel.

I had spent two wonderful years in Italy. I wished I could have stayed longer, but I needed to start my campaign. As I boarded the plane for New York, with sadness at leaving, I whispered, "Arrivaderla Roma," and began humming the victory march from *Aida*.

# 17

The US embassy in Rome, formerly known as Queen Margherita's palace, is just that, a palace. The five-story classical structure extends for a full city block. Four marble Corinthian columns mark the entryway. Each of the more than three hundred windows has a cornice. The rear looks out at the manicured gardens of the Palazzo Margherita. Inside, the facing of the walls in all important rooms is marble, the ceilings carved and painted, the floors inlaid with various rare woods.

I soon observed that grand buildings affect behavior. Inside the palace, we lowered our voices and minded our manners. It was not long before I noticed that visitors did the same.

No American businessman, no matter how rich, can achieve nobility. As ambassador to Rome, though, I came close. I was formally introduced as the Honorable Henry J. Wojecoski. A corps of foreign-service officers was at my beck and call. They were my court. A personal staff—a butler, chauffeur, and male attendant—waited on me. To them, I was a royal figure, at least a count.

There was just one problem: I couldn't speak Italian. I tried hard. Took private lessons, but never got beyond basic phrases. A true nobleman is not only fluent in the language of his country, but speaks it with eloquence and style. I was a faux nobleman.

New York was a letdown after the palace. Hudson House was spacious but not regal. Riverside Drive was a far cry from the Via Veneto. But the thrill of running for president made up for everything.

Pennsylvania Avenue and the White House surpass the Via Veneto and US embassy. "Honorable" is a nice title, but it doesn't compare with "Mr. President." I was abandoning a prestigious job for a chance at the ultimate job.

I began my campaign by calling Karl Rove. I asked if he would consider resigning as senior White House adviser and signing on with me. Putting on my best godfather accent, I said, "Bush is finished. I'll soon be boss. A large sum on deposit in a Swiss bank is yours if you agree to be my consigliere. It's an offer you can't refuse."

"I can and will. I'm under a cloud, being investigated by an independent prosecutor. He says I'm not a target, but I've been before a grand jury three times. I'm eager to work with you, but your first appointment shouldn't be someone who soon thereafter gets indicted."

I thought that was the end of our conversation, but after a pause, he doled out some free advice. "You have a lot going for you. You're five oceans and several continents removed from Bush and Cheney. Boy, are they pissed off at you, but that's good, not bad. They're both unpopular among rank-and-file Republicans, even more so within the organization. You're in a better position than any of the other candidates to claim that a vote for you represents change. Dramatic change. A candidate from a working-class family, not the despised eastern elite. You know, Henry, you might just make it. If you do, don't forget me. I want to be ambassador to Italy."

"If I make it, I'll see what I can do."

"Hire Steve Smith as your advisor. He's young, savvy, and vicious as hell. I've told him about you. He'll do it for one hundred thousand dollars down plus expenses and another hundred at the end of the year."

The meeting with Smith turned into a week-long skirmish (but not quite a battle). We fought over every point, but I liked the bluster and the give and take. Rove was right: Smith was a pit bull. But I wasn't sure I wanted him to be my pit bull. He wanted to micromanage the campaign, from the announcement of my candidacy to the last primary, and proposed opening offices in every primary state and hiring a ghost writer to write my memoirs. He called his plan a triple-A blueprint for a presidential campaign. Budget: fifty million dollars.

"I'm a maverick," I told him. "I'm sticking my toes in the water, not diving in head first. I don't want hundreds of campaign offices or fake rallies. The best way to test my candidacy is through a series of speeches on national television. Then we can take polls. If I'm in, I'll ask my supporters to contribute money, not to my campaign—I'll finance that myself—but to help poor people. I'll match every dollar raised from the public up to one hundred million dollars."

"Who are you, Lord Bountiful? As a practical matter, your one hundred million dollars is a drop in the bucket. It's nothing to you. Do you want to make a contribution that will resonate with the electorate? Up the ante to a billion."

Each of our ideas moved like a boomerang—out and back at us, a round trip journey to nowhere.

"It's my campaign, and you work for me," I said, "if I hire you for the long haul."

"Strategy and tactics are my bailiwick," he said. "Political campaigns are a form of war. They must be waged in the traditional way. You either engage fully or not at all. You can't skip the trappings. You must have an organization behind you."

I knew Smith was good and wanted him to stay on. But we were deadlocked. I proposed mediation, with Rove as the mediator.

Off we went to Washington. After listening to both sides, Rove gave his decision. "Henry came from nowhere. A high school education, a working-class background, and he made a fortune. He had no experience in diplomacy. Yet he was one of our most successful diplomats. We get calls from heads of state asking for more Henry Wojecoskis. Smitty, I agree with you. If I were running Henry's campaign, I would use the same strategy. Henry, however, may be smarter than both of us. The times call for a new approach. Henry has a record of success. Let's try it his way. If the polls show a low number and Henry decides to stay in, you can go back to the old ways."

Rove rose from his chair. His light brown hair was fast fading, growing even thinner. His only distinguishing feature was a round face. He pointed his finger at me: "Now see here, Henry, you have to go along with some of Smitty's basic strategy. You're a billionaire. Don't play the poor Polack. You'll need speech writers, media consultants, pollsters, advance men, and PR experts. Let Smith hire them. And Smitty, don't shop for bargains."

We accepted Rove's decision. Smith found the experts, with one exception. I insisted on Hertzel for PR.

On April 19, 2006, my campaign was officially launched. I preempted thirty minutes of prime time television. Right off the bat, I disclosed my plan to protect the country against terrorists: by winning the hearts and minds of those who hate us. Instead of dropping bombs on mosques, hospitals, and schools, we should instead provide food, medicine, school books, and the Koran to Muslims in Afghanistan, Iraq, and Iran. I asked supporters to contribute money over the Internet to www.MuslimHelpFund. org." Then I dropped the bomb. "I will match every dollar contributed up to one hundred million dollars. To ensure the money reaches the right people, the fund will be managed by leading statesmen from Muslim countries."

I also offered a solution to reverse the rising trend of unemployment. "I come from a working-class family. I know firsthand how important it is for men and women who can work to work. If elected, I propose to allocate hundreds of billions of dollars to build and improve bridges, tunnels, highways, and railroads. These projects will put unemployed, working-class Americans back to work. Infrastructure projects will, my experts project, create three million jobs. On the negative side, it will cause a deficit, one that will have to be borne by future generations. Very little, if anything, comes free. Our children, grandchildren, and great-grandchildren will, however, benefit from the improvements. In my opinion, it is fair for the cost of projects lasting twenty-five years or more to be spread among the ones who will use them."

I concluded by saying, "Better to run deficits for projects that improve quality of life than for the continuation of the war in Iraq."

The right-wing press was outraged. They denounced me as a liberal and mocked me for posing as a Republican. They suggested I run as a socialist.

I was angry. Some nerve calling *me*—a lifelong Republican, a big contributor to the party, one of Bush's self-proclaimed "constituents," a former ambassador, a billionaire—a socialist. That would be funny were this not a serious matter.

The other candidates were more nuanced. They called me "well meaning but naive, unsophisticated, weak, unrealistic, a Dr. Pangloss." But none said a word about my proposals. Their ad hominem attack and absence of constructive criticism or suggestions of reasonable alternatives helped me prepare my next national television appearance one month later.

"I'm for creating jobs," I said in that speech. "Are my opponents against that? They sure sound that way. Does a program of job creation to put people back to work disqualify me from running on the Republican ticket? Does it make me a socialist, a liberal, a Democrat? Are my opponents in favor of unemployment?" I used the same approach on the other issues, asking whether my opponents favored continuing the war in Iraq. "Who," I asked, "is a better candidate to lead the Republican party—one who stands for the best American traditions or the worst?"

The *New York Times* endorsed my ideas as a matter of principle but reserved judgment for further study. "Ambassador Wojecoski, a businessman cum diplomat," the editorial began, "proposes an abrupt change in our domestic and foreign policies. What he seeks is both idealistic and far reaching. We agree change is necessary. We also agree it must be radical in order to restore our country to a position of respect and leadership. Position papers on these points must be carefully studied before we can decide whether the ambassador's ideas are realistic or pie in the sky.

"What is undisputable: a Republican candidate has appeared with a clear mission—reverse the policies of the Bush administration and restore the United States to a position of respect throughout the world. We welcome Ambassador Wojecoski's candidacy and intend to follow it closely."

The polls showed me advancing weekly. From a base of zero, I was now challenging the frontrunner, former New York mayor Rudy Giuliani. The other candidates were mostly ignoring Giuliani, and for good reason. He had no money, little organization, a checkered family life. A scandal was rumored to erupt involving Bernard Kerik, Giuliani's former police commissioner and present business partner, whom Giuliani had backed for secretary of the Department of Homeland Security. His candidacy would self-implode. The other candidates feared me—or so Smith said. He predicted that during the upcoming first debate, I would be the principal target.

That night, Giuliani was the first to speak. He said the nation had to hang tough in the war against terror and accused me of being soft on terrorists—and otherwise ill equipped: "His lack of experience in running a state, a city, or anything other than a mortgage business means he lacks qualifications to protect our country against attack."

My answer came easily: "Mister Former Mayor and Present Lobbyist, let me begin with a correction that will place the issue in proper perspective. There is no such thing as a war on terror. Terror is a tactic, not a nation, not an ideology, not a cause. We must destroy Al Qaeda. We must make sincere efforts to convert militant extremist Muslims to peaceful activities. The road to victory over Al Qaeda lies in a concentration of our forces in Afghanistan, not in a diversion into Iraq. The way to convert extremist Islam is to understand and address the reasons for their hatred of the western world. Through education and good deeds, we may be able to remove the hate and thus convert our enemies into friends. You probably did not listen to my program for ending the war in Iraq that I first announced on *Larry King Live*. You, Mr. Mayor-Lobbyist, favor the war in Iraq. Your anger over 9/11 begins and ends your analysis. Without that fury, you would be speechless. Problems are not solved by anger but by reason. I fear for our country in your hands."

The audience erupted in applause. The moderator, William Walters, held up his hands and called for quiet. "I remind you. The audience must restrain from exercising any form of approval or disapproval. If it happens again, I will ask the security guards to clear the auditorium. The candidates must observe the rules, and so must the audience."

My debate with Giuliani was like a boxing match. I delivered a hard right hook to his jaw. It knocked him down. He barely got off the floor before the count of ten and stumbled to his corner.

Huckabee was next. He affirmed his belief in Christian values. He opposed abortion. His appointees to the Supreme Court would reverse *Roe v. Wade*. He stated unequivocally that atheists in America caused God to allow the World Trade Center disaster. He questioned my religious beliefs, asking me to state my position on creation and intelligent design. "Should they be taught to young children in public schools? Or should evolution alone be taught?"

I considered Huckabee and his views ridiculous. To me, he wasn't even a good Christian. Smith, however, warned me not to underestimate the man. He might wear blinders, but a lot of Americans, even more blind, supported him blindly. My reply was carefully crafted so as not to alienate that substantial bloc.

"I personally oppose abortion but would never force my beliefs on others. A woman bears the child. It is her right to determine whether to do so. Governor Huckabee, you are the governor of the State of Arkansas. Don't you know abortion is also a state issue? Many states legalized abortions before *Roe*, my state included. If *Roe v. Wade* were reversed, women in New York could still obtain abortions. So could women living in other states that allow it. Further, a woman living in a state such as Arkansas, which does not allow for a legal abortion, could obtain one by traveling to a state that did. *Roe v. Wade* simply prohibits states from barring abortions. If it were reversed, states would still be free to grant or ban them.

"I'm Catholic. My church speaks out against abortion. It speaks, however, for Catholics and cannot control the actions of women of other faiths. The law in this country is secular, not religious. Neither my church nor yours should determine our nation's laws. I believe in the separation of church and state. In selecting judges for the Supreme Court, I will pick the most qualified. Their views on constitutional questions will not be a factor. Your one-issue criterion for judges would saddle the Supreme Court with mediocre justices at best."

I then turned to evolution—and decided to tread softly. "I believe in evolution. It is backed by scientific evidence. About four hundred years ago, my church punished Galileo for saying the earth revolves around the sun. My church has since apologized for its error and has vowed not to contradict science. Like me, the Catholic church accepts evolution. That does not exclude the role of God. There has to be a first cause of everything. God is the first cause of evolution.

"Intelligent design is a theory not backed by scientific evidence. It is supported by faith. As I have already said, I believe in the separation of state and church. It is part of our Constitution. It must be observed. I oppose the teaching of intelligent design to young, impressionable students in public schools. It is not based on science."

Giuliani is a smart man. He recognized a lethal blow; Huckabee did not. "I'll wager the good people who make up the Republican Party will reject the godless, Ambassador Wojecoski."

Next up was Romney. He touted his Harvard education, his success in running a venture capital firm, and his term as governor of Massachusetts. Only then did he turn to me. "I admire Ambassador Wojecoski. He is a high school graduate with no advanced education. He made a billion dollars peddling subprime mortgages to institutional investors. He purchased his position as ambassador to Italy. In my administration, ambassadorships will not be bartered and sold. The job of president of the United States is the most powerful and demanding one in the world. Are we ready to turn our country over to an uneducated man? A man who has never been elected to office? Wojecoski should first prove he is capable of managing a state or city before running for president. These are dangerous times. Our next president must be experienced and well educated."

Giuliani and Huckabee endorsed Romney's attack. Each stressed his own academic credentials and public office. McCain was silent. Then it was my turn.

I congratulated Romney on his fine education. "I recognize the value of a Harvard degree. In my business, I hired a young graduate of the university and its business school. He was so smart and competent I made him my junior partner.

"Your father," I continued, looking directly at Romney, "headed a major automobile company before becoming governor of Michigan. You were fortunate to be born with a silver spoon. You had all the advantages. My father was a plumber. He could not afford to send me to Harvard. Instead, he enrolled me in the college of hard knocks. In that school, I learned the value of work. By hard work, I overcame my lack of a college education. Before I was thirty-eight, I was CEO of a company listed on the New York Stock Exchange. If elected president, I will apply the lessons learned in my college."

I then turned to my service as ambassador. "I have been a loyal Republican all my adult life. The sale of a public office is a serious crime. If, Governor Romney, you have any evidence that President Bush violated public trust by selling ambassadorships, I urge you to turn over the evidence to the attorney general. He and the Senate, which, by the way, approved my appointment, will determine whether President Bush should be impeached.

"I do not like to brag. Forgive me just this once. Did you know, Governor Romney, that in the long history of US diplomatic relationships with Italy, I am the only recipient of the Giuseppe Garibaldi Medal for Extraordinary Diplomatic Services?"

The audience remained silent, intimidated by the moderator. Their nonverbal signs, however, spoke loud and clear. The TV cameras captured smiles of approval on the faces of many and thumbs-up gestures by others.

McCain, a savvy veteran of political campaigns, praised me. He suggested that I would make a great running mate. I thanked him and said a "Wojecoski-McCain ticket might be even stronger than a McCain-Wojecoski ticket." That got a laugh. "Let the voters decide who should lead."

After a debate, it's customary for a campaign staff to declare its candidate the winner. Giuliani's, Huckabee's, and Romney's staffs were silent. No hype could possibly restore their wounded candidates. The results were all too clear. I was the winner, and McCain came in second. We both gained support in the polls; the others fell so far that for all practical purposes, they were out of contention.

Smith was ecstatic over my debating skills. He claimed my personality came through. I was a man of the people, an extraordinarily uncommon common man. "The voters are with you," he declared. "There is an outpouring of people volunteering to work for you. The support is growing like kudzu."

And indeed it did. Thousands of volunteers signed up to work for me. Offices were opened throughout the country, staffed by voters committed to my candidacy. I appeared on talk shows. I wrote an op-ed piece—someone on Hertzel's staff wrote it—for the *New York Times*. Riverhead, New York, became a tourist site. Banners flew from Riverhead homes declaring the town the birthplace of Henry Wojecoski. My face was known throughout the country. How did I feel? I felt entitled. It was earned. It was my due. Until I remembered a joint family dinner in or around 1994, when Mary was still very much alive.

Michael Markowitz had asked his mother the meaning of "hubris." She said it was a Greek word describing a condition that affects some people who think they're great. "It is excessive pride and arrogance. The gods played tricks on ancient Greeks who suffered from hubris, causing them to fall from grace in disgraceful ways. You can think of hubris as pride that cometh before a fall. The antidote is humility and modesty."

Mary spoke softly. Her eyes glanced around the table but fell more often on me. Was I too full of myself because of my success in business?

After the presidential debate, I was cocky, certain that I would win the biggest prize. My opponents were pushovers, no match for me. I was much more in the grip of hubris than at any previous time. I wondered how the gods would bring me down.

# 18

The primary was a horse race, and McCain, the leader, was hugging the rail. By some miracle—and twenty-five million dollars of my own money—I was on the outside, about a length behind and closing in. To McCain, it was reminiscent of the 2000 primary. He was in the lead when Bush made his final run. Bush hired Anthony Mazziola, a sensation-mongering journalist who specialized in sordid reporting and Bush sicced him on McCain. The strategy and the sleaze did McCain in.

As a navy fighter pilot in Vietnam, McCain was shot down by the Vietcong. He spent five years as a prisoner of war. When McCain returned home, he received a hero's welcome, one I thought he richly deserved. During the Bush campaign decades later, Mazziola dug up rumors that attacked McCain's character and patriotism. One claimed he'd divulged so many military secrets that his codename was "Songbird." A second was that the POW experience had "unhinged" him. A third claimed he fathered an illegitimate black child. In several states, McCain had campaigned with his adopted Bangladeshi daughter. The dirty tricks slowed him down, and Bush crossed the finish line first.

McCain feared I might pull a "Bush." He took preemptive action and got there first. He hired Mazziola with these orders: "Do to Wojecoski what you did to me!"

I would come to learn that Mazziola always wore a wire. When a story was dead, he peddled the tape to the victim. I know the "facts" he uncovered on me because I purchased the Wojecoski tapes for five thousand dollars.

Mazziola dug—and dug—for dirt. Affairs. Drugs. Whores. A queer fling in my past? Was I ever mean to a dogcatcher? Did I gamble? Did I drink too much or not pay my maid's Social Security—the worst social ill of all? Poor guy, he found not a hint of wrongdoing. He was inclined to quit but felt he owed McCain for the damage done in 2000. For his final foray, Mazziola went back to my childhood in Riverhead. It was a dead end. No one had a bad word to say.

Mazziola did come up with a wisp about a party that Mary and I had attended that was a farewell for a number of the guys off to Vietnam. I would soon learn that he asked several of our contemporaries about the party. None could recall anything, except for Diane Heaney, who volunteered that Janet Kiviatkovski "claimed to know something weird, too weird to mention." She said that Janet had married a man from Honesdale, Pennsylvania, named Joseph Keegan, and they lived in his home town.

Once he heard this, Mazziola gathered information on the Keegans and then drove the ninety miles to Honesdale, where he checked into the Wayne Hotel. He arrived at the Keegans' house at cocktail hour with a bottle of bourbon and introduced himself to Joe at the front door: "I'm under contract to write an unauthorized biography of Henry Wojecoski. Your wife, Janet, knows something about Henry and his sister—so everyone in Riverhead tells me. I'd like to take both of you for drinks and dinner at the Wayne. My publisher is willing to pay generously for your time. I have a cash advance of one hundred dollars; it's yours just for having dinner with me. If you provide helpful information, I'm authorized to pay as much as five thousand dollars."

Keegan turned and yelled, "Hey, Janet. We just won the lottery. C'mon here."

Keegan was well over six feet and weighed about three hundred pounds. His pants hung around his hips. He had a mop of black hair and was given to shouting.

Janet appeared, but it was her husband who spoke. "You know how you're always talking about the Wojecoskis? This guy wants to know all about that graduation party." He repeated the financial offer and waited for his wife to leap at the invitation.

Janet looked petite standing next to her husband. In fact, she was of average height, slightly overweight, with closely bobbed red hair. In a soft voice, she said, "Mary and I were not friends. I suspected something, but it was based on a fleeting moment. I doubt it's worth a dime."

"Never mind her," Keegan said to Mazziola. "She's naïve. Give her the one hundred dollars and let's go. Janet, get your coat." Mazziola handed Janet a hundred-dollar bill, and the trio set off for the Wayne.

Mazziola ordered martinis, and before dinner, husband and wife had two each; Mazziola drank water. At dinner, he ordered a bottle of wine and then a second. By the end of the meal, the Keegans were feeling no pain. Mazziola smiled at Janet and casually asked, "What happened that night between Henry and Mary?"

Her husband again answered. "She knows a lot. She isn't talking until we see the color of your money."

Mazziola reached into his pocket and pulled out a thin wallet. He showed the contents to the Keegans, who almost did a double-take. "You can see the money," Mazziola said. "You can touch it. It's not yours until Janet tells me what I want to hear. No ticky, no laundry. Once I decide you've given me something good, I part with the cash. My decision. You'll have to trust me."

Mazziola put the wallet in his pocket and then tantalizingly returned it to the table, within easy reach of Keegan. Mazziola was not worried Keegan might snatch it. The journalist carried a gun, and Keegan was too drunk to get far.

"C'mon, Janet," he said, "tell us about Henry and Mary at the party."

She protested at first, saying she knew nothing. Then she must have thought of the certified letter from the bank that held their mortgage. "Near graduation time, the boys threw a party. It was called the ides of March party. Henry was the organizer. He told the girls that the guys were going to Vietnam, risking their lives to defend democracy. Some would not return; others would come back missing arms and legs. We fell for it. At the party, almost all the guys had sex with girls, some guys with the same girl. Others, with more than one.

"The party was held in a large, vacant Southampton house. We staged a daring break-in. We danced, drank, and smoked pot downstairs. The kids got stoned, and things started to happen. You know what I mean. On the upper floors were lots of bedrooms. On each door were the cards they have on hotel doors. On one side, 'vacant,' and the other, 'occupied.' I went upstairs several times but never entered a bedroom."

"Yeah, sure," interrupted her husband. "The boys were banging you from the time you were fifteen. How many of the good ole boys did you have that night?"

"Shut up, Joe; you disgust me. I'm done talking. Keep your stinkin' five thousand dollars."

"I'm sorry, Janet," said Keegan. "Frank, I swear, Janet was a virgin on our wedding night. C'mon, Janet, we need the money. Otherwise, we lose our house. Do you want to live in a tent in the park?"

"I can see why the boys liked you," said Mazziola. "You're an attractive woman and must have been a knockout as a teenager. I'm sure you behaved yourself. I'm also sure you were a virgin on your wedding night. Please, continue."

Janet poured another glass of wine. "I went upstairs on two occasions. The first was early on; the second was when the party was about over. The first time, I noticed the sign was turned to 'occupied' on just one door, at the end of the hall. I didn't stay long, but I was curious who the fast ones were. I checked around and saw that Henry and Mary were missing. I kept looking for them, but they were nowhere to be seen. I asked several of the girls if they'd seen the twins. None had. As the party was ending, I went upstairs again. As I was standing in the hall, Henry and Mary came out from the room. They were joking around in a familiar way. They were also holding books. I was sure of one thing. They sure as hell weren't reading in there. Come to think of it, Mary was a reader. Valedictorian of our class. Not Henry. I didn't think he even knew how to read. The twins were very different. Maybe that's why they were attracted to each other. Years later, I read somewhere they lived together in a big house in New York with their families."

Joe Keegan started to talk. Mazziola motioned him to be quiet. He handed Janet the wallet, said it was late, and bid them good night.

The *National Enquirer*, the usual parking place for Mazziola's stories, insisted on corroboration. The requirement was easily satisfied. A recording, lending slight support, was sufficient. He had enough to satisfy a tale of incestuous lovemaking. The next day, Mazziola spoke with Alan Ellis, his liaison with the McCain camp. Mazziola relayed the gist of the story, said he had recorded the conversation and that the *Enquirer* would publish it. The only question: should he go public with it? Ellis asked for a draft. Mazziola said it was a bad idea, as the draft might be found in McCain's possession. It was better for the candidate to say, "I had never seen the story until it appeared in the *Enquirer*."

A few days later, Mazziola stopped to buy his daily papers. Ellis was there waiting for him. He handed him an envelope stuffed with bills. "It's a go."

The *National Enquirer*'s front page serves as a table of contents. Photographs of celebrities, usually five or six on the page, are featured with come-on captions. In the paper featuring Henry and Mary, there was only one picture, a photo of the twins taken from their high school yearbook. The caption read, "What were the Wojecoski twins doing together for two hours in a bedroom during a wild party?" The story said the partygoers had broken into an unoccupied Southampton mansion and there held a pot, booze, and sex party. Henry had organized the orgy, it continued, to provide a "heroes' reward" to the boys off to serve in Vietnam. The Valkyries readily responded. The many bedrooms were in use throughout the night. One room was sequestered for the entire evening. "Following in the Wagnerian tradition of Sigmund and Sieglinde, Henry and his sister spent the party together in bed. Many of the revelers questioned the absence of the dynamic twins. One observed them enter a bedroom, post a sign announcing the room was occupied, and exit the room at the end of the party. It is the policy of the *Enquirer* not to disclose sources, but because of the sensational nature of this disclosure, the paper will break from tradition. The eyewitness was Janet Keegan, nee Kiviatkovski."

The *New York Times* ignored the article. Not so the candidates. McCain denounced the story as a "pure fabrication." He ironically urged the Justice Department to bring criminal proceedings against the *National Enquirer*. "Let's find out who wrote the article and who sponsored it, and punish them along with that filthy newspaper."

Huckabee blamed the First Amendment. Freedom of the press should be circumscribed. "The *Enquirer* should be closed down for publishing blasphemous statements. As immoral as parts of this country has become, incest remains a taboo observed even by the irreligious."

Giuliani claimed he too had been vilified by the *Enquirer*. He ignored the article and advised Wojecoski to do the same. "As public figures, we are subject to intense scrutiny. The public understands our private lives should remain private, but only if we refrain from discussing it. Clinton could have avoided an impeachment trial if only he had refused to comment on the Monica Lewinski affair. Few people believed the president had sex with a White House intern until he denied it."

Romney incongruously said, "I refuse to give currency to the article by commenting on it. Henry Wojecoski is a moral man. I am sure he never had sex with his sister."

I was alerted to the story the moment the paper hit. I ran to the nearest newsstand. After reading it, I said aloud to no one and to all within earshot, "Fuck Henry Wojecoski." Then I said to myself, "I'm glad Mary is dead." I cursed myself again for thinking such a thing and came close to tears. I should never have sponsored that party. I should never have dragged Mary there. I should have thought about appearances. Poor dear Mary. *Wait*, I thought, *Mary is dead. It's* my *honor*, my *candidacy that needs protection.*

I had trouble recalling Janet. She was not part of the "in" group. She was at the party but only as a substitute for Peggy. Damn, if only Peggy hadn't been such a prig. Then I had an epiphany—or was it just a long-forgotten surfacing when I really needed it?

One day in the spring of 1967, my mother burst into my room waving the invitation to the party and the attached list of attendees. She had rifled through a metal box in my closet that had contained fishing paraphernalia and that I used to store personal papers. She had demanded to know why Mary hadn't been invited. When I said it wasn't a party for nice girls, she pointed to Peggy's name. Peggy, I said, had refused to attend, and Janet Kiviatkovski had replaced her. Elizabeth, who was frantic that Mary had no social life, threatened to tell my father about the planned break-in unless Mary attended. Mary agreed in order to save the party but imposed a condition: we spend the evening reading. And that was how it came to pass that on the night of the hottest party of my high school years, I sat in a room with Mary reading a book.

I had a habit of holding on to things, even those for which I had no use. Peggy accused me of "constipation of things." Now my habit was about to save my reputation and political career. The list of attendees would not contain either Janet's name or my sister's.

The box was on a shelf in my closet. I raced home. The invitation and original list of invitees in my handwriting was there. Just as I had remembered, neither Janet nor Mary's name was on the list. I said a prayer thanking Jesus for afflicting me with constipation.

I made a copy of the list and returned the original to the box. I then placed the box in a safe in my home office and immediately set out for Honesdale.

Janet answered the bell. When she saw who was at the door, she gasped, "What's a famous guy like you coming to my shack? Henry, you haven't lost your good looks. You're as handsome as ever. How's Peggy, that lucky girl?"

I asked to come in. I took a seat on a couch and motioned for her to sit next to me. I showed her the *Enquirer* and asked her to read the story to the end before commenting. Halfway through, she broke down.

Janet called Mazziola "a fuckin' liar. He bribed us and got us drunk." I brought her a glass of water and assured her that all would be well.

I asked her how she knew the reporter's name. "He introduced himself as Anthony Mazziola and said he was under contract to write an unauthorized biography of you. He asked for my help on the early years in Riverhead. My husband made him produce identification. He showed us his driver's license. He invited us to dinner. He gave us one hundred dollars just to have dinner with him. Henry, we mostly sit at home watching TV. Dinner out is a rare treat."

She pulled a tissue from her pocket and wiped her eyes. "At the restaurant, he ordered drink after drink and two bottles of wine. After dinner, he showed us a wallet with five thousand dollars in it. He said it was ours if we told him bad things about you, Henry. We've missed payments on our mortgage. We were about to be kicked out. The five thousand dollars saved our home.

"The next day, the bastard called. He said he was wired. 'Don't bother to deny anything; it's all on tape.'"

From Janet's living room, I made three calls. The first was to my campaign office. I asked for information on Anthony Mazziola. The second and third were to Robert Stultz, my lawyer, and Richard Hertzel, my PR man. We arranged to meet at Hertzel's brownstone. There, we could come and go with less chance of being spotted. I could be there in three hours.

I told Janet not to say another word, no matter who called or stopped by. "Just ask for their name. Then say 'no further comment.' Call me as soon as you can with the person's name. Here's a phone number where you can reach me or my assistant any time, day or night. It's important, very important, that you do exactly as I say."

I wanted to strangle her. It was the only time I could remember wanting to kill someone. Instead, I kissed her cheek and said, "Remember, Janet, say nothing more to anyone."

I arrived at the brownstone on time; Stultz was waiting in the living room; Hertzel had two staff people with him. I related the substance of my meeting with Janet. As soon as I mentioned Anthony Mazziola, my cell rang. I listened in silence, thanked the caller, and snapped the phone closed. "Guess what? It was

Mazziola who did the hatchet job on McCain in 2000. Do you think it was McCain who hired him this time?"

"Mazziola has more than one client," Hertzel said slowly, "but since there is a McCain connection, it's likely. Let's put that to one side for now. We have to respond to the story and quickly. It's on the evening news, and it'll surely be on the late talk shows.

"We got Charlie Gibson to denounce it. He called it 'incredible.' He said your campaign has denounced it as 'false, false, false' and promised to have 'irrefutable evidence' that it's an outright fabrication. Here's his last quote: 'What has happened to decency? What is the world coming to when such a horrific story can be published?'"

"It's not that easy to refute," I said. "Parts are true. We did hold a wild party. It was the sixties. Booze, pot, and the pill. Mary and I were both there. We were in a bedroom for most of the evening. Reading. The strange part is Janet's not on the list, but she still could have been there." I showed them the Xeroxed copy.

Stultz, ever the lawyer, was the first to speak. "The list is strong evidence, because it's in writing and prepared contemporaneously with the event. It tops contradictory oral testimony—that is, in a court of law. What about the court of public opinion?"

That was Hertzel's cue. "A lot of people will believe her. It's too fantastic to have been made up. We need a lot more than a playbill. We need to enlist Charlie Gibson to stay on this story. We'll get an expert to say the paper and the ink date the list to 1967. It has been untouched and unaltered. The expert must provide impressive evidentiary support for his conclusions. We'll get a former FBI guy to be a witness. Then, I propose a national figure should say, 'I will not read the names aloud. No persons today should be embarrassed because forty years ago they attended a party. I will answer a single question: whether Janet Kiviatkowski's name appears on the list. Nothing else. It does not.'"

Hertzel pointed to one of his assistants. "Taylor will provide the motive. He'll say Janet was paid fifty thousand dollars."

I interrupted. "Not fifty thousand dollars, five thousand dollars."

"I heard you," said Hertzel. "Can you imagine the *Enquirer* being so dumb as to say, 'We didn't pay her fifty thousand dollars; we paid her five thousand dollars'? Meanwhile, we get a free shot in the arm—fifty thousand dollars is not only ten times more but a figure large enough to entice. It's vital that Mazziola, the *Enquirer*, and Janet shut the fuck up."

Stultz said he knew the lawyer for the *Enquirer*. "I'll tell Phil Grossman to retain a criminal lawyer as we'll be seeking an indictment. Phil will get my message. As long as the *Enquirer* does not get into a pissing contest with us, we'll let the matter drop."

I said I had Janet's house under surveillance day and night. Her phone was tapped. She promised to stay mum, but just in case, I was ready to swing into action.

"Look," said Stultz, "Mary's name is also missing. She wasn't even there."

"Leave it alone," I said. "Mary was there all right, at our mother's insistence. Mary brought two books along, one for her and one for me. She made me spend the night in a bedroom with her reading *Oliver Twist*. She told the story so many times to so many people it has become part of the family lore. 'Poor Henry. I ruined his evening. His testosterone level was so high; he was ready to take on all the girls. Instead, he had to stay with me and read.' If we claimed Mary was absent because her name was not on the list, its integrity will be impeached."

"Keep it simple," said Hertzel. "It's enough the eyewitness wasn't there."

I was at home the night of *The Charles Gibson Show*. I told Peggy about the bribe, that the Keegans were about to lose their home, and Janet's cry that Mazziola was a liar. "Of course he's a liar," said Peggy. "Mary was about as far removed from a slut as her virgin namesake. She didn't even date. I didn't go to that party. I know Mary. Her account about the two of you reading was certainly true. She told me, 'I saved Henry for you.'"

The show faithfully followed Hertzel's script. The retired FBI witness was fantastic, Taylor was sensational, but the best performer was the national figure, none other than Jimmy Carter. That classy statesman played his part for free.

Then came the kicker. George Randolph, one of my political aides, handsome and articulate, appeared. "We have learned that the author of the false and defamatory article was hired in 2000 by a primary opponent of Senator McCain's. He wrote a mudslinging, blatantly false article asserting that McCain, in flagrant violation of the United States Code of Military Conduct, divulged so many military secrets during his five years as a prisoner of war that the Vietcong nicknamed him 'Songbird.' The article labeled McCain 'unhinged' by his POW experience and added that while a prisoner, he fathered a black child."

"Ambassador Wojecoski does not—cannot—believe that Senator McCain hired Anthony Mazzioli. He was, however, well financed. He induced his alleged source, a poor woman struggling to keep her home, to provide false facts by paying her a large sum. Whoever hired Mazziola paid him well and must have had a big stake in hurting Wojecoski. This is not the usual *National Enquirer* story. It's an attempted political assassination."

Gibson concluded the segment. "I offered equal time to Mr. Mazziola. He declined to appear. Now, folks, you have the facts behind this tale. Politics has hit a new low."

Peggy looked quizzically at me. "Are you sure Janet wasn't there? She was a perfect candidate."

I hated to lie to Peggy. "I'm sure she was not on the original list. I have no second list. What Carter said was literally true. I recall, however, her being there."

"When you were eighteen," said Peggy, "I wouldn't put anything past you, but touch Mary? Never! Janet's a vicious liar. She must have been desperate."

Did the program restore my campaign? According to the polls, about 10 percent of the populace believed the *Enquirer* story. Another 10 percent thought I'd taken a cheap shot at McCain. In a country heavily populated by cynics, less than 1 percent blamed McCain. For the first time since I had entered the primaries, my support fell. Smith, my campaign manager, compared the race to the tide. "Political campaigns ebb and flow. We'll come back even stronger."

Smith toiled long and hard. I appreciated his hard work. But I hadn't accepted his judgment when we started, and I didn't now.

# 19

*F*or a few weeks, it seemed that I had dodged a bullet. I'd outwitted the gods. They're fools to think a third-rate hack can beat a world-class guy. Damn, I was back in the grip of hubris. I got down on my knees and prayed for my will to be ruled by humility and modesty.

It was too late. Within a fortnight, the gods struck again. This time, they bombed me indirectly: the real estate market imploded. Its collapse brought down all other markets, and the world dropped into the chasm eventually dubbed the Great Recession. My political fortunes nosedived. Why? They blamed me—me personally—for the crash. Who was "they"? I can't name them, but that is the way it began to feel: the media, the public, the chattering classes.

From 1992 through 2004, in managing Wojo Partners, one of my tasks was taking the temperature of the real estate market. I met regularly with experts and with their help, charted trends. In the early years—1992-1994—the market was unchanged. From 1995 through 1999, prices rose steadily. In 2000, the index climbed until it reaching its high in 2005.

My partner in Wojo Management, James Watson, and I became wary. Markets that rise rapidly tend to fall rapidly. We were skittish. That was one reason we sold Wojo and AMG in 2004. I continued to watch the market afterward, but from a safe seat on the sidelines.

In the summer of 2006, the market began to decline. Ups and downs are common in real estate. They are usually not catastrophic; rather, they correct an overheated market. The market loses steam, it bottoms out, and the upward cycle starts again.

This time, the market not only failed to recover but collapsed. As home owners saw the value of their houses fall way below what they owed on their mortgages, they stopped making payments. Lenders foreclosed and sold the properties at fire sale prices. The forced sales exacerbated the decline.

People who had lost their homes were angry, frightened, and eager to blame someone—anyone. The search for a villain began even before the bleeding could be staunched. When the public became aware that many people had bought homes by borrowing 100 percent of the purchase price, homes they could never have otherwise afforded, the tail was pinned on subprime mortgages. This easy form of credit offended millions of home owners who had worked hard and done without luxuries, sometimes necessities, to make their down payments. Worse yet, the no-money-down people often had nicer homes than the many who had made a down payment. There was a torrent of name-calling. "It's the blacks, the Hispanics, the freeloaders, the druggies. And don't forget the bleeding-heart liberals who gave our money to them."

From the summer of 2006 through June of 2008, I had been locked in a primary contest. I knew my opponents would try to blame me for the collapse. How did I know? The instrument I invented, the subprime mortgage, was now being called "a weapon of mass destruction." And don't forget that I had made $1.5 billion out of it. If dirty politics allowed my opponents to twist an innocent evening with my sister into an incestuous liaison, what would the political tricksters do with hard facts? Before the collapse, I was untouchable. As a Washington outsider, I carried no baggage. I was not a member of the distrusted Eastern elite but a self-made man who had taken the ball capitalism handed me and run with it. Joe Six-Pack, the average guy, identified with me. With cries for change reverberating through the country, I was seen as someone who could lead us up and out of the quagmire—at least that's how I wanted to be seen.

My opponents had probed for a weakness—and it was no longer my scorching night with my dear sister. The real estate debacle exposed my Achilles heel. Wojecoski, they exulted, had invented subprime mortgages, made a fortune, and got out when the getting was good.

Romney was the first to lower the boom. "Ambassador Wojecoski invented the weapons of mass destruction that have wrecked the real estate market. He made a fortune and got out before the crash. He is running for the highest office in the land. He owes the American public a full and complete explanation."

Giuliani's attack was worse. "The tobacco companies don't smoke cigarettes; they only make them. Courts have rightly held them liable for injury caused by their product. Lawsuits are pending against manufacturers of handguns, seeking to hold them liable for injury caused by their products. If Wojecoski gave birth to subprime mortgages, he should be hanged, drawn, and quartered."

McCain had something to say too. "I offered to make Ambassador Wojecoski my running mate. I now withdraw the offer. It can be revived if Wojecoski establishes his innocence." McCain hammered home the ancient rule in politics: a candidate is guilty until proven innocent.

So did Huckabee: "Ambassador Wojecoski should seek redemption through prayer. Instead of running for president, he should minister to the countless millions hurt by his un-Christian activities."

I knew my business practices were sound. *My* subprimes had not defaulted. *My* borrowers helped, not hurt, the economy. They had bought uninhabitable houses, and through hard labor, they had made them into homes their families could be proud of. Those banker bastards stole my sound idea and gave subprimes to everyone who asked. They polluted a sound instrument for their own selfish benefit.

I wanted to mount a counteroffensive on national television. I had faith in the American public. When the facts were on the table, I would not be found a villain. Smith disagreed. "When a politician is touched by scandal, less is more. All you need say is, 'I have been out of the real estate business for three years. I know only what I read in the newspapers about the abuses in the subprime market. None occurred in my company while I was at the helm. I deplore the excesses and urge criminal action against those responsible.' End of the matter. Say nothing else. If questioned, refer to your statement or, if necessary, repeat it."

I received similar advice from others. I rejected it as quickly as I had rejected Smith's. I had done nothing wrong. Why hide? On talk shows and at rallies, I explained how I had run my subprime mortgage business. I contrasted it with the way others had managed theirs. The others were wrong; I was right.

In mid-December, 2007, I asked the family to watch me defend myself on TV. Regina, my eldest child, was the first to speak. "Dad, that's not you. You're not whiney, begging to be understood. You're also not arrogant. You're ineffective when you whine, and when you flip-flop and sound arrogant, it's even worse. When you knocked the stuffing out of the *Enquirer*, you stayed in the wings and let others deliver the message. Why don't you use the same script now?"

My older son, David, agreed and added, "I don't think anyone is buying your fine and dandy defense. Subprimes caused two trillion dollars to vanish. To restore voter confidence, you need a lot more than your *ipse dixit*—pointing the finger at others."

Peggy was silent in front of the children. When we were alone, she pleaded with me to withdraw from the race. "The campaign is taking a toll on your health. You tire easily, and you get angry too fast. You've accomplished so much in life. You don't need to be president. You're young. You can afford to wait. Make a deal with McCain. I know you hate him, with good reason, but there is precedent for rivals to become running mates. You're much younger than he is. When McCain's terms end, you can run uncontested for president."

"I hate McCain. I want to crush him. He besmirched the memory of my sainted sister. I can never forgive him; I can never work with him."

If my wife and children didn't swallow my defense, I was in trouble. And my poll numbers validated the family's opinion. They slipped. Okay, they plunged. I turned to Watson.

He too had watched me on television. "The message came through clearly," he told me. The trouble was the messenger. "Remember the film we showed when we were soliciting investors? Flesh-and-blood mortgagors who bought wrecks explained how through their own hard work, they now had valuable properties worth a lot more than the purchase price. Let's revise the film. Put in more mortgagors, especially white, blue-collar Christians. Have them thank God and you, in the same breath, for their homes. I know a firm that can quickly examine our mortgages and attest that the ones we show in the film were representative of our portfolio. Next, we have institutions that purchased our mortgage-backed securities say they made money, not lost it. Then we get a Buffett-type value investor to say, 'Wojecoski's mortgages were sound. If all lenders had adhered to his principles, the real estate market would not have collapsed.'"

"I don't know, Jim; I'm beginning to think that nothing I say can make a damn bit of difference."

"I'm not saying it will work, but you have nothing to lose. Your ship is listing. It's going to sink unless you change course. You've got too much at stake to quit now."

I adopted Watson's plan. He and Hertzel produced the film. They added ten new subprime mortgagors to the original five. All were working-class men and women from the heartlands.

They described the improvements made to their homes and thanked family members and friends for pitching in. The houses were shown before, in-between, and after. None had defaulted on their mortgages. All thanked God and *me*—by name—for the blessing of home ownership.

Two pension fund managers appeared next. They said they had made money on the mortgages purchased from my company, not so on other mortgages. Every subprime owned by them was in default except mine. If all mortgage lenders had been as prudent as Henry J. Wojecoski, they concluded, the present crisis would not have occurred.

The statistician, a chaired professor at MIT, said he had examined 15 percent of all the mortgages my company had issued. Samples, he said, are regularly used by statisticians as representative of the whole. In support, he read from a textbook he had coauthored with a professor from the University of Chicago. "Provided the sample is broad enough, a reliable conclusion can be drawn from a small number as low as 5 percent," he explained. He then compared the sample with the fifteen mortgages featured in the film and found them consistent with his sample—all of them supported by sweat equity.

The statistician next made a regression analysis. He took two hundred defaulted subprime mortgages unsupported by any equity—cash or sweat—and compared them with my subprimes. He found a direct correlation: the ones that did not default (mine) were supported by sweat equity.

The final speaker was not "a Buffett-type" but Warren Buffett himself. In making investments, he said, he looks for companies that have value in excess of their market price. Mortgages, he said, require a different kind of analysis, but the end result is the same: is the house worth more than the mortgage? Buffett distinguished between subprimes supported by sweat equity and the rest. He called the first group "value investments," houses improved by labor that were worth more than the mortgages. The others were not "value investments."

Buffett noted that one of his companies had lost a lot of money in the subprime mess. He wished, he said, Wojecoski had been running that company.

My family watched the show. When it was over and they had finished clapping, there were hugs and kisses all around. "Dad," Regina said, "when you get elected, make your family your kitchen cabinet."

News of the infomercial made the front page in many newspapers, including the *New York Times*, which also commented on it in an editorial. With an accompanying group photo of the fifteen mortgagors, the article detailed the improvements each had made. It stressed that all their mortgages were performing, and none were in default. Buffett's evaluation of subprimes supported by sweat equity was treated as a laying-on of hands by an *éminence grise.*

Although news stories generally refrain from expressing opinions, editorials do not. "Wojecoski's approach to subprimes helped working-class families buy homes without endangering the economy. His business plan improved deteriorated neighborhoods, transforming them into pleasant places to live. He performed a valuable community—indeed national—service," said the *Times*. "Hindsight, i.e., the ability to understand a catastrophe after it happens, is helpful in providing measures to prevent a recurrence. All the candidates seem blessed with that quality. Foresight, i.e., taking steps in advance to guard against disaster, is of a different and higher art form. Henry Wojecoski showed the kind of foresight possessed by a wise businessman."

The television production and the publicity that followed put an end to my opponents' public accusations, but the attacks continued sub-rosa.

McCain, who was well liked in the Senate, asked his colleagues to investigate the real estate bust, with special attention to my role. A bipartisan subcommittee of the Finance Committee was formed to hold hearings.

The Senate is a club; McCain is a member ; I'm not. Worse, I was in a primary race with a club member.

Although it must have been clear to the committee that I had no role in the debacle, I was subpoenaed to appear as the first witness. I turned the subpoena over to my friend and lawyer Robert Stultz.

"Henry, the world knows your practices were sound," said Stultz. "You did nothing wrong. You are nevertheless under suspicion. You profited from a system that failed almost everyone else. The other candidates are friends of committee members. You have no friends in Congress. Further, you're whipping the committee's friends. They will be out to get you. Keep in mind, the only rap that can stick is perjury. Time and time again, innocent people get nailed, not for the crime under investigation, but for perjury. I know a smart lawyer who advises his clients to take the Fifth Amendment. He tells them, 'It doesn't matter what you say; they won't believe you, so why open your mouth?' That's good advice, but as a candidate running for president, it would be suicidal for you to take the Fifth. So here is the second best advice. Make sure you tell the whole truth. No half truths. If you don't know, say 'I don't know.' Don't guess. But if you do know, speak the truth, and damn the consequences. I'll attend the hearings unless you don't want me to."

"What? Stultz, old boy, I only want you."

Stultz suggested a way to benefit from the hearing. "The committee will be polite. In fact, it will show you deference. The members will weigh the possibility that you might emerge as the next president. Politicians are careful. They won't want to offend you. At the opening of the hearing, you can request an opportunity to address the committee. The request will be granted. In your presentation, try to create the impression that you are being called on as an expert for advice on how to fix the problem. Make your speech short. Then request an opportunity to attach a copy of your full statement to the record. Your organization can then provide copies of your statement to the press. You may well get something positive out this."

I appeared before the subcommittee on January 11, 2008. After being sworn in as a witness, I asked for and was granted permission to read a prepared statement. It detailed what I believed to be the wrongful practices, the greed motivating mortgage brokers and bankers, and the laissez-faire attitude that had allowed a huge trading market to operate without government supervision. I concluded by proposing legislation to prevent a recurrence. "New laws are needed. They should prohibit mortgage lenders from selling subprime mortgages unless they are willing to guarantee them. Subprimes will then be granted only to creditworthy borrowers."

The committee listened politely. As coached by Stultz, I said, "I am able to make my talk short, because I have prepared a two hundred-page report. I know how hard senators work. I am sure you will read my report carefully. I ask that it be attached as an exhibit to this hearing." The committee unanimously granted my request.

Once questioning began, following Stultz's advice, my answers were short, nonargumentative, yet complete. The attorney for the committee established that I'd created the subprime mortgage and the consolidated mortgage obligation and used credit default swaps to create derivative securities. These tools were the very ones branded weapons of mass destruction and toxic assets.

It was now Stultz's turn. He told the committee he and I had met as young men and had worked together for many years. He acknowledged the proceedings were formal. "I should call the witness Mr. Wojecoski, but I can't. For too many years, he has been Henry to me. Mr. Chairman, with your kind permission, I request an indulgence. May I call Mr. Wojecoski 'Henry'?" The chairman smiled and said, "Permission granted."

Stultz had, with a swift stroke, made me a human being.

"Henry, do you have any basis in fact for believing the activities of Wojo Partners and its general partner, Wojo Management, contributed to the real estate decline? Please provide a full answer."

My answer ran on for ten minutes. I said none of my mortgages had defaulted. Even after the real estate market crashed, every one of them continued to perform. Those who purchased the subprimes from Wojo and its limited partners profited handsomely from the high interest rates. From 1992 to 2004, the year I sold Wojo Management, the limited partners had made four times their initial investment. "Based on the fact that my mortgages allowed hard-working blue-collar folks to own their own homes; based on the fact that my subprimes are all performing; based on the fact that my initial investors quadrupled their investment over twelve years; based on the fact that purchasers of my mortgage-backed securities lost not a penny, receiving instead generous returns; I can assure the committee and the American public that my mortgage business benefitted a whole range of individuals and institutions. We helped, not hurt, the economy."

The press ignored my opening statement and report, focusing instead on my testimony. "Henry Wojecoski, a candidate for president, admitted in hearings before a subcommittee of the Senate Finance Committee that he pioneered the use of sophisticated financial instruments generally blamed for the crash of the real estate market," said the *Times*. "Mr. Wojecoski made $1.5 billion; the rest of the world lost trillions." The article described each of the instruments and reminded readers that they'd been described by experts as "weapons of mass destruction and toxic assets."

The *Wall Street Journal* took a different approach. Although its reporters and editorial staff are generally at loggerheads, this was a rare instance of unity. The journal exonerated me in a page-one story and on the editorial page. The reporter quoted extensively from my testimony, calling my approach to subprime mortgages "prudent."

As for the claim that I was responsible for the disaster, the editorial called it "nonsense." "Is the inventor of the handgun responsible for the death of innocent people murdered by deranged individuals? Is the inventor of dynamite guilty of the atrocities caused by terrorists? Should the teeth of the inventor of gin turn bitter because drunks abuse the product? Of course not. Wojecoski is not accountable for the sins of others."

The debate raged on, in talk shows, letters to the editors, op-ed pieces. Paul Krugman's view, however, seem to stick. It was frequently repeated. "Causation is a familiar term in science, law, and life. Wojecoski should have foreseen the abuse his instruments, in reckless hands, would bring about. Other creators of dangerous instruments provide warnings. Cigarette manufacturers advise their products may cause cancer. Explosives are labeled 'handle with care.' Wojecoski offered not even a hint of caution. He flunked his duty of care by not warning that the highly sophisticated instruments invented by him were only as sound as the lowly mortgages embraced within them. Wojecoski knew or should have known of the potential of abuse. He sounded no alarm, either before, during, or after. Causation shines like a beacon. Wojecoski is reprehensible."

How is it possible that a brilliant guy could be so stupid? My face red with anger, I put a match to the column. Did I think that torched, it would be expunged from the record? Why was I being vilified? Putting the self-serving PR releases to one side, why did I invent subprimes? To help humankind? Don't make me laugh. I did it to make money. My father got it right when he accused me of profiting from the sweat of the working stiff. The greedy bankers, whom I scorned, engaged in the same practice for the same reason, only I acted responsibly, and they didn't. I didn't deserve to be hit by the backlash.

To the outside world, I called Krugman "a wrong-headed egghead. A guy who has no real-world experience. He should pontificate in the classroom and nowhere else."

McCain got some mileage from the Senate's investigation. It is never good to be the subject of a congressional investigation while running for office. It is especially bad if the investigation reveals that the candidate profited, and everyone else lost their shirts.

The newspaper reports on my Senate hearing sparked interest among a group of plaintiff's lawyers. To them, humongous damages and a deep pocket matter more than the criteria for liability.

Within two weeks of my testimony, a flood of lawsuits was brought against me by individuals whose pension plans had purchased mortgage-backed securities and lost billions. The complaints, almost identical, rested on Krugman's view of my failure to warn. They alleged I owed a duty of care to all purchasers of mortgage-backed securities. Over one hundred lawsuits were filed in state and federal courts across the country. The plaintiffs and their lawyers were blackmailers. They hoped to force me to settle to avoid further embarrassment.

Stultz maneuvered to get all the cases before one judge, the Honorable Lewis J. Birnbaum.

The lawyers for the plaintiffs, but not the flesh-and-blood litigants themselves, attended the important first pretrial conference called by the judge. Stultz anticipated that event and asked me to be present and sit next to him. "It will be a sign to the judge that you care but the plaintiffs don't."

Judge Birnbaum asked Stultz how he intended to proceed. Stultz read part of Krugman's words aloud. "His column," he said, "stimulated the lawyers to adopt the professor's metaphysical approach to the law. Whether it is sound philosophically is for others to debate. As far as the law is concerned, it is contrary to precedent. None of the one hundred plus complaints alleges that the plaintiff did business with my client. There is a good reason: none did. Accordingly, Ambassador Wojecoski did not owe them a duty of care. None of them alleges foreseeability, and all allege indirect injury. If the attorneys representing plaintiffs are not already aware of the controlling law, I intend to open their eyes.

"Court decisions are, in some instances, like the Bible: search hard enough, and you can find support for almost any proposition. There are, however, certain inflexible rules of law. In negligence, the alleged wrongdoer must foresee that his conduct will cause injury, and the allegedly injured party must have sustained injury directly from the allegedly negligent conduct. Absent these elements, there is no liability. *Palsgraf v. The Long Island Railroad* is one of the first cases taught in law school. The decision, by Judge Benjamin Cardozo, teaches just that. It is as binding today as the day it was issued. It mandates the dismissal of all pending claims. Unless the cases are voluntarily dismissed, I intend to make a motion to dismiss and hold the plaintiffs' lawyers liable for costs, including my firm's legal fees."

"I am, of course, familiar with Judge Cardozo's decision in the *Palsgraf* case," Judge Birnbaum said, "and the unbroken line of cases upholding that landmark decision. No complaint alleges that Ambassador Wojecoski intended to inflict harm. All rest on negligence—his alleged failure to warn. As does Mr. Krugman's diatribe. Mr. Krugman is not a lawyer, so he can be forgiven. Everyone here is an attorney. Mr Stultz has correctly stated the holding in *Palsgraf.*"

The judge gave the lawyers an option. Either they discontinue their cases or he would hear Stultz's motion promptly after it was made. "Mr. Stultz, how long will it take you to make your motion?"

"Less than a week."

The judge ruled that plaintiffs would have a week to respond. In the likely event that the motions were granted, costs, including legal fees, would be assessed personally against the lawyers.

By the end of the day, all the cases were withdrawn.

That night, together with our wives, we celebrated the legal victory at Per Se, perhaps the most expensive restaurant in New York. Our table overlooked the statue of Christopher Columbus in Columbus Circle. The dinner, nineteen separate small courses, including caviar and generous sprinklings of white truffles, lasted four hours. The champagne flowed freely. The bill, including tip, exceeded two thousand dollars.

A photographer, I thought employed by the restaurant, took pictures of us clinking champagne glasses and playfully feeding our wives truffles. I was wrong. The photographer worked for the *New York Post*. He and a staff reporter had bribed their way into the restaurant. They had somehow gotten a copy of the bill. The next day, photos and a story appeared on page 6. While the rest of the world lost their homes, Wojecoski was pictured eating and drinking like a king.

That photograph hurt more than the news a day later helped by reporting that the lawsuits had been discontinued. My prospects as a contender for commander in chief were fading fast.

Allegations of wrongdoing have a life of their own. The Old Testament likens malicious gossip to a pillow torn apart with its feathers scattered to the four winds. No amount of effort can gather all the feathers and put them back into the pillow.

My poll numbers slipped. With their decline, I lost my swagger. On TV and in personal appearances, I became defensive and nervous—a marked change from the cool, effective early campaigner. In the early primaries, I placed no higher than third. My own polling service now projected I would not win a single state.

In a televised speech on January 25, 2008, at New York's Symphony Space, before an audience filled with supporters, I announced the inevitable, the end of my candidacy. "My party has spoken. It does not think I have the qualifications to be president. I support the judgment of my fellow Republicans. I am withdrawing from the contest, effective today. I thank my supporters for their help. You deserve a stronger candidate."

When I mounted the podium, there were chants of "Run, Henry, run!" When I finished, the audience filed out silently.

My campaign headquarters was at 30 Rockefeller Plaza. I also had a home office in the basement of Hudson House and another in a room off the master bedroom. The office at 30 Rock had a switchboard, computers on almost all fifty desks, and a media room equipped with TVs and video and sound equipment. Since the staff worked from dawn to midnight, the office had a fully staffed kitchen and dining room. In my home, five additional telephone lines and two TVs had been added. There were over one hundred auxiliary offices throughout the country staffed by volunteers. All had direct lines to headquarters.

Experts had coached me on current events, history, and geography. I even was prepped on pop culture. I charted a jet and traveled all over the country. I made speeches in big cities and in small towns. I slept whenever and wherever I could, rarely getting more than five hours. And, yes, I kissed babies.

Within days of my withdrawal, the offices were closed, the equipment taken away by the truckload. My life was suddenly funereal, eerily silent. No more requests for public appearances, no more telephone calls. It was a rare stranger who greeted me by name. One who did, taunted me: "Hey, Wojecoski, can you spare a dime?" Another passerby spat but, lucky for him, missed me.

The campaign had many pluses and minuses. The pluses were the size and enthusiasm of my followers. At one point, my pollsters estimated my support at over twenty million. The biggest downer was the accusation that I caused the Great Recession.

During the most hectic days, I had neglected my family. I tried to make up for lost time, but it was hard. Kids are insecure even when they are young adults. In truth, mine were embarrassed by all the noise about me. I sensed they wanted to keep me at arm's length.

Overnight, metamorphosis. A national figure became a forgotten man. No longer wanted even by his children. Fortunately, my wife was more forgiving. In fact, she was happy to have me back.

# 20

The campaign cost me over thirty million dollars not counting indirect expenses: money spent subsidizing my ambassadorial budget, my matching contribution to the Muslim fund, and legal and PR expenses I otherwise would not have incurred. Do I regret it? You bet I do. Although I had a good ride, got a taste of success and an education in politics, the charges that I had an incestuous encounter with my sister and that I caused the Great Recession were unbearable accusations, the one as preposterous as the other. I didn't miss the money; I missed the peace of mind.

At times, I fantasized I was still in the race and plotted my strategy against the two candidates who were. I hated McCain, but he was the best of the bunch. Then he picked Sarah Palin. What a bonehead play.                                    Suppose he died in office? Maybe the rumors were true: five years as a POW had unhinged him.

At one point, he considered me for the number-two job. There's good precedent for choosing a rival. Kennedy picked Johnson. Bush opposed Reagan, who turned around and chose Bush. Clinton selected another primary opponent, Gore.

I could have helped McCain. When the Great Recession struck in October, 2008, McCain's earlier admission that he was not a financial expert hurt him. With me as his running mate, he could have said, "Henry Wojecoski is a world-class businessman. If elected, I will appoint him to spearhead a taskforce to restore the country to an unprecedented level of prosperity." He couldn't say that with Palin. She probably thinks economics is related to *The Communist Manifesto*—though that may be too intelligent.

I laughed when Obama fell flat on his face with the guy the papers called "Joe, the plumber." What fun I would have had with Joe. I'd have asked him, "Joe, what do you charge per hour, twenty-five bucks? That's what my father charged. My brother-in-law, David Markowitz, is a famous heart surgeon. He used to call himself a plumber. When arteries get clogged, he unplugs them, like you do and my father did with pipes. When a heart valve leaks, he replaces it. I called him a plumber for humans. You know what, Joe? He gets slightly more than twenty-five dollars per hour." I would have drawn laughs. By introducing my father and David, I'd have shown that my family was more than plumbers. I would also have revealed our diversity. It includes a Jew.

In an election, the Jewish bloc is more important than its actual numbers indicate because Jews vote and live in big cities, in states with large electoral votes. Their vote can swing an entire state.

I watched the debates and criticized both candidates for deflecting questions. I screamed at the TV, "The people want answers, not doubletalk." I would have talked straight.

Obama was smart and articulate, and exuded charisma, but he sure had a lot of weaknesses. Whoever heard of an American with the first name Barack, or worse yet, the middle name Hussein, or the last name Obama? McCain should have been an attack dog and not feared alienating blacks or liberals. They were going to vote for Obama no matter what. He should have focused on working-class whites and tried to get every single one of their votes.

I'm a loyal Republican, so I started out rooting for McCain. After the first debate, I was neutral, but true neutrality is rare. One is either neutral for or neutral against. I was neutral for Obama. Over time, Obama's cool made me a strong supporter. I even forgot he was black. I called Obama, told him I was for him, and was ready to go public. On the same day in October, Obama announced the support of two Republicans: Colin Powell and me.

For the first time in my life, I voted for a Democrat for president. To put an exclamation point on my vote, I pulled the lever for the straight Democratic ticket.

After the election, the new president called me. He thanked me for my support and offered me a post. "I would be happy to appoint you ambassador to Iraq. Unlike my predecessor, I'll listen to you."

I thanked the president for the offer and promised to get back to him promptly. "Four years ago," I told Peggy, "I would have accepted. Now, I'm tired. I promised you a long vacation, one that will last the rest of our lives. I don't want to get back in the harness. There's a time for everything. My time has passed."

Although I was only sixty, too much time in the spotlight and too little time relaxing and exercising had taken its toll. And Iraq was not exactly Rome. I tired easily, needed a nap in the afternoon. I needed to regain my strength. Exercise was the key. Peggy suggested long walks. She urged me to buy a dog and take him along. "There're lots of strange people lurking around the park. A big dog will protect you."

For my companion, I chose a red German shepherd raised and trained in a monastery in upstate New York. I named him Siegfried after the eponymous hero in Wagner's third *Ring Cycle* opera. These dogs are intensely loyal but only to one person. Siegfried bonded with me. Practically every morning, we walked from Hudson House to Grant's Tomb and sat on a bench overlooking the river and the monument. I read the *Times* and rested. Then we returned home. I grew so fond of Siegfried that I didn't mind picking up his mess.

One cold November morning, about a year after the election, Siegfried and I were alone on our bench. The park appeared to be deserted when two burly men in black overcoats and hats approached from behind the tomb. Both pulled guns. Siegfried jumped at them. A shot was fired, and he stopped in his tracks and fell to the ground.

"You killed my dog!" I screamed.

"No, mister, we just put him to sleep. He'll wake up soon. The only one we're likely to kill is you, that's if you don't come with us."

"What about my dog?"

"See those guys with a stretcher? They'll take your dog to your backyard. By the time he wakes up, you'll be home. If you cooperate."

How did they know I had a backyard?

I was shoved into a tan SUV and blindfolded. My first thought was that I was being held for ransom. For the first time in my life, I felt vulnerable, terrified. How could I alert the FBI?

An eternity later, my abductors pulled me out of the SUV through a doorway and then yanked the blindfold off. I was pushed into a chair at a simple wood table. The men took seats on either side of me. About ten feet ahead was a raised platform and, on it, a high-backed judge's chair. Sitting in the chair was a man I had met twice before, once in my office with his banker, John Paulsen, when the Cosa Nostra invested in Wojo Partners, and again when I presented my credentials to the Italian prime minister. He appeared to be the judge. Seated at a table next to mine was a middle-aged man in a double-breasted black suit, a white shirt with French cuffs, and a red and black tie. I guessed he was the prosecuting attorney. Sitting near the wall, on the right-hand side, were six men. The jury? Where the hell was I? A basement? There were no windows, and the air stank of moisture and mold. Along the walls were hundreds of bottles of wine. Were we below a restaurant?

I was a captive of the mafia. But what had I done to offend them? I remembered my doubts about letting the mob invest. I should have said no. It looked as if I was about to be tried by criminals, just like the sex offender played by Peter Lorre in the movie classic *M*. What would happen if I demanded my rights? I decided to try.

"I am unrepresented by counsel," I said to the don. "I want my lawyer present. As the head of the Cosa Nostra, if you are to be the judge, as you appear to be by your position in the room, you are biased. I demand an impartial judge. One learned in the law. Judge Birnbaum, for example."

"You are entitled to a lawyer," said the don. "We have two men stationed outside the office of Robert Stultz. Call him. Tell him to come quietly with my men. No harm will come to him. As the head of the organization, I preside over all internal disputes. You agreed to serve us. You accepted one hundred million dollars from our pension fund. You invested the funds for the benefit of members of our family. You are a de facto member of the family. I am trained in the law. In accordance with our custom, I will preside. You will get a fair hearing. We will adjourn to await your attorney."

I called Stultz at his office. "The Costra Nostra," I said, "plans to put me on trial for the losses its pension fund incurred in Wojo. I've been abducted and am in what I think is the basement of a large restaurant. There are two men waiting outside your office to bring you here. The don has promised safe passage. You will be blindfolded. I need your help, but I'll understand if you say no."

"I wouldn't miss the show for anything. I'll bill double rates because there's an element of danger."

I also got permission to call Peggy. I said I was fine and would be home late in the day.

"Henry, what happened? Are you all right?"

"Is the dog with you?"

"He's sleeping in the back, but what is going on? I demand to know."

"I'll tell you when I get home." I hated to do it, but I hung up on my frightened wife and returned to *The Godfather*, part 4.

While we were waiting for Stultz, I asked why Siegfried was still asleep. "He won't wake up for at least another hour, but he's fine," said one of my abductors.

"Thank you," I said automatically. I was grateful they hadn't killed the dog. I had actually treated this goon like a human being. What else would I do by the end of this living nightmare?

When Stultz arrived, he asked to be alone with me, and we were taken to a bathroom. "It's a matter of money," Stultz said.

"Lehman and Bear Stearns, which had bought Wojo before going belly-up in the fall of 2008, leveraged the company to the hilt and bought shoddy subprimes with the borrowed funds. Wojo was wiped out. The Mafia wants its investment back with interest," Stutz said. "If you refuse, you will probably be shot. We've dodged other bullets, but this is a real one, and it's aimed right at you." The prosecutor made his opening remarks. He noted that over a hundred civil actions brought against me had been withdrawn. The plaintiffs in those cases had had no direct dealings with me. "Our family did," he said. "Our family invested one hundred million dollars. Our investment was worth five hundred million dollars when Wojecoski sold his interest to a consortium of unscrupulous thieves. We lost our entire investment; he"—he pointed at me—"made a billion dollars and an extra five hundred million dollars from the sale of AMG to Merrill Lynch. But that's not all he made.

"In 2006, Wojecoski sold short a billion-dollar collateralized debt obligation. He covered the short sale in December 2008 at a cost of two hundred dollars. He made another billion. Did he invite his former partners to participate in the deal? No. Fairness and equity require the payment to us of five hundred million dollars plus 50 percent of Wojecoski's profit on the short sale—another five hundred million dollars."

Stultz had not heard about the short sale. He looked at me. I nodded. That was all he needed. "Your organization accords honor the highest of ranks," my lawyer began. "Keeping principles of honor in mind, I address first the short sale made in 2006. At that time, Ambassador Wojecoski had no relationship with you. It was severed on notice two years earlier. If the market had turned the other way and Wojecoski had lost a billion dollars, would your family have been willing to share in the loss? If not, is it honorable to demand a share of the profits?"

The don, who was looking directly at Stultz, dropped his eyes and stared at the bench at which he sat. Stultz had hit a sensitive nerve.

"Wojecoski did not secretly redeem his interest in Wojo Partners," Stultz continued. "He wrote to all the partners advising them of the proposed sale and adding that the deal allowed all partners the right to turn in their interests. At that time, your interest was worth five hundred million dollars. You could have cashed out as Wojecoski did. You had your own financial adviser whom you asked, or should have asked, for advice. You chose to stay with the new managers. You made that decision in the full knowledge that Ambassador Wojecoski had made a contrary decision. Is it honorable to hold the ambassador liable for an investment decision you alone had discretion to make?"

The don frowned. He motioned to Stultz to stop and asked the prosecutor in Italian whether what Stultz had just said was true. I had learned enough of the language to understand the question. When the prosecutor answered, "*Que vera es*," I suppressed a smile. The don asked Stultz to continue.

"Ambassador Wojecoski regrets that you lost your investment and the twelve-year return he made for you, but . . . who is to blame? You or Ambassador Wojecoski? Are you acting honorably when you ask my client to reimburse you for what turns out to be a gross error made by you? No, no, no. You are acting dishonorably."

The don addressed the six-man jury. They talked softly in Italian. Stultz and I could not make out what was said, but we sensed a disagreement. The jury left the room with the judge. They returned in about an hour, and the don declared, "Wojecoski owes nothing to our family on the short sale. He must, however, pay one hundred million dollars representing the loss on our initial investment. He does not have to restore the profits. Our decision rests on the ground that Wojecoski owed a fiduciary duty to warn us that the new management group were high-risk players and took an imprudent approach to investing. His failure to alert us to danger violated his duty. We rule that it is fair and honorable for Wojecoski to make us whole. He has thirty days to satisfy the judgment by wire transfer to our bank account. Here are the instructions for making the transfer. Court adjourned."

Stultz and I were again blindfolded and taken back to his office. "You have no alternative but to pay," he said. "If you don't, they'll track you down and kill you. It shouldn't be difficult for them."

"But, Robert, don't you think that—"

"There's a way to make this less expensive. The tax code permits a deduction on contributions made to accredited charities in foreign countries. If the Cosa Nostra Pension Fund is recognized by Italy, your payment will qualify for a charitable deduction." Stultz called an office of the IRS. He posed the question and smiled when a few minutes later he heard the answer. The Cosa Nostra Pension Fund was an accredited charity.

"They sought one billion dollars," I said. "You persuaded them to reduce the amount to one hundred million dollars, which after taxes will cost me about sixty million dollars. You know my motto. One doesn't have to do the best. Good enough is good enough. The deal is good enough."

When I got home, I heard Siegfried barking. He came right to me. I kissed his nose and rubbed his underbelly. "You love that dog better than me," Peggy said. "I was getting worried about you when you called. I'm so happy to see you. I didn't even mind that your first question was about Siegfried."

"Despite what you might think, I love you and Siegfried about the same."

"That's not funny," said Peggy. "Tell me what happened." I related the events of the day; she listened with her hand over her mouth. "How do you know it will end if you pay them the money?"

"We can't afford to find out. Stultz thinks it's over, based on what the family's US banker, John Paulsen, told him. He said, 'The don's decision is final.' I got that impression too. They're vicious criminals but observe a strict code of honor. If they wanted to extort more money, they would have done it after the trial. I should never have turned Wojo over to Lehman and Bear Stearns. They had much too much debt. The slightest dip in the market and both were finished. The don's proceedings were as illegal as hell, but they did reach a fair result."

Peggy was up most of the night. I slept fitfully. She claimed she had nightmares in which I was tortured and shot. "Let's leave New York and spend a long time in Southampton. Several of our old friends have retired from the police force. We can hire one or two as bodyguards. You and Siegfried can walk on the beach. It's after Labor Day—quiet and restful. The fresh sea air, long walks, and days away from the spotlight is just what you need. We'll keep a low profile. If we stay here, every time you leave the house, I'll worry. Last night, I thought I heard someone breaking in. We'll come back when we feel safe."

Our Southampton house turned out to be the perfect sanatorium. The ocean moderates the extremes in temperature. At the beach, winters are milder, and summers are cooler. I walked practically every day except when it rained hard, and I took pity on Siegfried. Peggy and I also took up golf.

We joined the unrestricted Southampton Golf Club. Some members were summer people—rejects from the nearby Shinnecock Hills and the National. They hung out with each other. By an unwritten rule, the summer people took no part in the management of the club. The locals ran it. Roman Warzelbacher was honorary president, having served as president for twenty years. His son, John, my former lawn-mowing partner, was the president. As soon as we joined, they asked me to become a director. I turned it down, but it was nice to feel so welcomed.

Golf looks like an easy game. You have all the time you want to hit a stationary ball with a big club. I hit the ball all right, but never straight. It either went flying far right or took a line drive left. When I tried to put it in the air by swinging under it, it rolled along the ground. When I hit down, trying to run onto the green, it flew into the air. The harder I tried, the worse I did. And then there were the lessons. Whatever grain of confidence I gained from hitting balls at a driving range, I lost after a lesson. To me, the game was diabolical, a mystery, a conundrum, a paradox.

Peggy was better. Her balls went mostly straight though not far. At first, we got lots of invitations to play but declined. "We'd love to play," Peggy said, "but our game is terrible, and that's an overstatement. When and if we get better, we'll call."

Peggy and I played together late in the afternoons. We developed a golf attitude. When we hit a bad shot (almost always), we laughed. On the rare occasions when we hit good shots, we also laughed but out of astonishment. Golf served a therapeutic purpose. We were so involved in trying to hit the ball our other concerns disappeared.

By Labor Day, Peggy had gotten over her fears, and I was my old healthy self. With regrets, we left the camaraderie of Southampton and returned to New York.

Peggy had missed our New York friends. She arranged a series of dinner parties. When conversation turned to the economy, she declared, "Money talk is off limits. We've had enough of that to last for the rest of our lives and part of eternity. Henry and I are interested in opera, theater, art, films, good books, and music." It was more than dinner conversation.

We attended opening night at the Metropolitan Opera. Our seats were the best in the house: parterre, center box. The evening began with a stirring rendition of "The Star-Spangled Banner" by the Met orchestra led by James Levine. The opera was a new production of Wagner's *Das Rheingold,* reputed to be a difficult opera. I don't know why it's considered hard; I followed the story and loved the music. And I'm a neophyte. My only problem was that there was no intermission. The one and only act lasted three hours.

Afterward, we had dinner on the grand tier. Seated between Peggy and me was the star of the performance and one of the world's leading bass-baritones, Bryn Terfel.

Next, we saw Verdi's *Rigoletto*. What a lot of fun, until the final act. The music was hummable. I bought a CD and played it over and over again. I hired one of the Met's assistant conductors to tutor me in all things operatic. She laughed at my comments, and I didn't understand hers. I cancelled after the first session.

I was eager to see more operas until we went to *Boris Godunov*. Five hours! I fell asleep during the first act. I didn't like the book or the music. One pretender to the throne of Russia battling another faker. The music was dour, not melodious. I was offended by the portrayal of a Polish priest as lascivious and scheming. I thought it sacrilegious and anti-Catholic.

"Let's take a break from opera," said Peggy. "It's an acquired taste. We're going too fast." *Boris* was the last opera we saw.

Peggy was still on the board of MoMA. That fall, the museum had a major retrospective of the New York school of abstract expressionists. We went to the opening and returned two more times. I tried. I really tried but remained bewildered. Jackson Pollack dripped paint on a canvas while waltzing around it. Mark Rothko painted red and black geometric shapes. Wilem de Kooning had a painting titled *Woman*! If it were not for the title, I would not have known that the central character was a woman. "The only reason these meaningless markings are called art,"

I said, "is that a small coterie of experts have given them that label."

Peggy made an effort to explain why these works were considered art, but even she couldn't change my mind. I wouldn't want to own anything in the exhibit.

Peggy and I saw two movies, back to back, about the financial crisis. One was a fictional tale titled *Wall Street: Money Never Sleeps* about a young man in love with a very rich woman. He wants to turn her money over to a mad scientist working on a harebrained project to free the world from fossil fuels. There were tales of Wall Street firms failing or prospering and scenes of government bailouts. To me, the movie was science fiction.

The next night, we saw *Inside Job*, a documentary examining the causes of the Great Recession. It exposed stupidity and corruption among economic advisers, particularly academics, but not the real causes of the crash.

"When a team loses a game," I said to Peggy, "the players, not the owner, the manager, or the umpire bear the brunt of responsibility. Let's say you had a team of apple growers who grew a billion apples, all rotten. The apples were sold and resold in different-sized packages all over the world. Insurers, for a fee, guaranteed holders that the apples were wholesome. Speculators, who owned no apples, placed bets that the apples were rotten by purchasing insurance that a particular package contained good apples. Substitute rotten subprime mortgages for apples, and you've got the cause of the debacle."

"The government," said Peggy, "could have stopped the sale of the apples. Then only the growers would have suffered."

"You're right. The government could have stopped trafficking in apples. But we're talking causation, not accessories to the crime. The culprits were the mortgage brokers who inflicted their fraudulent product on the world at large. Since I was a mortgage broker, I got tarred with their brush. Lucky for me that the movie concentrated on regulators and economists, not the real culprits."

In the fall of 2010, Peggy and I wallowed in culture. How did I enjoy my emergence? Not nearly as much as I'd enjoyed business and politics.

# 21

*W*hoever invented the consolation prize deserves a Nobel Prize.

If we didn't get the White House, we had promised ourselves a farm house in Tuscany. However, Italy was no longer viable. Peggy would be frightened every time she saw men in black coats. We needed a safe home in a neutral country. What better place than Switzerland? I called a former US ambassador to Switzerland for a recommendation. "Before you buy," he said, "spend time at the Victoria-Jungfrau in Interlaken. It lies between two lakes and the snowcapped Jungfrau Mountain. The hotel's spa is world class. It will provide a good base from which to explore Switzerland."

Before leaving for Interlaken, we had to find a temporary home for Siegfried. A commercial kennel was out of the question. Instead, we drove to the upstate monastery where Siegfried was raised. The dog seemed to know we were separating. We looked at each other eyeball to eyeball. The monk asked that I make a sign that Siegfried could go with him. Tearfully, I pointed to the monk and said, "Siegfried, it's all right to follow him. I'll be back soon." The dog hesitated, turned, and went with the monk.

We booked the tower suite at the Victoria-Jungfrau. It sits atop the roof enclosed in a distinctive dome and occupies the entire floor. It has two terraces, one facing the Thurn River; the other, the River Buenz. The bedroom and living room have direct views of the Jungfrau. The hotel combines old-world elegance with every modern convenience. The swimming pool is vast, with marble columns topped by a glass roof about fifty feet above the pool.

Every morning, we swam in the pool, had a massage, and ate a wholesome spa breakfast. After breakfast, we walked along mountain trails, drawing deep breaths of clear mountain air. In the afternoon, we turned our back on the town's many tourist attractions, horse and buggy rides and a tour of the town on a "nostalgic" train among them. The buggy rides were for tourists, unseemly for senior diplomats. The train was brand new, disguised to look quaint. It was worse than touristy; it was false. Instead, we took advantage of Interlaken's central location and the excellent Swiss railroad.

The train station was near the hotel. In less than an hour, we were in Bern, the capital of Switzerland, a medieval city designated as a world heritage city by UNESCO. It is easy to see why: it has hardly changed in five hundred years. The city is a peninsula surrounded on three sides by the River Aare. It is home to the Paul Klee collection containing over four thousand paintings representing over 40 percent of the artist's oeuvre. Klee was Swiss. "His early paintings," Peggy said, "are watercolors in the expressionist style. His later works transform natural sights into geometric forms. Those paintings, Klee's major works, represent cubism. I have a better sense of this major modern artist from seeing the landscape of his country."

Another day, we went to Basel. There, on the elbow of the Rhine, three countries meet: Switzerland, France, and Germany. The city, the cultural capital of Switzerland, is the home of Art Basel, the premier international art fair for modern and contemporary art. It was held in June several months after our visit. On a bright clear day, we strolled through the alleys and lanes of the old town. The museum buildings, about thirty in number, provided an exciting outdoor show of design and architecture.

Despite our clean living, my health declined. My neck sprouted a bulge. I had difficulty breathing and swallowing and was short of breath. My voice was hoarse. Most disturbing of all, I developed a cough and spat up blood. We had spent about a week in Switzerland when Peggy packed our bags and announced we were leaving the next day. She had called David. He said come home right away. "It's probably nothing that we can't fix, but time is important. I'll arrange for tests at my hospital."

I protested. There were doctors in Switzerland. Why interrupt our vacation? Peggy said she only trusted David. "As soon as you're better, we'll return."

With David at my side, I took a series of test including a CT scan and a thyroid biopsy. They showed I had an advanced case of anaplastic thyroid cancer, which had metastasized to my cervical lymph nodes and lung. A tube was inserted in my windpipe to ease my breathing. My cancer was deemed inoperable. External-beamed radiation eased the pain. Four times a day, I took medicine. It made me drowsy.

For the next six months, I was in remission. The oncologist told me to take full advantage as the cancer would reemerge with a vengeance.

I knew I was dying but refused to believe it. I asked the doctor whether I could possibly live for five years. "How can I know that?" he said. "I don't know whether I'll live for five years." The doctor didn't say there was no chance, so I continued to hope.

One thought kept reoccurring: *How can my family get along without me?* I gained solace from the adage that if a child is on the right path, there is no need to interfere. My kids were all headed in the right direction; they would do fine. But what about Peggy? We depended on each other for the essence of life. I wouldn't want to live without her, but if she were to predecease me, I would manage. So would she if I died first.

My home office looks out over our garden and on to the Hudson. One day, I saw Peggy sitting on the bench under the Camperdown elm where Mary's ashes were scattered. She was sobbing. Peggy returned there again and again. I knew then, if I had not already known, that my days were numbered.

Seeing Peggy on Mary's bench turned my thoughts to my sister. Would we be reunited? I know it sounds foolish—it sounds foolish to me—but dying does that to people, or so I learned, rather earlier than I thought I'd have to. The question cannot be definitely answered this side of heaven. If we were to meet, I wondered what Mary would say about the *Enquirer* story.

She had read *The Holy Sinner* by Thomas Mann and had asked me to read it. Twins, a brother and sister, lived together as man and wife during the middle ages and ruled a kingdom. The sister became pregnant and gave birth to a boy. The brother joined the Crusades and died a Christian soldier's death. The child was abandoned but returned as a grown man to the kingdom. He made love to his mother, spent many years on a rock repenting, and was elected pope. I imagined Mary saying, "That's the only story more preposterous than Mazziola's tale."

Remission ended after six months. As the illness claimed my life, I shrank and lost about one hundred pounds, going from over two hundred to one hundred without dieting. My full head of hair was reduced to a few wisps of gray. The pain, when it was not abated by drugs, caused my face to twist and contort. I apologized to guests for subjecting them to witness the change in me.

My children, nephews, and nieces, Stultz, Watson, Hertzel, and of course Peggy and David were regular visitors. You would never have guessed I was dying by their forced cheeriness. I wanted to tell them that fake laughter rolled off me. But what would I want to take its place? Idle chatter, jokes, smiles were probably the best you could expect from people who loved me while they watched me die.

Siegfried did not leave my room except for trips to the backyard to do his business. When I first got him, Siegfried was a lively, happy dog. Now, he was sad. Was it possible his sense of impending doom was as sharp as a human's? A dog's sense of smell is sharper than ours. Maybe a dog's sense of death is also sharper.

I thought about suicide, but my religious scruples precluded it. When you are dying, you don't want to agitate God. Also, if I took my life, my church would deny me a Christian burial. I was born Catholic and would die Catholic. I wanted a full Catholic funeral. Did I believe I'd see my beloved sister Mary? I didn't want to do anything that would ruin my chances.

I had purchased thirty burial plots in the Catholic cemetery in Riverhead. Two at the head of the section were reserved for Peggy and me. The rest, if they wanted them, were for my children, their spouses, and my grandchildren. I knew the dead hand cannot rule the living, but I hoped three generations could be buried together.

# 22

*P*eggy gave me the manuscript, the pages you just read, and said, "Dick, you were not just Henry's PR man; you were his friend. Please finish this. Henry said he wanted you to write the last chapter." I had my work cut out for me. Henry's obituary in the *Times* was an abomination to his memory.

At Madoff's sentencing hearing, his lawyer invoked the usual tactic of mentioning lenient sentences that were imposed on worse criminals, a difficult assignment since Madoff was the arch-financial swindler of all time. The lawyer was overzealous: "There is a man, free as a bird, enjoying life and his ill-gotten billions who defrauded the world of one trillion dollars. My client's crime pales next to that committed by Henry Wojecoski."

The judge dismissed the comment with a wave of his hand and, in disgust, turned his chair so that his back faced the lawyer. Soon after, he imposed a sentence of 150 years. The *New York Law Journal* speculated that an additional fifty years was added for the jab at Wojecoski.

The *Times* obit referenced the remark.

Peggy said to me, "Your last assignment for Henry is to restore his reputation—for his children, me, and his father, and for the truth."

I had an idea. We would hold a party in Henry's honor several months after his death. Everybody mentioned in his memoir would be invited and, of course, family and friends. The party would celebrate Henry's achievements. I would see to it that it was well publicized.

People are affected differently by the approach of death. Some block the knowledge, hoping that denial will forestall their fate. Henry was a realist. He knew his death was imminent, so, as he did throughout his life, he took matters into his own hands. He discussed with Cardinal Dolan, the archbishop of New York, the Catholic way of dying. Together, they planned the rites and rituals culminating in burial. Just before his death, the cardinal administered the last rites.The wake was held on the first floor of the Frank E. Campbell Funeral Chapel. The body reposed in a mahogany casket bedecked with flowers. Candles, at its head and foot, were kept burning throughout the two-day vigil. A rosary was placed in Henry's hand and a cross on the wall above his head. Hundreds came to the viewing.

Peggy sat beside the coffin. Although she had had a year to prepare for this moment, she seemed in a state of shock, barely coherent when she spoke. Prompted by David, she would murmur, "I thank God for the thirty-six years I spent with him. I'm sorry there weren't more." And then she would cry.

David said it was good for Peggy to show emotion. After Mary's death, he said, he had kept his feelings bottled up, with horrendous consequences. He didn't want Peggy to sink into a similar deep depression. He encouraged the children to talk to her. "Say anything that comes to your mind, but talk. Don't let her dwell on death."

On the third day, the casket was carried by hearse to St. Patrick's Cathedral. Cardinal Dolan greeted the coffin at the church door and sprinkled holy water on Henry's corpse. Inside the sanctuary, the cardinal conducted a requiem mass. In front of the archbishop was a sea of black: men in dark suits, women in black dresses, and the clergy covered in black robes and hats.

Following the service, the coffin was transported seventy miles east to the Riverhead cemetery. The hearse led the way, followed by four black stretch limousines carrying members of the family. Others tailed along in private cars. Peggy, her children, Cardinal Dolan, and Andrew, eighty-seven, the sole survivor of the original Polish-town home, were in the car immediately behind the hearse, followed by the cousins and David. Cardinal Dolan conducted the burial ceremony, leading the crowd in prayers and hymns. Henry's funeral, as he had wished, conformed to Catholic protocol.

In January, I turned to the party and proposed the Plaza as the site. Peggy objected. "The Plaza," she said, "has no connection with Henry."

Andrew suggested Riverhead: "Henry was born and raised there. He could have erected a mausoleum in a fancy New York cemetery, or anyplace else he wanted, but he chose Riverhead as his final resting place. He lies near his mother and where I will come to rest. Henry was a veteran. Let's hold the party in the VFW hall. It's located in Polish Town, a short walk from our home. It has a large party room big enough for four hundred people."

David Markowitz supported Riverhead but objected to the VFW. He said Henry despised his service in Vietnam and referred to the war as "the cause of the fucking pigs."

"Henry hated that war all right," said Andrew, "but respected his fellow veterans. I'll never forget the Memorial Day parade led by me and Henry. Afterward, we celebrated in the hall. Henry was happy and at home."

David, Peggy, and I drove to Riverhead. The VFW rang true as a place to celebrate Henry's life. A contribution to the VFW's scholarship fund sealed the deal.

Invitations went to friends, family, and the notables mentioned in the book including George W. Bush, Silvio Berlusconi, Rudy Giuliani, John McCain, Mitt Romney, Bill and Melinda Gates, Karl Rove, and Paul Krugman. John Paulsen, the Costra Nostra banker, was also invited. In a handwritten note, he was asked to invite the don. None of the public figures accepted, and only a few even bothered to reply. *Sic transit gloria mundi.*

The response from family, friends, and business associates was overwhelmingly favorable. All five surviving members of Amalgamated's board of directors accepted. So did most of the pension fund managers, Henry's partners in Wojo. Overall, there more than three hundred acceptances.I suggested five speakers: three from the family and two from business. I relied on Peggy to choose the family members. She selected their oldest child, Regina, a graduate of Columbia College and its law school, saying that she was a good public speaker and very close to her father. Peggy also named her nephew, Michael, who worked for a large advertising and PR firm. The third, Andrew, was self-nominated. He insisted on going last.

From the business side, I selected James Watson and Robert Stultz.

I hired a cinematographer to record the occasion and to splice photos of Henry and his family into a video. We dubbed it "The Henry Show."

On the night of the party, the heavens and the earth were in sync; the weather was mild and dry, and traffic in Riverhead was light. At the VFW, there was a crush of guests, security guards, and town police. After drinks and food, I mounted the podium. "I admired Henry Wojecoski," I said. "Like Abraham Lincoln and Andrew Jackson, Henry rose from humble origins to seek the highest office in the land. He was denied a chance to run for that office by dirty politics. Henry made his fortune by helping working-class families buy their own homes. Only opportunistic politicians (that may be an oxymoron) had the gall to accuse him of responsibility for the Great Recession.

"In my opinion, Henry Wojecoski would have made a great president. I regret that he never had the chance. "The first speaker will be Regina Wojecoski, Henry and Peggy's oldest child."

Regina's eyes were her most striking feature. When she wanted to (she did not always) she could light up the room. Well, her lights were on. "I used to greet my dad," she began, "by imitating his dance step. He fancied himself an accomplished disco dancer. Here's the way it looked to me." She flung her arms about, shuffled her feet, and jumped up and down. Everyone roared with laughter. Then she began her speech.

"Dad was the most generous, selfish father who ever lived. How could he be selfish and generous at the same time? In the early years, it was no fun being with him. He was distracted, thinking about business but not about us. All that changed when Dad started doing what made him happy. Instead of taking us to the playground, watching us in the sandbox or pushing a swing, or going to kiddie movies or puppet shows, he took us to places he was interested in. He also took us on adventures that were fun and, we thought, sophisticated.

"I remember the wonderful Saturday mornings we spent shopping for the perfect chevre. We went to cheese stores in the Village, on Madison Avenue, and along Broadway. We bought artisanal chevres made in France, Italy, New York State. To go along with the cheese, we bought apples and wine. Dad would give me a sip of wine, claiming it would sharpen my sense of taste. When Mom found out, she was furious. 'You'll turn Regina into an alcoholic.' 'No,' said Dad, 'into a connoisseur of fine wine and chevre.'

"Dad took me to the ballet, concerts, and plays. We had lunch in fancy restaurants. I loved it. And so did he. He did what he wanted to do and took me along. I developed interests that, but for my dad, I never would have had.

"Once, I asked Dad to take my best friend, Helen, with us on a Saturday excursion. He suggested tea at the Plaza. Helen and I pretended we were debutantes planning our coming-out party. We walked into the Plaza with our noses pointing up at the ceiling. Dad told the maître d' we were high-society young women and asked to be seated at an appropriate table. The maître d' played along. He took us to a round table in the middle of the room. Helen and I nibbled on pastries, drank tea with milk, and discussed in loud voices the boys we planned to invite to our coming-out parties. Helen said, 'We must invite Pierre du Pont; he's so cute.' I mentioned Peter Rockefeller and John Morgan. I know we were being silly, but it made us happy. Dad laughed a lot.

"As we grew older and went our own ways, we still enthused over outings with Dad. He took us to the World Series—but only when the Yankees were in it! We screamed our heads off and came home hoarse. We saw movies and plays. It's hard to imagine life without Dad."

Regina tried to repress her tears but could not. She wept, walked off the podium and straight into Peggy's arms. They both cried.

Michael, Henry's nephew, spoke next. I introduced him by saying, "In reply to my question as to what he wanted to be, Michael answered, 'You. The highest-priced PR man in America.'"

Michael mounted the podium. He stopped directly in front of me. "Just call me Richard Hertzel, PR man to the stars." Over the laughter, Peggy's voice could be heard. "So typically Michael."

"He was Uncle Henry to his five nieces and nephews," Michael began, "but he was more than that. He treated us no differently than his own children. To us, he was a second father. Uncle Henry owned a big house on the ocean in Southampton. The place was open house all summer long for all the children. It was just down the block from the Meadow Club, which we could see but not join. 'They don't like folks whose ancestors didn't arrive on the Mayflower,' Uncle Henry would say. 'We're not pure enough to join their sterile society. They venerate their ancestors, whom they consider more worthy than they are. They're probably right. People whose ancestors are better than the present generation concede they're worth more dead than alive. Never forget this. Different kinds of people invigorate a country, a group, a club. America's strength is its ability to absorb all kinds. A sterile society doesn't change, doesn't grow. Under principles of evolutionary biology, it's doomed to extinction.'

"One hot July Sunday, Uncle Henry decided we should mix but not blend with the folks at the Meadow Club. As most of you know, Poland's flag has two broad stripes, white on top and red on bottom. Uncle Henry had ten bathing suits made to order, with bright red trunks and white tops. He appeared in his own suit and handed out the rest of them to the nine of us, whom he always referred to as his 'kids.' We took a group picture; you can see it on the video. We went into the ocean and swam to the Meadow Club beach. When we got out, the kids formed a single line facing Uncle Henry and the clubhouse, right in front of the club members on the beach. Uncle Henry took out a tuning fork, sounded it, handed us Polish flags, and then led us in singing the Polish national anthem. We sang loudly and waved the flags. They tried to ignore us, but how could you ignore ten people all dressed the same singing loudly and off-tune? There was nothing they could do. All beaches in New York State are owned by the public up to the mean high-water mark. We were within our rights."

Michael paused to look up at the video screen, looking for a particular shot, gave up, and continued. "When we finished singing, we joined arms and walked home. We wanted to do it again, but Uncle Henry said no. 'We showed them we were proud to be Polish Americans. To repeat would make us pests.' Uncle Henry is dead, but a part of him lives on in all nine of his kids."

The twelve video screens showed twenty different pictures in twenty-second intervals. At the end of Michael's talk, the flashing screens paused for five minutes and showed only one picture: Henry and his kids in their red and white Polish bathing suits.

Robert Stultz was up next. I introduced him as Henry's close friend and lawyer. "By way of full disclosure," I said, "Stultz is my own lawyer, as well."

Stultz said Henry was his only friend who had not graduated from college. "Henry did not need a college education. His ability to understand, analyze, and apply his native ability to solve complex issues put him, in business matters, at the top of the class. He knew, however, that being smart in business is not the same as being an intellectual. He felt disadvantaged, even cheated, because he had had no formal background in the liberal arts. 'Stultz, old buddy, have you ever heard of St. John's University in Maryland?' he asked me. 'The students learn by reading great books. You and me, or, rather, you and I, are going to form a book club, read the great books, and thereby enroll by proxy in St. John's. We're going to begin by reading English novels of the nineteenth century. We'll start with Dickens, and then on to Trollope and Austen. I'll suggest a book. We'll both read it and meet once a month at the Harvard Club, to discuss the book over drinks and dinner.'

"We met first in the tap room. The conversation there is mainly social and business gossip. Our conversation stood out. Others overheard us and asked to join in. By the third meeting or so, our group grew to ten members. We had to move two tables together so all could participate.

"Henry faithfully read the assigned book. In a session on Dickens's *Dombey and Son,* he discussed the theme of succession. Dombey owned a profitable business. He intended his son to succeed him, cared only about him, and neglected his daughter, Florence. When the boy died at an early age, Carker, Dombey's assistant, sought to replace the dead son. He also sought to replace Dombey. His method was to seduce Dombey's second wife, the young and beautiful Edith, and through an embezzlement scheme, to gain control of the business. Henry discussed the Oedipal implications of a man seeking to become a son by sleeping with his putative father's wife. He also pointed out homoerotic implications of Carker transposing his desire for Dombey onto his wife. Then Henry made another outstanding point: the son in *Dombey and Son* is, ironically, Florence, the neglected daughter. Later at dinner, one member of the group asked Henry what year he'd graduated from Harvard.

"Henry never said so, but I suspect that was one of the high points of his life—that question.

"Our monthly meetings ended when Henry announced he was leaving our club to join a Shakespeare group led by a Columbia University professor. He asked if I wanted to join. I said no and jokingly remarked that Shakespeare, in my opinion, was overrated. Months later, Henry confessed he had dropped the Shakespeare club. 'I repeated your line: Shakespeare is overrated. The professor said if I felt that way I should not return. Then he said my presence would not be missed. You know, Stultz, old buddy, me and you, you and me, could do Shakespeare better than that pseudo-intellectual professor.'

"'Henry,' I said, 'I truly love you, but I draw the line on Shakespeare. The Bard is not for us. Let's go back to novels.' Henry agreed, but we never got around to it. He went off to Italy and then began his ill-fated run for president.

"Henry called me the day he learned he had a fatal form of cancer. He asked to meet to review his will; he made no mention of the doctor's verdict.

"He came to my office leaning on a cane. I hadn't seen him for several months. He looked sick and weak. I asked what was wrong. He said, 'Chief Justice Rehnquist and I have something in common; the same form of cancer that killed him will shortly kill me.' I lost the power of speech for a full five minutes and began to cry. 'Henry,' I said to him, 'you are my kind of guy. A workaholic, street smart, big hearted. I had dreams. If you'd been elected president, I might follow you to Washington. Maybe as counsel to the president. I think of us as brothers. Now you say you are going to leave me. Promise me after you die you'll come back to visit.

"'Don't laugh, Henry. I just finished reading a book by Jose Saramago, *The Year of the Death of Ricardo Reis*. There, Fernando Pessoa, a dead Portuguese poet, visits regularly with Ricardo Reis. Pessoa says that all dead people have the right for nine months to call on friends. Henry, you must promise me, if at all possible, you will call on me.'

"Henry was a good man. My best friend. I will miss him."

Watson, who was to speak next, asked Stultz if Henry had reappeared. Stultz said, "I can't say for sure. It's confusing. One day as I was just waking up, I thought I heard Henry say, 'It's not so bad here.' But I heard nothing else. I looked at the spot the sound had come from and saw only a blank wall."

I introduced Watson as Henry's business partner, friend, and confidante.

"Henry was a hard-working man, a stickler for detail. I am not, however, going to talk about his work ethic but rather how he relaxed when he had downtime.

"One day, early in our partnership, I was eating lunch in the Amalgamated cafeteria. Henry approached with his lunch tray and sat down. I was reading *Chess Life*, a monthly magazine published by the US Chess Federation. Henry asked to see it and flipped through the pages, saying his kids were learning chess and that he too would like to play. I said a good way to begin was to find a good chess teacher. I recommended Lev Alburt, a grandmaster from the Ukraine who defected to the United States, was a three-time US chess champion, lived in New York, and gave lessons.

"In addition to teaching, I told him Alburt had published many instructional books on chess, including his two volumes on the once-secret Russian method.

"Six months passed with no further talk of chess. Then, late one afternoon, Henry asked me to meet him. We met in a conference room next to his office. On the table was a plastic chess set, a green and white cloth board, a chess clock, and pads and pencils to record our moves.

"Henry said he had finished reading the two chess books I'd recommended and had called Alburt for lessons. He suggested that Henry play a game and record the moves. Alburt would review the game, spot weaknesses, and be in a better position to teach.

"In my youth," Watson continued, "I was a tournament player; in college, I played first board on the chess team. We played one game that afternoon. I showed Henry no mercy. He complained, 'You won so quickly; Alburt will learn very little from the game. Let's try another. Try to play on my level this time. Okay?' I laughed and gave him the chess player's standard comment when asked to play down. 'Sorry, Henry, I can't play bad chess. To be competitive, you'll have to raise your game to my level.' Henry stared hard at me before replying, 'You'll regret that arrogant remark. The gods strike down guys afflicted with hubris. One day, you'll be a victim. I, a beginner, will beat you.' I said I looked forward to that day, though I doubted it would ever happen. Taunting Henry, I added, 'In chess circles, you're what's known as a *patzer*, a beginner.'

"Several months passed before we played again. This time, Henry set aside the entire afternoon. We played five games. I won all but one easily. In that game, Henry made me sweat. He was improving. My game was rusty. There was a chance Henry might one day call me patzer. To forestall that evil day, I renewed my membership in the Marshall, a chess club in the Village; purchased the latest edition of Fritz, a computer program; and studied the games of the grandmasters.

"We played about twice a month after that. During the game, we concentrated only on chess, never talked about anything other than chess, never interrupted the game for even a phone call. Afterward, we discussed our games. Henry also brought in the score sheets of games he'd played against his kids. Michael showed real talent.

"Henry discussed Alburt's analysis of our games. Although I invariably had the better position, Alburt found winning moves for Henry. 'Alburt probably considers me a patzer,' I said.

"'Not at all,' said Henry. 'Alburt said your game has improved. Watson must be studying chess in his spare time.'

"It was strange. Two men consumed by business took a break only to become consumed by chess.

"After we sold Wojo Partners, we played one more time. While Henry was serving as ambassador, I was in Rome, and Henry invited me to dinner. After we ate, Henry suggested a game of chess. We walked across the hall to Henry's study. There, on a game table, was a chess set and board. The chessmen were the traditional Staunton design, just like the plastic set we used in New York. There the similarities ended. The pieces were made of ivory. One side natural, the other stained red. The chessmen were large, heavy, and carved by hand. The knights were standouts; they had muscles and teeth. After the game, I asked Henry about the set. He said it was an antique made in the nineteenth century by an English company called Jacques and Son. He turned the king over and showed me the company's mark on the underside of the stand. The sets were originally sold in mahogany boxes lined in velvet. Inside, there were thirty-two precisely sized compartments, one for each piece. He then showed me the box his set had come in. 'Nothing made today compares to the wonderful Jacques sets,' he said. 'The chessmen and the box are regarded by their owners as items held in trust for future generations. That explains why my set is in excellent condition, although used for play, almost one hundred and fifty years after it was made.

"'Some people,' Henry said, 'collect antique chess sets. Most old sets are decorative; you can't play with them. Some collectors have more than five hundred sets, many old and valuable. The collectors formed an association called Chess Collectors International. It holds biennial meetings in cities in Europe and the United States. Reflecting the nationality of the members, two are held in Europe for every one in the United States.

"'At a recent convention and auction held in Rome, I bought this set. The box and this folding chess board came with it.' At that point, Henry opened the box, placed each piece in its proper pocket, closed the box, and folded the chessboard.

"'You introduced me to chess. More important, you are a real player, not a patzer like me. You deserve to have this beautiful set. Please accept it with the box and board.'

"The chess set is on display in my home. I continue to play chess, but not with Henry's set. Some evenings, however, I do use Henry's gift. I take the score sheets of one or sometimes two of our games and replay them. As I move the pieces, I sense Henry's presence. At times, I believe I can actually see him."

Andrew was the last speaker. I knew father and son had had a tumultuous relationship. Henry had spurned a plumber's life, and Andrew held "money lenders and paper pushers" in disdain. The family was anxious about what Andrew might say, and their anxiety was heightened by his request to have the final word. I decided on a short but flattering introduction. "It is my pleasure to introduce our last speaker, the patriarch, Andrew Wojecoski, the head of the Wojecoski family."

Andrew strode briskly to the podium, holding his handwritten speech. He was so eager to begin that he started before I could leave the podium.

"Blood is the strongest tie in the world. You can divorce a wife or abandon friends, but a child is your flesh and blood, bound to you for as long as you both live.

"I'm that unhappy parent who has survived his children. If Jesus made bargains, I would gladly have exchanged my life so Henry could live. I am as powerless to do that as I was powerless to make Henry follow in my footsteps.

"Yes, I wanted Henry to become a plumber and work with me for what I thought, at the time, was in Henry's best interests.

"A plumber like me lives in two worlds. Riverhead, where I live, is a nice, friendly, stable community. My neighbors work hard, earn a living, and raise their families. My second world is populated by the rich people I serve. Their lives look good except when they fail. Several of my customers committed white-collar crimes and spent time in the slammer. Others went belly-up or ran away, unable to face the music. One committed suicide.

"I wanted Henry to become a plumber. Why? To make sure that his life would be secure, that he would never be a failure.

"How could I have known that my son, the child of a dumb Polack plumber, would succeed mightily, almost getting elected to the highest office in the world? He left others who had had a big headway soaking wet in his wake. Henry succeeded to the point that Wojecoski, a hard name to pronounce, became a household word.

"I asked the librarian to help me find a saying from a famous person that described Henry. None was good enough, but this one by Theodore Roosevelt, a soldier like Henry, a politician like Henry, and a man like Henry who wasn't afraid to compete in the world arena, was the closest:

"'It is not the critic who counts; not the man who points out how the strong man stumbles, or where the doer of deeds could have done them better. The credit belongs to the man who is actually in the arena, whose face is marred by dust and sweat and blood, who strives valiantly; who errs and comes short again and again; because there is not effort without error and shortcomings; but who does actually strive to do the deed; who knows the great enthusiasm, the great devotion, who spends himself in a worthy cause, who at the best knows in the end the triumph of high achievement and who at the worst, if he fails, at least he fails while daring greatly. So that his place shall never be with those cold and timid souls who know neither victory nor defeat.'

"Henry, you were the man Theodore Roosevelt praised for striving valiantly and daring greatly, and I, the cold and timid soul.

"I regret that I lacked the courage to tell you how brave you were. Instead, I mocked you, buried your achievements under a bushel of hay, safely hidden, and ignored them. Now, in front of our family and your friends, I declare: 'Henry, you were the man in our family.'"

When Andrew left the podium, the grandchildren engulfed him. Theirs was a private convocation. I heard the word "catharsis" followed by its definition. Later, I learned that Andrew used a metaphor: "My speech purged my soul like a snake clears a clogged pipe."

I made the closing remarks. "The word *unheimlich* is a German word. It has no precise equivalent in English. The closest we can come is 'uncanny' and 'supernatural.' After listening to the speeches, seeing the video screen, hearing Henry's voice on the tapes, I get the unheimlich feeling that Henry is right here in this room with us. If I am right, I am sure he appreciated the evening."

# Conclusion

*H*enry's book was published six months after the party. It made the *New York Times* bestseller list and stayed there for ten weeks. I got credit for rescuing Henry's reputation, much more than I deserved. The book attracted the attention of a Madoff associate, who said, "Do for Madoff what you did for Henry," and suggested a title: *Bernie Baby Boy: An Unauthorized Biography of Bernard Madoff.* He offered a million dollars, but there are assignments not even a PR man will take on.